Also by Susanna Shore

House of Magic
Hexing the Ex
Saved by the Spell
Third Spell's the Charm
Magic by the Book

P.I. Tracy Hayes
Tracy Hayes, Apprentice P.I.
Tracy Hayes, P.I. and Proud
Tracy Hayes, P.I. to the Rescue
Tracy Hayes, P.I. with the Eye
Tracy Hayes, from P.I. with Love
Tracy Hayes, Tenacious P.I.
Tracy Hayes, Valentine of a P.I.
Tracy Hayes, P.I. on the Scent
Tracy Hayes, Unstoppable P.I.
Tracy Hayes, P.I. for the Win

Two-Natured London
The Wolf's Call
Warrior's Heart
A Wolf of Her Own
Her Warrior for Eternity
A Warrior for a Wolf
Magic under the Witching Moon
Moonlight, Magic and Mistletoes
Crimson Warrior
Magic on the Highland Moor
Wolf Moon
Magic for the Highland Wolf

The Reed Files
The Perfect Scam

Magic by the Book

House of Magic 4

Susanna Shore

Crimson House Books

Magic by the Book
Copyright © 2023 A. K. S. Keinänen
All rights reserved.

The moral right of the author has been asserted.

No part of this book may be reproduced, translated, or distributed without permission, except for brief quotations in critical articles and reviews.

This is a work of fiction. Names, characters, places, dialogues and incidents either are the product of the author's imagination or are used fictitiously. Any resemblance to actual events, organizations or persons, living or dead, except those in public domain, is entirely coincidental.

Book Design: A. K. S. Keinänen
Cover Design: A. K. S. Keinänen
Cover Image: Sergey Myakishev

ISBN 978-952-7061-61-9 (paperback edition)
ISBN 978-952-7061-60-2 (e-book edition)

www.susannashore.com

One

WHEN YOU KISS YOUR BOSS ON Saturday, and don't hear back from him on Sunday, going to work on Monday is nerve-racking. Take it from me.

Not that I habitually kissed my boss, Archibald Kane, the owner of Kane's Arts and Antiques. Or had, in fact, kissed him. He kissed *me*. But I'd participated, enthusiastically.

And then he hadn't acknowledged it in any way since.

As his assistant, I was used to keeping a respectful distance, and after-work calls had almost never happened. Or in-work calls for that matter, especially those that informed his poor assistant where he was when he didn't show up at the office, having gone for one of his days-long hunts for antiques.

But these past couple of months we'd grown closer and begun to socialise outside work, so I'd sort of hoped he'd call. If for nothing else, then to apologise for acting so out of character. It seemed more his style than ardent declarations of love.

I won't lie though. If he brushed the kiss aside, I would die.

The new phase in our outside-work relationship had started when I moved in the House of Magic in August. It was a shop in Clerkenwell, Central London, that sold tarot cards, healing crystals, and herbal teas among other witchy New Age things, with housing in three storeys above it.

My room was perfect and came with meals, and my new housemates were wonderful. I'd been amazed with my luck of finding lodgings in London after being evicted from my previous place, let alone one reasonably priced and within fare zone 1.

And then I'd learned that luck had had nothing to do with it. Magic had.

That's right, *magic*. The House of Magic wasn't merely a cute name for a charming shop and the house above, it was a home for people who could do magic. And not card tricks either; actual transmute-the-elements, shoot-lightning-from-your-fingers kind of thing.

My landladies, Amber Boyle and Giselle Lynn, were mages. It wasn't a thing you could simply become, you had to be born one for the spells to work. There were entire families of mages all over the world, and London was one of their largest communities. They were well-organised and highly secret.

Incidentally, the magic shop also sold real spell and potion ingredients for those in the know.

The room next to mine was rented by Ashley Grant, a firefighter a few years older than my twenty-six. She was also a werewolf, as in transform into a huge wolf during the full moon—and pretty much whenever she wanted. Also something she'd been born with.

The basement was occupied by Luca Marlow, a vampire who looked my age but was at least a hundred.

Magic by the Book

I'd never seen him transform into anything—I was hoping for a bat—but he could fling battle spells and was averse to sunlight, but not to garlic or holy objects. I'd asked.

I'd barely begun to process that what I'd thought belonged to urban fantasy books with bare-chested men on their covers was real—with great disbelief, I might add—when I learned that my boss, the always elegant and proper antiques dealer, was a mage too. He'd been their leader at the time even, but currently he was studying to become the archmage of London, which was the most skilled you could become mage-wise.

Well, there were warlocks, but they were evil and dealt with death magic; no respectable mage wanted to have anything to do with them.

Together with my housemates and him, I'd been plunged into a series of harrowing events that had tested not only their skills as "enhanced humans," as they called themselves, but my abilities and resilience as well. I'd been cursed, twice. We'd thwarted a warlock bent on taking over London, twice—though we'd only faced him the second time. I could only hope that he was gone for good, but I wasn't holding my breath.

Then I'd found out to my utter amazement that I, Phoebe Thorpe, was a mage too. I should've learned about it much earlier, but because my Great-Aunt Beverly, who was the previous mage in the family, died before I was in a suitable age, it had never happened. I'd begun to learn spellcasting, and after a lousy start—I kept creating accidental fires—I was finally getting the hang of it.

Last week, we'd defeated a vampire warlock on a revenge spree. We'd been celebrating surviving the final showdown with him when Kane had kissed me.

And then he hadn't called me.

Now I didn't know how to take it. Had he merely been swept up by the emotions of the moment, expressing his relief that we were both alive? Or was he, like I hoped, romantically interested in me?

That he didn't show up at the House of Magic on Sunday seemed to indicate the former. He'd started to attend the Sunday lunch regularly, lured in by Giselle's excellent cooking, so missing it had to be deliberate. I could only hope that, like me, he'd slept most of the day. It wasn't the late-night partying, it was recovering from all the magic we'd wielded—he more than I, naturally. It tended to completely wring out a mage.

Not knowing for sure had messed up both me and my morning routines. I'd slept poorly, which made me cranky and distracted. I agonised over my clothing and tried several hairdos, only to leave my long cinnamon hair down in the end. I left for work early, having skipped breakfast, and then I zoned out in the Tube, forgetting to switch lines at Liverpool Street station and found myself at Aldgate. Instead of heading back, which would have been the sensible thing to do, I switched to Circle Line, rode it to the Monument, and took a bus to the Bank where I could take the Central Line to Bond Street.

Needless to say, I was late arriving at Kane's Arts and Antiques at the edge of Mayfair and Marylebone, north of Oxford Street. I somehow managed to switch off the correct alarm to the offices upstairs, leaving the shop's alarm on as we weren't open on Mondays. I gathered the mail, only dropping it once, and carried it to my desk in the lobby outside Kane's office.

That's as far as I got. I slumped in my chair, mail unsorted, my laptop unopened. I was supposed to make tea for Kane for when he arrived at nine, but I couldn't muster the energy to even fill the kettle.

As the clock crept towards nine, the pressure to get my act on made my skin tighten, but I was more nervous than before a dentist's appointment and I couldn't decide which task I should do first. My stomach was in a huge knot that would've pushed my breakfast up if I'd had any.

Frustrated, I picked up a pen, but instead of doing something useful with it, like writing a to-do list, I tried to levitate it. Amber had taught me a simple levitation spell the previous day, but what had seemed easy yesterday wasn't that easy today. Spellcasting required concentration that I simply couldn't muster, and more energy than I had to give.

I should've called in sick and stayed in bed.

But practising the spell was better than obsessing about the kiss and agonising over what Kane would do, so I prevailed. Gritting my teeth, I forced my mind to calm, and coaxed the spark inside me that was necessary for casting spells. I made the correct movements with my hands and fingers and said the spell aloud.

The pen rose into the air, hovering a hand's width above the desk. It wasn't much, but even that made my head sway as a dizzy spell washed over me.

"I thought I told you not to strain yourself."

The spell cut as I lost concentration. The pen dropped. I'd been so engrossed in my attempt that I hadn't noticed Kane arrive.

Archibald Kane, or Kane as he'd asked me to call him, was thirty-five, with a lean, handsome face, deep blue eyes, and thick black hair that I itched to sink my fingers in. He was tall, lean, and surprisingly muscled underneath the precise three-piece suit he was wearing, thanks to long daily jogs.

I had colourful fantasies about those muscles that I'd witnessed first-hand once. I'd been attracted to him ever since I started as his assistant a couple of years ago, to his serious demeanour and precise, slightly old-fashioned manners coupled with great intelligence and occasional glimpses of a lighter side. And that was before I knew about magic.

After witnessing him fight magical battles with warlocks, I was pretty much completely smitten. He transformed into a fierce and strong warrior, capable of anything.

Though not this morning apparently. He'd halted at the door, a shoulder propped against the frame, hands pushed into the pockets of his suit trousers, and was watching me with a kind of adorable confusion from under his dark brows. I wasn't the only one thrown off by the kiss.

He removed one hand from the pocket and ran fingers through his thick hair, as if searching for words. "Sorry, I … didn't mean to sound so harsh."

I hadn't noticed the tone, the spell taking my attention. "Amber is much harsher."

He flashed me a smile that brought out an elusive dimple on his right cheek. If I'd been casting a spell, something would've caught fire for sure—and not because that used to happen every time I was spellcasting.

"In that case, good morning, Phoebe."

Magic by the Book

It wasn't the dreaded talk, but I couldn't relax yet. "Good morning, Kane. I'm sorry, but I'm running a bit late this morning, and your tea isn't ready."

He cocked an amused brow. "Too busy learning the levitation spell?"

It was as good an explanation as any—and would make me seem more competent than the truth—so I nodded and rose up, steadying myself against the desk as the strain of the spell made me sway.

"I'll start the tea immediately."

He halted me by lifting a hand. "I'm not staying. I need to go visit a few clients, and I'll be away the whole day."

My heart plummeted to the pit of my stomach. "Oh…" I managed to say with great intelligence. "Thank you for letting me know so that I…"

…won't work myself into a panic thinking you hated the kiss so much you can't come to work…

"…won't worry."

"Phoebe…" He took a few steps closer but paused before reaching me. He ran fingers through his hair again, his forehead knitting slightly, and I braced myself for a talk about how we should ignore the kiss or something. Then he straightened, tilted his head, and gave me a questioning look.

"Would you like to come with me?"

EVER SINCE I STARTED working at Kane's Arts and Antiques, I'd wanted to learn the practical side of the antique business. I wanted to hunt through old homes, barns, and county fairs for old furniture and paintings, knickknacks and books that had been forgotten. I dreamed of finding the hidden gems, preferably as bargains that showed how clever I was recognising them, and making a good profit in the process.

I'm not saying I'd watched too much *Lovejoy* as a child, but it was my mother's favourite from before I was born. She had all six seasons on DVD that we watched together between reruns.

I'd studied art history in university, and trained in auctioneering at Sotheby's, so I had the theory side covered. But while I had a fairly free hand at organising exhibitions and auctions we held, most of my duties consisted of office work.

Kane handled the acquisitions we sold at the shop, travelling up and down the home counties—and sometimes farther. He had never asked me to come with him before. I was giddy with excitement, the kiss almost forgotten, as I followed him to his car. If he didn't want to bring it up, I could ignore it too—for now. I didn't want to ruin my first opportunity with awkward conversations.

To my disappointment, he wasn't driving his Jag this morning. It was his old, faded-blue Land Cruiser that was roomy enough for transporting anything smaller than sofas and dining room sets. The engine was in good condition, as were the seats.

"Where are we headed and what do you expect to find?" I asked as he drove out of the garage near the shop where he parked during the day.

"Brighton. We should be there before midday."

The distance wasn't terribly long, under ninety kilometres to the south, but it would take us close to an hour to drive through Central London to Brixton and Croydon on the south side of the Thames, no matter what the GPS tried to say.

"And then down the coast to Portsmouth, with maybe one stop on the way," he added, joining the heavy morning traffic.

"Sounds exciting."

He shot me an amused glance. "Well, don't get used to it. I still need you to handle the office chores."

I could've told him he should hire an actual office person, but I didn't want to push my luck. "With the right tools, most of that stuff can be handled anywhere."

"Hmmm..." was all he said. I hoped that meant he was considering giving me the right tools and not that he wouldn't invite me again.

The traffic eased a little once we were past Croydon, but the speed remained low. The Land Cruiser couldn't really do high speeds anyway, so it didn't matter. I was in no hurry, and Kane seemed comfortable driving.

But I couldn't sit in silence all the way to Brighton. Well, I probably could and Kane likely wouldn't even notice, but I was brought up better.

My hands were getting a little clammy as I tried to come up with a neutral topic that didn't sound like I was desperately trying to come up with one. I couldn't very well point at every cow on the fields we passed, even if, as a city girl, I always found proof of their existence satisfying.

"So ... should I do research in preparations for today's meetings?"

Kane shot me a baffled glance. "Like what?"

"I don't know, eighteenth-century sea chests typical of the area or something."

He tilted his head. "Won't hurt, even if those aren't the target. The first meeting is about snuffboxes. Richard Walters was a known collector of them. He passed away recently, and his estate wants to sell his collection. I'm getting the first look. I went to school with his son Patrick."

Of course he did…

The most aggravating feature of the antique business in England—or any business, really—was that it tended to hang on who one knew. This, more often than not, was synonymous with men one went to Eton or Harrow or some other expensive private school for boys with, which effectively kept women out. Kane had the right background and connections, which in part made his shop successful.

If I wanted to make it in this business, I needed to cultivate those connections every opportunity I had. At the auctions and exhibitions we held, and at antique fairs and conferences, I tried to make the acquaintance of the people in our business, so that one day a person selling something would think of me first.

Kane already knew many of those people, which was why it was so important to me that he had taken me with him.

"Snuffboxes are your thing…" I said with a smile.

"Not so much a thing as something our clients are always interested in." He thought for a moment. "But if you're bent on researching something, you could look up Northney House and the Hayling family."

"Are we visiting them too?" I asked, taking out my phone.

"If we have time. It's near Portsmouth."

There wasn't much. The house was a Grade II listed Georgian limestone rectory near a twelfth-century church on Hayling Island, east of Portsmouth. It had once stood alone at the end of Church Lane, but the gardens, orchards, and meadows had long since been sold to developers, and it was now surrounded by late-twentieth-century cottages.

"I'm guessing the family needs money for a renovation?"

Kane smirked. "That's the official word. But I hear Mrs Hayling is paying off Mr Hayling after a tempestuous divorce."

Ooh, that was interesting. But wherever he got his intel from, it wasn't public enough knowledge that I could've found anything about it online. I did find a few mentions of the couple, with photos showing an elegant woman in her early forties and a slightly older husband, standing in front of paintings showcased in their art gallery.

But there was nothing that would tell us what Mrs Hayling might be selling, whether it was art or antiques. "We'll have to go in blind," I noted, putting my phone away as we approached Brighton. I could check auction records to see if the couple had purchased anything interesting they might be selling now, but that would have to wait.

"Which is why I'm not exactly interested in going," Kane said.

I kind of was. "So why were you considering it in the first place?" But I figured out the answer immediately. "They're a mage family, aren't they!"

He nodded. "She is, and her family-line, but her husband isn't."

"Is that why they divorced?"

"I have no idea, but it doesn't make for an ideal marriage if one has to keep such a secret."

"Is that why you've never taken me on these purchase trips?" I asked, the sudden insight making old upset ease deep inside me. "Because you occasionally meet with other mages and buy items I wasn't allowed to learn about?"

A small smile hovered at the corner of his mouth. "Something like that."

He shot me a quick glance but didn't elaborate. And I was too much of a coward to ask.

Two

NOVEMBER HAD EMPTIED Brighton of tourists, and we had no trouble finding parking on Marine Parade that ran along the south side of the town, with Regency terraces on one side and sea on the other. There was nothing but water from here on; it looked like we were at the edge of the world. Only the Brighton Pier cut the emptiness, but even that had quieted for the winter.

The sky was grey, and the sea was restless with high waves, but it wasn't raining yet. It was horribly chilly though, the wind blowing hard from the sea. "I didn't dress for this weather," I said, shivering as I exited the car.

I'd wanted to look good and had dressed in a sleeveless, knee-length shirtdress. It was dark grey wool, so technically warm, but I only had a sheer, powder-pink blouse underneath it that didn't warm my arms at all. Thick, black stockings and boots completed the look, and I wore a raincoat over everything, but I was regretting ignoring Giselle, who had reminded me to take a scarf and gloves when I left home that morning.

Kane gave me a concerned look. "Do you want to wait in the car? I won't be long."

"No. I came with you to learn."

Richard Walters had lived in one of the cream-coloured Regency terraces by Marine Parade, an elegant four-storey house in the middle of the row. Short steps led up straight from the pavement, and the door opened before Kane had a chance to ring the bell.

A man in his mid-thirties stood on the threshold, dressed in jeans and a white shirt. He was tall and stooping, with a ruddy complexion and dark-blond hair that was thinning a little. He spread his arms, delighted, as if wanting to give Kane a hug. Was he even English?

"Archie! Wonderful to see you. Come on in."

He stepped aside and Kane gestured for me to enter first. The man's face lit up impossibly more. "And who have we here? Have you married again and didn't tell me?"

"I'm sure you'd be the first to know," Kane assured him, shaking the man's hand as I stifled my annoyance for being reduced to a girlfriend—even though I did want to be Kane's girlfriend.

It was complicated, okay.

"This is Phoebe Thorpe, my assistant. She's learning the ropes of antique acquisition."

"Excellent! I'm Patrick Walters," the man said, shaking my hand with great enthusiasm. He looked so cheerful that I didn't dare to offer condolences for his father's passing, but luckily Kane did it for me.

"I was sorry to hear about your father. How are you holding up?"

Patrick brushed the concern aside. "It was his time. He was old already when I was born, and positively ancient at his death. It was peaceful. My children were devastated though, and consoling them has helped me get over the worst. Now I'm ready to tackle this mess."

He led us deeper into the house and I could only stare with my mouth hanging open. The rooms on both sides of the entrance hallway were filled with so much antique furniture, art, and curious items like fossils and taxidermized animals that there was barely any room for people to walk between them. It wasn't organised in any fashion I could recognise, everything piled on each other in a happy jumble. It was like the cabinets of curiosity of Renaissance collectors had come together and multiplied.

"Oh my," I said aloud. "It'll take months to go through all this."

Patrick flashed me a smile. "Luckily Dad kept catalogues, so I have an inkling of what's here. I'll have to hire a professional to handle everything, but I wanted Archie to have a first look."

Kane smiled warmly. "Thank you. Pity I can't devote the time it would take to find everything interesting here."

Pity indeed…

This was exactly the kind of place I'd dreamed of visiting and having a free hand in. My fingers were itching to start rummaging. "Is every floor like this?"

"Goodness, no. The rest of the house is perfectly liveable."

Patrick led us up a flight of stairs to a small parlour that overlooked the sea. It was a beautifully appointed, pale-yellow room. There were art and exquisite items there too, like vases and an ornamental French Louis XV style wall clock, but carefully selected to fit the interior. Every furniture and piece of art was something we could've easily sold in our shop.

Kane looked around, nodding. "You won't have trouble selling this."

Patrick shook his head. "Everything will remain as is in the upper stairs. It's the mess downstairs that needs to go."

He gestured at a Sheraton seating group upholstered in striped, yellow chinch, where several wooden cases were placed on a mahogany coffee table. "This is what I wanted you to see."

I wasn't interested in snuffboxes, but our clients were, so I took a seat next to Kane on a sofa that would've fit two Georgian ladies in pannier dresses, and watched keenly as he opened the first case. Nine small, round porcelain or enamel boxes rested on black velvet, each in their small slot. They were from the eighteenth century and finely painted with pastoral scenes that weren't remarkable even to my inexpert eye.

Kane picked one up and opened it. His brows shot up and I smirked too. The inside of the lid had a painting of a naked lady, in the very classical style that one sees in larger paintings of muses and goddesses in a museum. Inside of a snuffbox though, it was decidedly naughty, especially when it was without strategically placed drapes. Aristocratic Georgian men would've shown these off to each other in the corners of respectable salons and tittered.

The side of Kane's mouth quirked up. "I can definitely sell these."

Patrick looked relieved. "Good. At least half of these are like that, and I feared people would find them inappropriate. But they're genuine. I have provenances for all of them here." He patted a manilla folder at the corner of the table.

"I have a couple of clients who will fight over these. I'll get you a good price."

Magic by the Book

Kane opened every case and checked the quality and authenticity of each snuffbox. They were different shapes and sizes, and some were silver or gold, with better quality paintings and ornaments, especially those without naughty pictures. All of them were old. They would sell well among the regular snuffbox enthusiasts who weren't into Georgian pornography.

When he was done, he closed the cases, piled them, and stood up. "I'll let you know when they're sold."

"Thank you," Patrick said, getting up too. We followed him back downstairs and Kane began to take his goodbyes, but I wanted to linger and study everything. Kane noticed and smiled.

"We're not in a hurry if you want to take a look."

While he carried the boxes into the car, I slowly walked through the rooms. There was so much to look at that it was impossible to see anything interesting, but I took it as an exercise for my antique-hunting skills.

Maybe it was about intuition. Or maybe the special item would call me.

Amused by the thought, I closed my eyes, and lacking better options, concentrated like I did before casting a spell. I reached inside for the spark, and finding it sent it outwards, away from me.

A pulse pinged back to me. It was faint, but so surprising it broke my concentration. I turned towards the source and concentrated again, keeping my eyes open. This time I was expecting the pulse and was able to follow it to the corner of the room.

It was as full of curiosities as the rest of the room, and nothing immediately caught my eye as the source of the sensation. So I closed my eyes again and hovered my hand over the items. This time the sensation was clear.

My hand had paused over a wooden case much like those that contained the snuffboxes. I opened the lid and the contents turned out to be similar looking small ornamental items too, but they were flat.

My heart skipped a beat in delight. "Are these compact mirrors?"

Patrick came to look. "I have no idea. I haven't gone through the catalogues yet." He picked one up and opened it to reveal a darkened silver mirror. "You're right. Do you think there's a market for these?"

"People collect everything," I said, distracted, my attention taken by an art deco mirror with obsidian, silver, and blue enamel stripes inlaid on the cover to create a geometric decoration typical of the style, like a triangle or beams of a rising sun.

It was square with rounded edges and about the size of my palm. I picked it up and it zapped me, almost making me drop it. Had this been calling me? It had to mean something, even if it wasn't the remarkable find I'd hoped for.

"We could probably sell them one by one for tourists looking for something inexpensive."

Kane appeared by my shoulder. He studied the mirrors. "You do know people can get these online for a twenty?" But I gave him an eager look and he smiled.

"Fine. We'll take the lot."

AFTER A LUNCH WITH Patrick in a restaurant near his father's house, we were on our way to Portsmouth. I was holding the case of mirrors and was eagerly studying them for gems, but Kane was right. They were fairly ordinary, if genuinely old.

"I'm keeping this one for myself," I said, holding the art deco mirror. It wasn't the most beautiful mirror among the lot, or the oldest, and the mirror was slightly darkened at one edge, but it had called to me. None of the others zapped me when I touched them.

"Fine. You can consider it your finder's commission."

"I get commission?"

He smiled. "I don't see why not. But with knickknacks like these, it won't be more than that mirror."

I was fine with that.

The distance to Portsmouth west of Brighton along the coastline was the same as to London, but with less traffic, so it went faster. It had begun to drizzle, but the sturdy Land Cruiser could take any kind of weather.

I passed the time reading about antique compacts. Early to mid-twentieth century factory-made mirrors were sold by the dozen on Etsy and Amazon, with prices from ten pounds up, and most of them were even genuine.

But Walters Senior hadn't been taken with cheap copies. All these mirrors were older, and most were handmade. He'd been a very thorough collector too, and had made notes about each mirror, even if most contained guesswork about the age and provenance of the item.

My mirror—I'd already started to think of it as that—was English from the 1920s. It had a silver stamp at the back that would help to date it, and even the maker's name engraved there: Foster & Son, London.

I googled the name and found a match, but I couldn't be entirely sure I had the right company. There was one with that name still operating, but another one had gone out of business when the "son" in Foster & Son had died in the Second World War. I would have to pay the existing shop a visit one of these days.

I emerged from my research only to see Kane drive past the exit to Hayling Island. "I take it we're not going to visit Mrs Hayling after all?"

Kane cursed. "I forgot the whole thing." He glanced at the GPS, but it wasn't showing any turning points nearby. "I'll visit her some other time."

"If I were trying to pay off an ex, I'd want it to be done sooner rather than later," I pointed out dryly. He grimaced, likely remembering his own divorce from "the Bitch," aka Danielle Mercer, the dark lord in the making.

I wasn't being jealous; she really was studying to become a warlock—the reason for their divorce.

"Fine. We'll make a detour on our way back from Portsmouth."

I studied the map. "It's hardly a detour. A3 to London starts pretty much where the exit to the island is."

Happy with this, he drove us to Portsmouth. It was technically on an island too, though the canal that separated it from the mainland wasn't very wide. It was a hub of naval activity, old and new. The oldest part was on the southwest side, and Kane navigated us across the island there.

I'd been to Portsmouth a couple of times when I was a child, but not in recent years. The place had changed considerably, the old wharves transformed into a modern shopping and business hub that improved the neighbourhood but destroyed the old-world charm.

Our destination was on High Street—so named—behind the twelfth-century Romanesque cathedral. It was an antique shop that occupied one half of a four-storey Georgian house that had the street level painted in bright blue and the upper floors in grey, making it stand out among the redbricks and Regency whites.

Magic by the Book

The other half was taken by an inn, and the two shared an entrance. On each side of the door was a wide bay window, one for the inn and the other for the antique shop. Judging by the window display, the latter specialised in nautical antiques, which wasn't our field at all. I really should've studied up on those sea chests.

"So what are we doing here, again?" I asked as Kane opened the paned glass door and I entered the shop. Delicious scents hit me and my stomach growled even though we'd eaten before we left Brighton.

On the left was a small taproom and reception of the inn, and on the right the antique shop. Between the two halves was a wide staircase of polished wood leading up.

"I've asked around for an eighteenth-century occasional table that our client is looking for, and the owner said he has one. We're here to see if it's suitable."

This I could handle.

A woman about my age greeted us from behind the shop's counter, flashing a smile at Kane that was a bit warmer than I was happy with, though I tried not to notice. Kane kissing me didn't give me the right to shoot daggers at every woman who smiled at him.

"Good afternoon, Mr Kane. Are you here to see Mr Riddell?"

Kane nodded. "Is he upstairs?"

"Yes, go right ahead."

I followed Kane up, practically feeling the woman sizing me up behind me. I ignored the sensation. She was likely envious that she wasn't taken on antique hunts.

Yeah, right…

Upstairs, the duality continued, with one half being a dining room and the other the antiques shop. A sign pointing upstairs said "rooms." We didn't climb up there.

Kane led me to the back of the floor to an oak door of an office. He knocked on the door and entered.

Mr Riddell was in his sixties and portly, filling the space between his chair and desk completely. He smiled when he saw who had entered. "Archibald! Good of you to come."

They exchanged some pleasantries and Kane introduced me. Then Mr Riddell pushed up, nimbly, considering his size. "Let me show you the table."

We followed him to a storage room next to his office where a beautiful mahogany side table stood on a wooden crate it had been stored in. It was rectangular, wider than deep, with a drawer at the narrow end instead of the front, so it was probably a middle part of a dining table, meant to be taken apart and stored at the sides of the dining room when not in use. The panels on the sides and the drawer had gilded edges, but otherwise the ornamentation was simple, with fluted legs and skirt.

It was in great condition, or carefully restored, with the signs of age and handcraft still visible. It was old, but was it genuine? There were beautiful nineteenth-century reproductions that were in the antique category and sought-after too, but our client wanted a genuine eighteenth-century piece.

I glanced at Kane, who nodded, encouraging me. I opened the drawer, holding my breath. One can tell a lot about the age of a piece by how a drawer is put together: with fitted joints or nails and glue. Reproductions often cheated with the drawer as no one would see it anyway.

This one had beautiful, fitted joints that took great skill, with markings from hand-operated tools, and there were several layers of paintwork visible in places where it had been fixed during the course of its history. I let out the breath and smiled. That was one hurdle passed.

"I do have the provenance," Mr Riddell said. "Down to the maker. You can see the maker's mark at the bottom."

Kane turned the table upside down and the branded stamp was indeed still faintly visible. Nevertheless, we studied the table and the paperwork carefully, before Kane was satisfied enough to start negotiating the price.

In due course, we returned to the car with the table, Kane looking happy with the price he'd paid. I was happy too. I felt like I'd shown him I could do more than push papers at the office.

"Do you want to return to the inn for a cup of tea?" he asked when the table was carefully stored in the back of the car.

I sorely needed a cup, but I glanced at the sky that was fast darkening with intensifying rain. "Maybe we should push to Mrs Hayling and hope she'll offer us a cup." According to the GPS, it was a half an hour drive. I could wait for tea.

The rain began to pour in earnest as we were driving out of the town. By the time we were on the A27, it was coming down in a grey sheet that the windshield wipers were struggling to clear. We could barely see the red fog lights of the cars in front of us. The road was soon filled with several inches of water, pushed in by a heavy wind from the sea.

Traffic in our lane slowed to a crawl, the fast lane reserved for idiots who pressed on unheeding of the conditions. Kane relaxed slightly when we exited the dual carriageway, but the wind hit us with gale force on the

Langstone Bridge to Hayling Island, almost pushing the car against the baluster.

"I'm starting to think we should've stayed at the inn for the night," Kane said through gritted teeth, as he struggled to keep the car in the correct lane. I nodded, too tense to speak.

It was only late afternoon, but it was so dark he had the headlamps on, for what good they did. The wind didn't ease even after we turned inland, and flooding made the narrow road even more difficult to negotiate. Branches had fallen from trees on both sides of the road, creating treacherous obstacles.

We almost missed our turn to Church Lane, but luckily we'd been driving slow enough that when Kane hit the brakes it didn't send us careening into the brick wall lining the lane. The lane was barely wide enough for our car, but the wall and trees on both sides blocked the wind and much of the rain.

That was until a bend in the lane. Behind it were open fields all the way to the sea, and the wind hit us with the force that made the trees bend and sway wildly. Kane crawled the car forwards as slowly as he dared, struggling to see where he was going.

"There, on the left!" I exclaimed, having spotted lights in that direction.

Kane turned into the courtyard of Northney House and paused. We glanced at each other, smiling in relief, when a loud, violent groan sounded behind us. A huge tree fell down across the entrance, blocking us in.

Three

WE SAT TENSE AND STILL FOR A few heartbeats, waiting for something to fall on the car. Then Kane kicked the throttle and the car jumped forwards, spewing mud. He eased off the pedal and drove the car at a more sedate pace to the front door.

The door opened and a silhouette of a woman appeared in the yellow light at the doorway, but it was raining too heavily to see who she was. Kane cut the engine and we dashed out of the car, umbrellas pressed against the wind, but we were both pretty much soaked by the time we were inside the house and out of the rain.

The woman stared into the darkness, dazed. "Did the old oak fall? How's that even possible? It's ancient. The roots are deep."

"It's a gale out there," Kane answered, closing the door for her, as she seemed incapable of doing it, struggling to push it against the wind. In the short while it had been open, a puddle had formed on the limestone floor and there were spatters of water on her clothes.

The moment the door thudded closed, she startled from her stupefaction and faced us. I recognised her from the photos: Mrs Hayling. She was a bit older and less elegant than in the latest pictures I'd found, with a few strands of grey in her brown hair, and gaunter, as if she'd stopped eating. The shoulders of her tweed jacket bagged a little, no longer fitting her, and her tweed skirt sat low on her hips.

"Right. You must be Mr Kane." She offered him a hand. "I'm Letitia Hayling. Thank you for coming, especially in this ghastly weather."

"It wasn't this bad when we left Portsmouth," he said with a polite smile, shaking her hand. He introduced me and the woman nodded. Assistants didn't merit a handshake.

I was peeling off my soaked coat, so I didn't mind. The umbrella had been all but useless, the rain falling sideways, and I didn't want to keep it on a moment longer. Kane took off his suit jacket too, the superfine wool having survived the rain fairly well.

"You can hang your coats in the mudroom. There's a heater there."

She turned to cross the entrance hall and I pulled off my muddy boots, not wanting to soil the floor. Kane wouldn't deign to take off his shoes. He wiped them carefully on the red doormat and then we followed Mrs Hayling.

I looked around curiously. The eighteenth-century rectory hadn't been kept in its original form, the limestone floor of the entrance hall being an exception. The walls in the hall were whitewashed, the classical panel wainscotting typical of Georgian houses removed, and it was completely unfurnished except for a red umbrella stand by the door and a grey antique table in the middle, with a tall vase and a single red calla on it.

The rooms we passed had the half-panelling in place, but everything had been painted in translucent white, with the original grey showing through a little. Floors were bare, polished oak that looked new—that is, less than twenty years old. Each room was furnished in an ultra-minimalist style, with a Le Corbusier settee and a red rug in one, and an acrylic escritoire and chair in another, a white Mac screen on the desk and nothing else. All this to make sure the attention was on the large, colourful contemporary art that covered the walls.

It was like living in an art gallery.

After we'd hung our coats in the mudroom, and I'd dried and cleaned my boots to put them back on—the floors were cold—Mrs Hayling led us to a morning room that was mostly taken up by a modern oak dining table. It was comprised of three wide and thick sheets of wood forming half a box, two at the ends and one on the top, with similar chairs. The contrast between the old house and modern furniture worked surprisingly well.

The room continued as a Victorian conservatory through open glass doors. It was at the back of the house, and the wind didn't hit it with a full force, but the glass panes were shaking and chiming, and a puddle had formed on the redbrick floor as the deluge ran down the slanted glass ceiling.

For a conservatory, it didn't have many plants, only a couple of potted palm trees and a few smaller plants in an artful display. The space was mostly empty but for a white, cast-iron garden group. We took seats there. It was not comfortable.

"I'll bring in tea," Mrs Hayling said, disappearing in the adjoining kitchen.

It was chilly, the conservatory not a match for November storms. I would've preferred the morning room, with the French doors to the conservatory closed, but I didn't dare to suggest it. Luckily, Mrs Hayling soon arrived with the tea and poured us fragrant cups.

I concentrated on getting warm while Kane conversed politely with our hostess. I wished they would get to the point so that we could leave for home. And then it hit me—so abruptly that I exclaimed it aloud:

"How are we to get past the tree?"

Mrs Hayling gave me a baffled look for the interruption. "A neighbour will come in the morning to cut it."

"Morning?" I said, upset. Kane looked uncomfortable too. "But … we can't spend the night here."

"You can't drive in this weather either," she stated, as if the matter were decided already. "Don't worry. I have plenty of room. My boys are at school until Christmas."

I turned to Kane with a beseeching look. "Couldn't we try to, you know…" I wiggled my fingers. I knew Mrs Hayling was a mage, but I found myself unable to say the word *spell* aloud with a stranger present.

"You mean the levitation spell?" Kane asked, looking like he was considering it. "We might be able to make it work with the three of us."

Mrs Hayling pulled back and studied me like an odd specimen. "You're a mage too?"

"Yes," I stated, even though I wasn't much of a one. "Could we try it?"

Mrs Hayling shook her head, very decisive. "I won't stand in the rain and storm merely to move a tree, not to mention that it would be very public, even with the storm covering us. Besides, a fallen tree is unpredictable. If it's bent from the roots and not broken, it's like a tense bow, with huge amounts of energy that can do immense damage if it releases uncontrolled."

Kane and I exchanged glances and I nodded, shoulders slumping. I could spend a night here. It wasn't like my boss would miss me at work in the morning. But I wished I had a toothbrush and clean underwear with me.

Since we would be here all night, Mrs Hayling was in no hurry to bring up the reason for our visit. We emptied the teapot discussing modern art—I was too frozen to properly participate, though it was a topic I was an expert in—and it wasn't until we refused a second pot that she rose, and we headed upstairs.

It wasn't quite as sparsely furnished as the ground floor, but it would make Marie Kondo proud. It was also slightly warmer, and I finally began to thaw. Or maybe climbing the stairs had made my blood course faster.

She led us to a library on the first floor, a small room facing the front that actually looked like what it was, though I wouldn't have chosen the unvarnished, thick, birch plywood bookshelves, custom-made to fit the space. I half expected the shelves to contain only pieces of art and antique, but while there were those at artfully random spots, the shelves were mostly filled with books, though nothing as gaudy as paperbacks.

"I want to sell the family collection of grimoires and other books on magic," she said, surprising us both.

"Are you sure?" Kane asked carefully. "They won't fetch much."

She huffed. "Don't be crass. If I need cash, I'll sell something from downstairs through Sotheby's. I have a Francis Bacon my dad bought as new that will easily fetch me ten million pounds. Minimum."

Apparently we'd been wrong in our assumptions. She didn't need money for renovations or paying off her ex-husband.

Kane dipped his head in a small, apologetic bow. "Let's see the books, then."

She crossed the room and gestured in front of one of the shelves. I recognised magic being wielded when I saw it—had witnessed Rupert Barnet, the archmage, cast the same spell—so I wasn't surprised when books appeared on a previously empty shelf.

"All of these," she said, slightly breathless. Maybe she wasn't a strong mage, or it was a straining spell. I got dizzy after trying to levitate a pen, so I couldn't exactly judge.

Kane and I went closer to have a good look. There were six books, old leather-bound prints with gilded letters on the spines, and they looked to be in good condition. I recognised a couple of names from Amber and Giselle's shelves, basic starter opuses from the seventeenth and eighteenth centuries. Apart from their age, they weren't terribly valuable.

Kane didn't look impressed. "Why do you want to sell these? They're not rare or in great demand."

Mrs Hayling sighed. "I'm the last mage of my line. Neither of my sons have shown any signs of being mages, and their children likely won't inherit it either. It's matrilinear, you know. It's straining to keep it a secret, so I want the books out."

I could understand that. "Sometimes it makes an unexpected generation skip," I said. "I inherited it from my father's aunt, which shouldn't have been possible if it were purely matrilinear."

She tilted her head. "It's possible. But if that happens, they can find their own bloody books."

I could've told her it wasn't that easy. Mages held tightly to their books, and since they were a secret, I couldn't simply ask around for available copies. But I held my tongue and pulled out the closest book, skimming it to check its condition.

"I can certainly take these off your hands, but there's no demand for them at the council library in London, and I doubt other councils need them either," Kane said, studying a book as well.

"Maybe Amber could sell them in her shop," I suggested. "She's more likely to have customers who are interested in these than we are."

He pursed his lips. "Hmmm…"

"Or…" I said hesitantly, as a thought formed, "maybe I should buy these myself."

I HAD A GOOD JOB, but I didn't exactly have extra money for an impulse purchase like this. London is an expensive city to live in. Whatever remained after rent and food tended to go to clothes and bags. Moreover, my accounts had recently emptied because I'd needed to pay for the renovation of my previous flat after my flatmate had flooded it. Nick didn't have that kind of money.

But the lack of funds was largely a personal choice. I came from money, and I only had to call my parents and ask for a couple grand for a thing and they'd deposit it in my account. I wouldn't even have to tell them what it was for or pay them back.

I seldom did it though, and not because at my age I should get by with what I made. It wouldn't be free money. My mother especially would expect me to earn it, which would be fine if her ideas for it earning it weren't attending charity functions or—worse—dating someone of their choosing, marrying him, and becoming a good society wife who didn't work or have a life of her own.

The mere thought gave me a rash, but for these books I would be willing to endure it. Now that the idea had taken root, I really, really, really wanted them.

Kane looked surprised, but he nodded. "That would be the best solution. They're a good starter library for any mage. Normally, you would've inherited your great-aunt's books, so these will compensate for that."

It hadn't occurred to me to ask what had happened to her books. Had they been thrown away, stored somewhere, or had some mage salvaged them after her death?

"Would that suit you?" Kane asked Mrs Hayling.

She brushed a hand dismissively. "Absolutely. I don't care who buys them, as long as they end up with a person who knows what to do with them."

Yay!

I held the book in my hand more reverently now, knowing it would be mine. Kane and Mrs Hayling negotiated the price, and while I should've paid attention, both for personal and professional interest, I couldn't quite muster the focus. I kept petting the books like a weirdo.

"Is it fine with you, Phoebe?" Kane asked, claiming my attention.

"Huh?"

He grinned. "The price?"

I had no idea what they'd agreed on. "Umm ... what was the number again?"

"Two thousand for the lot."

It was at the upper edge of what I'd been willing to pay—or what the books were worth—but I could handle it, so I nodded and he smiled.

"Excellent. I'll arrange the transaction through the shop's account and invoice you later—with a commission fee."

There was a glint in his eyes that told me he wasn't entirely serious, but I wasn't about to complain.

Transaction settled, we had dinner that Mrs Hayling cooked. She was a good cook, and we had it in the kitchen, ultramodern but warm enough that I was able to enjoy the food without shivering constantly.

Afterwards, she showed us around the house. I didn't warm up to the cold, minimalistic style that made the place look like a museum instead of a home, but she had some truly excellent art on her walls.

Even the rooms of her two sons, fifteen and thirteen, currently at Eton, were in the same style. Nothing cluttered the surfaces of their desks, every item hidden inside plywood drawers and cabinets. I pulled one open after I retired for the night and saw that the contents were organised to an obsessive perfection.

Mrs Hayling had probably done it the moment her sons had left for school.

Kane had the other son's room, and we shared a bathroom that connected the rooms. Knowing we were only separated by such an intimate space made me incredibly self-conscious. Should I take the opportunity to bring up the kiss? Or would it make the shared bathroom even more awkward?

One would think I'd never had a boyfriend before with the anxiety this situation caused me. But I'd never kissed my boss before. This had too many repercussions if it went wrong.

I strained my ears to detect any movement from the bathroom, but it was quiet, so I opened the door—just as did he from his side.

We stared at each other for a moment, embarrassed. "You go ahead and use it first," Kane said, backing up.

"I actually thought to take a shower to warm up," I said. "If you're not showering, maybe you should go first."

"If you're sure?"

I nodded and backed out. I closed the door and slumped against it. That wasn't awkward at all…

He didn't take long, signalling with a knock on the door on my side as he left. I peeked in to make sure that he was gone and noticed his toiletry bag by the sink. He'd come prepared.

I hadn't. Before I climbed into the tub to take a shower, I washed my knickers quickly and hung them on the radiator in my room. With any luck, I'd have dry underwear tomorrow.

I was halfway through my shower when the electricity abruptly cut, leaving me in the dark. I switched off the shower, wondering what I should do now. If I'd been home, I would've known my way back to my room, but here, with my luck, I'd end up naked in Kane's.

A knock at his side of the door startled me. "Phoebe? Are you covered?"

"Yes. I think. I can't see anything." I couldn't remember where the towel was to wrap it around myself, but the shower curtain was opaque.

"Can you cast the light spell?" He sounded amused.

"No. Or fire, for that matter." I'd only learned four spells so far, and a fire spell wasn't among them, even though I'd constantly lit everything up before.

"I'll bring you a candle."

"Thanks."

The door opened and a small light appeared, silhouetting Kane against the shower curtain. "This should hold you until the electricity returns. You can take it into your room. I can create my own light."

I waited until he left to finish showering, quickly before the hot water ran out. I dried fast and brushed my teeth with the toothpaste by the sink, using my finger. It would have to do.

I took the candle to my room and placed it on the nightstand—plywood—and crawled under the duvet. It was heavy and warm, and for the first time that evening I stopped shivering.

I didn't want to blow off the candle, as I had nothing to light it with again if I needed it later. But fearing I'd burn the house down, I snuffed it anyway.

I was certain I wouldn't be able to sleep. The wind was still heavy and loud, throwing rainwater rapid-fire against the window. But the day had been long, and I dropped off the moment I closed my eyes.

I woke up with a startle, my gut tight. It wasn't dark anymore, but not because the lights had come on. There was a soft glow around the pile of magic books I'd placed on the writing desk, blue and cold.

There was nothing natural about that light, but I was too tense to get out of the bed to investigate, so I pulled the duvet over my head, and after a while fell asleep again.

The storm had ended by the time I woke up in the morning, and the electricity had returned, indicated by the ceiling light I'd forgotten to switch off before going to bed. The books didn't glow anymore, and by the time I'd cleaned myself, dressed, and made my way to the kitchen, I'd forgotten all about my night-time fright.

Four

WE RETURNED TO LONDON LATE in the afternoon. It had taken hours for Mrs Hayling's neighbour to chop the fallen tree and remove large enough pieces for the car to get through. The sky had cleared, and it was a fine November day, but the roads out had been only nominally driveable.

Our hostess had mostly been outdoors after breakfast, examining the extensive damage the storm had caused to her garden and neighbourhood, and then paced the courtyard impatiently, as if wanting us to leave as soon as possible.

I could relate.

Kane and I had spent the morning catching up with work. I'd also called Dad and asked for the money to pay for the books. I hoped he wouldn't tell Mom, but I didn't explicitly tell him not to. The only saving grace was that they didn't live in England anymore, having moved to South France and its warmer climate after Father had a heart attack. Mom couldn't personally come and drag me to a society event.

She could send Aunt Clara though.

I'd face that hurdle if—when—it arrived.

Kane drove the car down the pedestrian court to the shop and we carried our purchases in, excluding my books that I left in the car even though it pained me to part from them. Mrs Walsh, our shop clerk, didn't need to see a pile of spell books. It would cause too many questions I wasn't prepared to answer, and I didn't want to lie to her.

We'd informed her where we were, so she hadn't been worried, and she only gave us a curious look when we entered. She was an elegant woman in her early fifties who always dressed in designer clothes and very high heels to compensate her lack of vertical reach. It still didn't bring her close to my five-seven.

"Did you find anything interesting?"

We placed our purchases on the counter that doubled as a display case. "Snuffboxes and antique compact mirrors."

"That's not much." She knew perfectly what would sell, having worked at the shop before I joined the firm.

"Well, there's an eighteenth-century Hepplewhite side table a client commissioned," I told her, opening the wooden cases one by one for her to see the contents. I even showed the naughty snuffboxes, although those wouldn't go on display, amusing her.

I studied one of the mirrors. "Maybe I should polish these a bit so they will sell better. They've been held in these boxes for who knows how long."

I fetched my laptop from upstairs, and Mrs Walsh and I spent the rest of the day dusting and cataloguing each item. There weren't many customers, and we were able to work in peace.

Mrs Walsh put a couple of snuffboxes and mirrors on display. "It won't do to show them all at once. Leaves room for demand."

Magic by the Book

She would know what worked best.

The job finished, I was about to head upstairs when a customer entered the shop and gave the usual glance around to take everything in at once. He was in his late fifties maybe, with rusty hair and haughty face, and dressed in a tweed suit like a country squire. Many of our clients looked like him.

Since Mrs Walsh was in the back room, I smiled at him. He didn't smile back. "I'm looking for an old book."

My anticipation deflated. "I'm sorry. We don't sell books."

He looked around again, more officious now, as if trying to find the non-existent books. "Are you sure. I was told you have some ... special books."

He put a slight emphasis on special, but I had to shake my head. "Not even rare and expensive ones. But I can point you to the shops that sell them. There are quite a few in Mayfair alone."

His mouth tightened. "I was told this is the right place for the kind of unique book I'm looking for."

"I'm sorry, I don't know what to tell you except that your source is wrong," I said, spreading my arms as if to show I wasn't hiding any either.

Mrs Walsh emerged from the back room and gave me a questioning look, so I explained what the customer wanted. Her professional smile was much better than mine.

"I'm afraid we don't sell books," she repeated what I'd already told, but her tone was firmer. She'd raised three sons, and had the experience of dealing with difficult customers. "But we do have some rare prints. And we received early Georgian snuffboxes today. You'll get the first look."

"No," the man said with a firm slash of his hand. He twirled around and headed out of the door without another word.

Mrs Walsh and I exchanged amused looks, and she went to lock the door. It was time to close the shop. I went to fetch Kane so that he could give me a lift home as he'd promised.

It wasn't until he pulled over outside the House of Magic and I took out the pile of books from the back seat that it occurred to me what the man had meant by "special" books. He must have wanted books about magic. I told Kane about the client.

"It's entirely possible," he said as he followed me into the shop. "Some of those books go through my hands occasionally, but never through the shop's accounts. He should've contacted me directly."

"Maybe he'll do that later."

We entered the shop and I inhaled the scent of herbs and incense sticks that gave the place a unique scent that I'd started to associate with being home. There were no customers, so I marched to the counter at the back and placed the books in front of Amber, who was manning it.

She was in her late thirties, tall and thin, with a head full of red curls. They gave me serious hair envy, especially now that I'd had to cut bangs after burning some of my hair with botched magic. She gave us a wide smile.

"Quite an adventure you two had."

"Not so much an adventure as a brief fright," I said, shuddering as I imagined what would've happened if the tree had fallen on us. "But look what I got for my trouble." I dug out the mirror from my bag and placed it on the pile of books too.

She gave it an amused look. "The books I can understand, but the mirror?" She picked it up and startled.

"You feel it too?" I asked, baffled. "I kind of thought the mirror called me."

Amber opened it, her gaze inwards as if she was trying to sense the magic in the mirror. "I don't know what it is." She shook her head and gave it to Kane, who startled as well.

He hadn't held the mirror before, and he studied it now, turning it around in his delicate fingers. "Is this why you wanted the mirrors?"

"Yes. I thought it was intuition, but if you and Amber can feel it too, it's maybe something else."

I stifled disappointment that it hadn't been something in me that had detected the mirrors, but it had been a childish thought in the first place. The mirror had simply reacted to the magic feeler I sent out.

"Maybe there's a spell on it," Amber suggested.

Kane's eyes narrowed as he considered it. "Could be. But why would anyone spell a mirror?"

"You spelled a pen to track Rupert," I reminded him. "Maybe this is similar."

"Possibly, but those spells dissipate when the person is found."

"Maybe the owner of the mirror was never found."

The thought made me sad. It was a hundred-year-old mirror. If the spell had been tracking the original owner, it would be too late to find them now.

Kane shook his head. "The sense of magic is fairly strong. How long had it been in the collection?"

I took out the sheet of paper from my bag that had the information about the mirror. "Mr Walters added it to his collection less than a year ago, but there's no price so maybe it was a donation."

"Who's the previous owner? Maybe they're a mage."

"Justina Lewis." I gave him and Amber questioning looks, but they both shook their heads.

"Not a name I recognise," Kane said. "But if she's a mage from outside London, I wouldn't."

"It's not like we keep a national register of mages," Amber added. "However, everyone needs to present themselves to the nearest council to be officially granted permission to call themselves a mage and practice magic, so there are lists. Which reminds me, you'll have to start preparing for your presentation, Phoebe."

My stomach tightened into an instant knot. "I do? What do I have to do?"

I'd never met any mages outside our small group, if you didn't count the handful that had tried to attack us in recent months. I had no idea what to expect.

"You need to cast four basic spells to show that you have the skills. You already know those," Amber said. "All you need is to practice your concentration so you don't freeze."

"And you have to be able to cast the four spells back-to-back," Kane added. "It's more straining when you're new."

"I've noticed," I said dryly. But I'd held my shield up against the magical onslaught of a vampire warlock. I could probably handle four basic spells in a row. "How soon do I have to do it?"

"The next council meeting is next Tuesday," Amber said. She was the current leader of the Mages' Council, having been thrust into the position so that Kane could concentrate on becoming archmage, as one person couldn't be both.

My worry intensified. "Isn't that a bit fast?"

She shrugged. "It's not a life-or-death test. Only the simplest spells are allowed."

"Need I remind you that only last week I set everything on fire with my spells?"

Kane grinned. "You've come far since. The levitation spell you showed me yesterday worked beautifully."

It seemed like a week ago that I'd sat anxiously waiting for him. At least I was past that—if I didn't think about the kiss.

KANE COULDN'T STAY for dinner. He had to meet with Rupert for his archmage studies, to learn as many of Rupert's unique spells as possible before Rupert died. He was ancient, so it could happen quite suddenly.

Everyone living in the House of Magic was present, even Ashley, whose shifts as a firefighter kept her away every other day or so, and Luca, who could be out and about more freely now that the sun stayed behind heavy clouds most of the time.

I carried my purchases to the kitchen slash living room on the floor above the shop, too tired to take them two more floors up to my room. Like the entire house, the room was long and narrow, with two bay windows facing the street below. Half of the room was crammed full of Victorian furniture that had come with the house, a wonderfully witchy collection of plump sofas, tasselled lamps, and crocheted doilies.

The other end was a functional, cosy kitchen with a large stove and an oak table that could seat ten. Giselle was at the stove, and the moment she saw me she abandoned her cooking and came over to pull me into a tight hug. She was in her early forties, short and a little plump with pixie-cut grey hair, and her hugs always smelled like freshly baked bread.

"Welcome home. Did you have a ghastly time? I couldn't believe how bad the storm was in the south when I saw the news. We barely had any rain here."

Luca and Ashley were roused from their respective sofas by her concern, though I was sure they'd smelled me enter. Their noses were creepy good.

Luca reached me first and pulled me into a hug too as if I'd been away for days instead of one night. He was only a bit taller than me and tightly muscled, with surfer-blond, messy hair and twinkling green eyes. For a vampire over a hundred years old, he was laidback like a surfer too.

"You smell weird," he declared, stepping aside to let Ashley hug and sniff me too, which wasn't weird at all.

Hugging her was like hugging a wall. She was over six foot tall, with an athletic body and bald-shaven head. She scrunched her regal nose, making her piercings sway.

"Almost wasn't sure it was you who entered."

"Thanks," I said dryly. "I had to wash with a different shampoo last night."

Amber closed the shop for dinner, and we settled down to eat. I told them about my adventure, such as it was, and showed off my purchases. Everyone had to try the mirror, and they all sensed some sort of vibe from it, but no one had anything worthwhile to suggest.

"Maybe we should run some tests with it," Amber suggested. "Maybe it'll tell us something about the caster."

"Maybe you could give it to the council as a gift when you present yourself," Giselle added. "It's customary to give little something curious and inexpensive."

I snatched the mirror and held it close to my chest. "I'm not giving it up. Couldn't I give one of the books?"

They hadn't been exactly inexpensive, but I was already emotionally attached to the mirror, unlike the books. They were in a pile at the empty end of the dining table. Amber tilted her head and read the titles on the spines, her lips pursing. She pulled out the bottom one and skimmed it. "This is curious and clearly unique. It would do for a handsome gift."

I knitted my brows, studying it over the table. Upside down though it was for me, I couldn't recall noticing it before, and I'd purchased the books only yesterday. It was older than the other books, and handwritten. I stared at the pile—and then it hit me.

"There are seven books!" I was met with baffled looks, so I elaborated: "I only bought six. Where did seventh come from?"

Had Mrs Hayling added a book in my pile without me noticing? But why?

"Are you sure you only bought six?" Luca asked. "Those two books at the top are thin. Maybe you mistook them as one?"

I looked at him miffed. "I know what I bought. And I have a receipt to prove it."

"Maybe you took one of Archibald's books from his car by mistake?" Giselle suggested. I couldn't imagine he would keep valuable books in the car, but since it was the only explanation that made sense, I nodded.

"I'll ask him tomorrow."

After dinner, Amber sent Luca to man the shop and I headed to the attic with her, leaving Ashley to help Giselle to clean the kitchen. The attic had been converted to a workspace for Amber and Giselle's magic work. It was an open space that ran through the house from the street side to the back yard, with a polished wooden floor and a slanted ceiling with skylights. Shelves lined the long walls, and at the short end towards the street was a large wooden workbench on which they prepared the ingredients for complicated spells and potions they sold at the shop. I hadn't even begun to learn those.

Amber took a piece of chalk from a shelf where several of them were neatly stacked, and opened a book of diagrams of protective and other kinds of circles that were used in spellwork. She located the one she needed and drew it on the floor with the chalk. It wasn't large, but it was complicated.

"I should probably start learning drawing these things too," I noted, and she nodded.

"Let's get you through the enrolment first. Now, place the mirror in the circle."

I did as she asked, and sat on the floor outside the circle. "How does the spell work?"

She shot me a mischievous grin. "I'm not entirely sure. I haven't tried this before. It's not complicated, but I need you to feed energy to the circle. Do you remember how?"

I nodded, as we'd gone through it many times. She indicated she was ready, and I concentrated on the spark of magic inside me. When I found it, I nodded, and we began to chant the words of gathering magic.

As I did, I sent my magic out, much like when I'd located the mirror in the first place. This time it remained in the circle and didn't go searching for resonating magic.

I kept feeding the energy while Amber chanted in the language of magic, her eyes closed, her concentration unwavering. The mirror began to glow faintly, but other than that, the spell had no effect.

After a while, Amber ended the spell, sighing, and the mirror stopped glowing. "I don't know what it's supposed to do. It doesn't trace anything or anyone. But I think it connects to somewhere or with someone."

That was vague. I took the mirror from the circle, and it zapped me so hard I dropped it on the floor. Luckily not from high up, so it didn't break.

"Maybe it's connected to you," Amber suggested, getting up.

"How could it be? I only got it yesterday."

I got up too and went to fetch a mop. I'd already learned that it was the job of the junior mage to clean up after spells.

"But you searched for it with magic. Maybe the connection formed then," Amber reminded me.

"Maybe. But I'll search for the previous owner to learn more."

"How will you do that when we don't even know if she's a mage?"

I gave her an amused look. "There is this thing called the internet…"

She grinned. "Right. Old-school."

Laughing, we headed back downstairs.

That evening, I arranged the books on the shelf in my room. It was getting crowded. I only had one bookshelf and many books, but I cleared room for them. I didn't shelve the extra book and instead began to skim it.

It was a handwritten workbook bound in leather, and maybe from the sixteenth or seventeenth century, as the paper was made of cotton instead of wood pulp. The pages were filled with diagrams and magical symbols, some of which I recognised but didn't know the meaning of. The handwriting was old enough to make it near impossible to understand the words, as it wasn't in the style used in England at the time.

After struggling for quite a while, I realised it was written in a language that looked completely made up, like cypher. But I didn't get any vibes from it, and it didn't zap me or pulse when I handled it.

I placed the book on the desk to remember to take it with me in the morning, with the compact on it. Antique or not, and even with a darkened mirror, it would stay with me. Satisfied, and more tired than I ought to be, I curled into my bed, happy to be home.

I woke up with a start in the dead of the night, panting and sweating, as if I'd had a fright. I sat up, leaning against my arms until my heart stopped racing. Grizelda, the grey cat who was the queen of the house and went wherever she wanted, jumped off the bed, indignant for being disturbed.

I ignored her. Something had woken me up. I looked around and my heart jumped.

The book on my desk was glowing cold blue again.

Five

GRIZELDA HAD FROZEN IN THE middle of the floor, and she was staring at the book like she'd sheen a ghost. Her back was arched, her fur stood up, backlit by the blue glow, and her tail was double the normal size. She was hissing.

This couldn't be good.

Confident that she would defend me should anything untoward happen, I threw the duvet aside and rose from the bed. I crept to the desk as silently as possible, as if the book could sense my approach, and peered at it.

It was definitely the workbook that was glowing, and it had wrapped the mirror in the blue light too. It didn't make any noise, hum like electricity or something, and it didn't smell like anything. I didn't sense anything evil or nefarious.

I didn't dare to touch the book though—or the mirror for that matter. I'd already been cursed twice; I didn't need another go. But I needed to investigate.

I reached inside me for the spark of magic, struggling to concentrate as my heart was beating too fast. I sent it at the book and felt a familiar pulse as the mirror responded. But the book might as well have not existed for all I sensed from it.

I couldn't understand it. Surely a self-glowing book about magic would be full of magic. There should've been some kind of response, like from the mirror.

Baffled, I fetched my phone from the nightstand and took a couple of photos. The phone's camera had trouble focusing on the book in the dark and the pictures came out blurry, but at least the glow was visible.

Satisfied that I had proof of the odd phenomena, I reached for the lamp on my desk and switched it on. Warm yellow light filled the desk—and the book stopped glowing. Interesting.

I switched off the lamp, but the book didn't begin to glow again. I waited for a while, in case it needed a moment, but nothing happened. Disappointed, I returned to the bed.

Griselda joined me, calm now that the light was gone, but she was restless the rest of the night, and her search for a perfect sleeping spot kept waking me up. Every time I did, I checked the book, but it didn't glow anymore.

"I discovered something odd about the workbook that may or may not belong to Kane," I said to Amber and Giselle the next morning when I came down for breakfast. I held the book in front of me, showing it to them. "It glows in the dark!"

They gave me baffled looks over the rims of their teacups. "You mean it's phosphorescent?" Amber asked, putting her cup down and reaching for the book.

"I don't know. I thought it was magic, but maybe it's something natural. That would explain why it didn't respond to magic."

Heads pressed together, the women studied the book. "Leather isn't usually phosphorescent," Giselle noted.

"Maybe it's coated with something that is?" Amber suggested. She lifted the book to her nose and took a sniff. "Smells like leather to me."

Ashley came downstairs and heard the comment. She gave them an amused look. "Are you doing scent testing? With your noses?"

Amber gave the book to her and she began to meticulously sniff it. "What am I trying to detect?"

"Whether it's coated with something that'll make it glow in the dark," I explained, opening the photos I'd taken on my phone. I showed them around, and blurry though they were, they proved I wasn't making it up.

"That doesn't look like it's photoluminescent," Giselle said. "It's dark, and the light warps at the top."

"That's my mirror. The light spread over it too." I inhaled as I remembered: "And the night before last, the entire pile of books glowed, but the rest of them were on the shelf last night and didn't glow." Had the book been in the pile already then? In that case, it couldn't belong to Kane.

Amber shook her head, baffled. "I've never encountered anything like this. You'd best show it to Archibald. And maybe Rupert too."

"It doesn't smell of any chemicals or anything manufactured," Ashley said, finishing her olfactory inspection. "Only leather and people who have touched it. Maybe a hint of mould, but not so much that it would make it glow."

"It didn't feel evil or anything, really, when I poked it with magic," I told them. "And it stopped glowing and didn't start again when I switched the light on."

"Doesn't mean magic isn't involved," Amber stated. "Especially since it's a book about magic. Does it have the name of the author?"

I opened the front pages. "No. It's a workbook, someone's notes on magic in a weird language. And it's old."

"Every mage keeps those. Even I do. Hundreds of such books exist," Giselle said, sighing. "It'll be impossible to find the author, even if he's someone from London."

"Didn't you say mages are registered?" I asked Amber, who nodded.

"There isn't a national register, but each council keeps track of their own. Those registers go back for ... I don't even know how far."

The antiquarian in me was instantly intrigued. "What would be the chance of ever getting to study them?"

She smiled. "Since I am the leader of the council, fairly good, but you need to be looking for something specific."

I didn't have anything specific yet, but that might change in the future. It was good to have that option.

I was more coherent and alert heading to work than on Monday, and arrived at the usual time. I had all the morning chores finished and Kane's tea brewing when he arrived.

His smile was warm. "Good morning, Phoebe. Have you recovered from our trip?"

"Yes, but there's been an interesting development." I got up and followed him to his office with the book. "Is this yours by any chance?"

I gave him the book and he studied it, curious. "No. I don't think I've seen it before. Where did you get it?"

"It was in the pile of books I bought from Mrs Hayling."

He frowned. "I would remember if there had been a handwritten workbook among them. This is much more valuable than the other books put together."

"That's not even the oddest thing about it." I told him about the glow and showed him the photos. While he studied them, I poured him his tea. I placed it on his desk, where it grew cold as he pondered the photos and studied the book.

"I'm stymied," Kane said, giving the phone back. "I've never encountered the language. It must be the mage's own invention, maybe to keep their studies a secret. It looks like an alchemy study. I recognise some of the symbols. Alchemists were notoriously secretive as they didn't want anyone else to figure out how to turn lead into gold. Maybe the glow is a residue of his experiments."

I had a sudden urge to scrub my hands clean. "Could it have remained all these centuries?"

"Probably not," he admitted.

"Amber suggested we take it to Rupert."

He nodded. "I think it's wise. In the meanwhile, I'll call Mrs Hayling and ask her where the book came from."

But Mrs Hayling didn't answer the phone, and didn't the whole day. The mystery of the book kept bothering me as I went about handling my actual job, but there was nothing I could do about it. Eventually I had to settle for waiting until the evening and Rupert's expertise.

Besides, there was the mystery of the mirror to solve too. Justina Lewis, the previous owner, proved to be elusive. I couldn't find any traces of her online, and she had no social media presence. I was stymied, too, for a moment, until I realised that just because the purchase of the mirror had been recent, it didn't mean it had belonged to a person who was young or even alive.

The mirror was likely originally purchased by, or for, someone who had been grown-up enough to own such a mirror during the 20s when it was made. It probably hadn't been Justina herself though, as that would've made her around a hundred and twenty at the time Walters Senior acquired the mirror from her.

Luckily, *The Argus*, the local paper in Brighton, published death notices online. I didn't have to search long. Justina Margaret Lewis, eighty-eight, had died about six months after Walters got the mirror. Since they'd been roughly the same age—there was the death notice for Walters Senior too—they might have been old friends.

Miss Lewis had been unmarried and childless, and her estate had gone to a charity. It seemed like a dead end. There was no one I could ask if she'd been a mage. But I wasn't about to give up. Maybe the mirror had been spelled from the start. Perhaps finding who had made it would lead me to something.

"ARE YOU READY FOR lunch?" Kane's voice roused me from my research. He seldom asked me, and I was briefly flustered. But we were in a new phase in our relationship, whatever it meant, so I nodded.

"I am, but I need to run an errand while I'm out."

He lifted his brows in polite inquiry. "May I join you?"

"It's a silversmith in Mayfair that maybe made my mirror."

He smiled. "Sounds interesting. Lead the way."

Everything in Mayfair was at a walking distance from our shop, and since the weather was fairly nice—meaning it wasn't raining, though the day was grey—we set out on

Magic by the Book

foot. I was wearing a scarf and gloves today so I wouldn't freeze, and walking was faster than trying to catch a cab. I spent the walk telling Kane about my research so far.

He nodded when I finished. "If Walters' collection weren't in such a chaos, it might be worth checking if Miss Lewis sold him other items, and if those are touched by magic too."

"I would give my left arm to get a chance to go through his collection," I said, making him laugh.

"No need for such drastic measures. Other opportunities will rise."

Foster & Son was located on New Bond Street, about a ten-minute walk from our shop. It was an elegant, two-window shop in a late eighteenth-century building in a district of several other gold and silversmith shops. The shop's façade was polished, dark grey marble, with the name of the shop debossed on it in large gold letters.

I half expected the shop to be open by appointment only, but the door opened when Kane pushed it. Inside, it looked like all high-end jewellery stores—and much like our store—with hardwood and glass display cases, and a polished hardwood floor. Only the extra cameras and a guard in a dark suit in one corner indicated that the wares they sold here were more desirable to customers and thieves alike than ours.

Foster & Son may have started as a silversmith, but judging by the contents in the glass cases, they now sold high quality diamond and other precious stones jewellery, like necklaces that cost more than my decade's pay, and engagement rings that would make all my girlfriends envious.

An elegant woman in a wine-red suit appeared from the back room and smiled politely from behind the desk that blocked access to the back. She gave Kane a brief once-over and judged him affluent enough, because her smile widened a little.

"Good afternoon. How may I help you?" She addressed Kane, which annoyed me so much that I stepped to the desk and placed the mirror on it with a large, decisive move. My smile was forced but polite—I hoped.

"I'm trying to trace the provenance of this mirror. It may have been made here in the 1920s."

Her smile froze and she eyed the mirror like it was something unsavoury a dog had dragged in. "We don't sell trinkets here."

I turned the mirror around and showed the engraving at the bottom. "It says Foster & Son."

"Let me get Mr Harbour." She disappeared into the back room, and a moment later a man in his early sixties arrived. He looked more delighted by our presence than the woman.

"You wanted to trace an old item?"

I smiled more naturally now, and showed him the mirror. "Is this the Foster & Son that made and sold this mirror about a century ago?"

"Yes and no," he said, without even looking at the mirror. "The original silversmith stopped operating after the Second World War when the elder Mr Foster retired. But the firm was revived a decade later by his daughter and her husband. They kept the original name."

"And the records?" Kane asked, leaning his hip at the desk next to me.

"We have them all. If I could study the mirror? I'll go check the records."

Magic by the Book

I gave it to him, and judging by the lack of reaction it didn't zap him, so he wasn't a mage. I felt oddly anxious when he disappeared into the back room with it, as if I'd never see it again. I passed the time studying the contents of the cases, but while they were all pretty and definitely expensive, I wasn't impressed. Nothing was unique, and most of it was either factory-made or by a luxury brand.

"Nothing like the mirror," Kane noted too.

"Handcraft isn't valued anymore," I said with a sigh. I preferred antiques partially for that reason. I could always trust that the items we sold had been lovingly manufactured by a skilled master.

"May I interest you in anything while you wait?" the woman asked. She gestured at the array of diamond rings in the most prominent display, where customers couldn't fail to notice them.

Kane and I glanced at each other, and stepped apart as if on cue. Our reaction was so funny that I couldn't help laughing, and Kane grinned too.

"No thank you," he said politely to the woman. "As an antiques dealer, I prefer jewellery with more history and character."

His response made my chest warm. We had that in common at least.

Mr Harbour arrived before things got more awkward. "I'm sorry it took so long, but the old registers aren't digitalised. And you're in absolute luck. It turns out the item originally belonged to old Mr Foster's daughter, the same whose family later continued this company. The father made it for her as a confirmation present in 1923. May I ask where you got it?"

"I purchased it from an antiques dealer, who bought it from one Justina Lewis, in Brighton."

He pulled straight. "That's marvellous. Mr Foster's daughter married Frederick Lewis. Justina was their daughter. The mirror has been in the family all this time."

For an antiques dealer, a provenance like that was golden. "Does the Lewis family still own this firm?"

"No, Justina and her sister sold it in the 80s when their brother who had run the shop passed away without children, and no one in the extended family was interested in continuing. The shop wasn't doing very well in those days."

Another dead end. I was ready to give up. But Kane wasn't. "Are there any Fosters or Lewises left?"

Mr Harbour pursed his lips, searching his memory. "Justina's sister or her progeny might be around. She married a man named … Mercer, I believe. Maybe you can track them somehow."

"Thank you, we will," I said warmly, taking the mirror and turning to exit. Kane took a beat to follow, and he was tense even after we were out of the shop.

"The name meant something to you?" I hazarded a guess when he kept silent as we headed to a pub offering lunch in the nearby corner.

"Of course it did, and it should mean something to you as well."

I was denser than normally, because it took me a moment. "Mercer, as in Danielle? Your ex-wife?"

"Yes. It's not a common name among mages. Justina Lewis's sister must be Danielle's grandmother."

I gave it a thought: "So the odds that Justina Lewis was a mage are pretty good."

"Yes. Danielle comes from a strong line of mages, and her grandmother, most likely Justina's sister, definitely is a mage."

"So maybe one of them put the spell on the mirror. Amber couldn't tell what it was or did, but maybe it's been there from the start. Maybe there's someone alive who could tell us more."

Kane groaned as we entered the pub. "Fine ... I'll call Danielle's father."

I felt a bit bad for forcing him to contact his ex-father-in-law, but I really wanted to know. I was carrying around a spelled item, and I didn't want any surprises from it.

Kane was able to contact Danielle's father later that afternoon after we'd returned to the office. "We're in luck. Danielle's grandmother is still alive and isn't suffering from dementia. Maybe she knows about the spell."

I smiled gratefully. "Thank you for indulging me. I know it's not an important matter, but I really want to know all about the mirror."

His smile was warm in return. "Of course you do. Unfortunately, we can't visit her today. She lives in a retirement home, and Danielle's father wants to come with us when we visit. We'd best concentrate on your other mystery purchase, the glowing book."

So, after work, he drove us to Rupert's. Rupert Barnet, the archmage of London, lived in one half of a grand Victorian villa in Highbury Crescent, a few miles north of the shop. But we ran out of luck there too, because he absolutely refused to see us or even let us in so that we could do research in his library.

"He's too tired," his housekeeper, Mrs Turner, said apologetically, barring the door.

Kane rubbed his face with both hands, but let the matter be. Rupert was old and eccentric. "Tell him we'll be back tomorrow with an intriguing mystery. That should cheer him up."

I felt slightly dissatisfied and restless the whole evening. My research on the mirror hadn't really led to any breakthroughs, and we were no closer to figuring out where the book had come from or why it glowed.

"Maybe you should leave it in our bedroom tonight," Amber suggested. "Maybe it'll wake us up with its glow too, and we can try to study it closer."

Since I didn't want to be woken up by it again, I agreed. She drew a containment circle on their bedroom floor and placed the book inside it. "That should hold it, if it's up to no good."

"But what if it prevents it from glowing?" I asked. But she shrugged.

"That's a result too."

Satisfied, I headed to bed, certain that I would have a good night's sleep for a change. But an insistent beeping woke me what felt like only an hour later. I fumbled for my phone to shut it off and saw it was one in the morning. Then I read the automated message sent by the antique shop's security system and was instantly wide awake.

Someone was breaking in.

Six

LUCA AND ASHLEY WERE WATCHING TV in the living room when I rushed down the stairs five minutes later. Luca usually closed the shop at midnight and then, naturally nocturnal, spent the rest of the night either playing pro poker or night trading. Ashley kept him company when she couldn't sleep, or if she was on call.

They abandoned Netflix and rose from their sofas when I emerged into the short hallway that separated the stairs from the rest of the floor. I'd pulled on leggings and a hoodie over my nightclothes, and I paused for long enough to pull on my wellies and grab a coat from a rack where we kept our outdoor clothes.

"Where's the fire?" Ashley asked, concerned, crossing the room to me with Luca.

"Someone broke into the antique shop," I said, dashing down the stairs—a bit risky in the wellies, but I hadn't had time to lace my trainers.

"We'll take my car," she said, speaking so close to me that I startled and almost tripped. She could move incredibly fast and silently. Luckily she had fast reflexes too, and she steadied me before I plunged face-first the rest of the way.

I didn't waste breath arguing or thanking her. I didn't have a car, and without her help I would've needed to call a cab. Well, I could've borrowed Amber's car, but in my mad dash down I hadn't remembered to take the key from the bowl in the hallway.

At the foot of the stairs, I had to wait for Luca to switch the alarm off and back on after we'd exited through the back door. Then we filed into Ashley's large Land Rover and she sped off down the quiet streets as fast as she dared.

I was glad she was behind the wheel. She knew how to handle a large vehicle at high speeds, and she was calm and composed in emergencies. I was a nervous wreck. I kept trying to call Kane, but he didn't answer. Either he had the phone on silent, or he was already on his way to the shop and had left his phone at home.

There wasn't any traffic and Ashley made the five kilometres from Clerkenwell to Mayfair in under ten minutes, having ignored all the traffic lights and speed limits. I could only hope there hadn't been any speed cameras monitoring the route.

She drove down the pedestrian court straight to the shop. Two other cars were already there, Kane's Jag and a black Audi with the logo of a security firm on its doors. Kane was by the door, and a man even bigger than Ashley had just exited the other car.

I opened the car door to dash out, and she stiffened. "Shit."

I gave her a baffled look. "What?"

"That bloke is a wolf. He belongs to a different pack than me, and our packs aren't friendly."

I could barely discern his face in the dimly lit court. "You can tell?"

"I can smell."

Of course.

"Will it cause trouble?"

"Not unless he does."

She exited the car and the strange wolf's attention was instantly on her, his body tensing and his eyes glowing eerily in the dark. She ignored his reaction and covered the distance to the shop's side door in confident strides, pausing outside his reach to assess him with calm arrogance.

He was a couple of inches taller than her, around six-three, wide-shouldered and tightly muscled in black cargoes and a long-sleeved T-shirt with the company logo on it. He seemed to be a few years older than her, mid to late thirties, but it was difficult to say for sure, as his hair—lush at the top, cropped at the sides—and neatly trimmed full beard were silver-grey. His features were strong, with a large Roman nose and grey brows, but I couldn't say anything about the colour of his eyes because they were still glowing.

Luca and I paused behind Ashley's back, wary of having the strange wolf's attention on us. Vampires and werewolves didn't get along at the best of times, and my reaction was primal. I'd only ever met one other werewolf than Ashley, her brother Ronnie, who had been laidback compared to this guy—and he hadn't really been laidback at all.

If Kane noticed the tension, he ignored it as he turned to greet us. He was wearing black sweatpants and shirt, with a parka thrown over it to block the chill of the November night. His hair was endearingly messy.

He smiled at me. "I see you brought the cavalry."

"They kind of brought me. Is the burglar still inside?"

"No," the wolves and Luca said simultaneously, startling Kane and me.

"We can smell them entering and exiting," Luca clarified.

"They're not far. Luca and I will follow the trace," Ashley declared, making the other wolf growl.

"I'm in charge here," he stated, his upper lip curling like he was snarling. His voice was low and gravelly, but that could be because of the growl that reverberated in his chest.

"Absolutely," Ashley said, but not like she was backing off an inch. "You'll stay here and secure the crime scene. We'll chase the burglar."

She didn't wait for his reaction, but took Luca by the arm and dragged him to the door, where they spent a moment sniffing around. Then, in a few economical moves, she stripped, unheeding of us watching or the cold. She crouched, and before my unbelieving eyes, shifted into a wolf.

I'd never witnessed it before, and I hadn't known what to expect. Pain, maybe. But it was almost instantaneous, a brief, bright flash and there was a large grey wolf where the woman had been, shaking her fur to settle it. She sniffed around a little more, and then the wolf and the vampire were running side by side down the pedestrian court towards Oxford Street, the wolf with her nose pressed down.

The strange wolf didn't stop growling until they were out of sight and scent. Then he shook himself, as if casting the unpleasant encounter aside, and gave Kane a sharp nod.

"Marcus Grady, Grady Security. Let's switch off that alarm." He sounded calmer now that Ashley wasn't here, but the voice was still deep.

He didn't seem quite as intimidating anymore, so I ventured past him to collect Ashley's clothes and put them in her car. He pulled on vinyl gloves but didn't immediately open the door that was slightly ajar. Kane and I stood side by side, watching as he sniffed the door like Ashley and Luca had done. Only after he was done did he push the door open, careful not to touch the handle.

"Can you tell us anything about the burglar?" Kane asked as Grady entered the code that switched off the blinking light.

"Human. Male, judging by the aftershave. A mage, I'd say. I can smell magic. Probably used it to unlock the door, because there are no signs of a break-in."

Kane's brows furrowed. "And to unravel my wards too, because he wouldn't have got beyond the threshold otherwise."

"Do you want me to call the police?" Grady asked.

"Let's see if he's stolen anything that I need to claim insurance for. Otherwise it'll be difficult to explain how he got in without making us seem incompetent or like accomplices."

Kane switched on the lights in the shop and we entered through the connecting door. Everything seemed to be in order. Nothing was broken, there was no mess of things thrown on the floor, and nothing was so obviously missing that I would've spotted it right away. Grady went through the shop, sniffing everything.

"The burglar has definitely been here, opening every cupboard."

"He was looking for something specific," Kane noted.

"But what?" I asked, baffled. "We don't sell magic items. What sort of antique could possibly be so interesting that it would lure a mage to steal it?"

"Whatever it was, it had to be small enough for him to flee with it on foot before we got here," Grady said.

Kane nodded. "Or he didn't find it."

We went through the backroom and the storage, but while most of cabinets' doors had been left open, their contents hadn't been disturbed.

"I don't think we have to call the police," Kane noted after we'd gone through the ground floor. "Nothing's been broken and nothing's stolen."

"What about the safe upstairs?" I asked. "Or the computers there?"

Grady headed up before us, but halted on the landing at the top. "He didn't come here. No scent traces." He switched on the light, peeked into the office lobby and shook his head. "Nothing's been disturbed. Computer's still there."

Kane climbed to the door too and traced with his hand. "My wards are undisturbed."

"Maybe he didn't realise upstairs has its separate alarm, and triggered it when he tried to go up, forcing him to flee," I suggested. Grady nodded, descending the stairs.

"It would explain how he'd managed to go through the entire shop before we got here. He'd only disabled the alarm to the shop." He studied the alarm system. "I could take the fingerprints on this and the door. I have the kit in my car, in case you change your mind about the police."

We exited the shop as Ashley and Luca returned, she still in wolf form. Grady growled instantly, and the wolf halted, Luca next to her, his hand on her back as if to hold her in case she decided to attack. She didn't look aggressive though. She looked arrogant, insofar as a wolf could.

"It's not polite to growl at my friends," I said to Grady, not even knowing how I had the courage to scold him. He shot me an incredulous look, as if not believing I'd spoken either.

"I'm sorry?"

I fought to meet his gaze, but it was a struggle. His eyes—grey, I'd noticed in the shop—flashed the eerie light again and I all but whimpered. Ashley growled, and Kane placed a hand on my shoulder. Encouraged by them, I pulled up straight.

"You heard me. I don't care what sort of power struggle you have going on here. You're being rude. Ashley and Luca are here to help."

"I am the alpha of the most powerful pack in London. She should heed me and fear me. And you should know your place."

That sounded impressive, but I couldn't back down now. "When you singlehandedly kill a hellhound to save me, I'll be as impressed with you as I am with Ashley. Until then, please, behave."

I had the satisfaction of seeing him look stunned before I marched over to Luca and Ashley. Turning my back to Grady probably wasn't wise. My spine tightened in fear, and the hairs on the back of my neck stood up for anticipating teeth to sink in, but he remained put.

"Did you find the burglar?" I asked them.

Luca shook his head, but his attention remained on the alpha. "No, he got in a car at the Marble Arch, after having led us through half of Mayfair, all the way to Grosvenor Square."

I ran the route in my head. I'd never taken such a bizarre detour to Marble Arch, as it was less than a kilometre straight down Oxford Street from the shop, but I estimated it was about fifteen minutes at a regular walking speed. With their supernatural speed, even the detour slowing them, they'd made it there and back in twenty.

"The burglar was running?"

"Most likely all the way there."

"So someone fit," Kane concluded. He should know; he ran five kilometres a day, occasionally ten.

"Still, the detour was really odd," Luca noted. "If he was in a hurry to flee, why didn't he head straight to his car?"

"Maybe he doesn't know London well and simply ran in a random direction first," I suggested. "A Londoner would've parked the car closer to the shop too." At that time of night, there was plenty of space.

"So, a fit non-Londoner mage. Is that who we're looking for?" Grady asked. Kane nodded at him.

"Closest we can guess anyway. Is there any way we can access traffic cameras to see what kind of car he got into?"

Grady sneered. "There is indeed."

Probably illegally, but I wasn't about to complain. Luca had all sorts of accesses that he wasn't supposed to have as well. They'd come in handy a few times.

Grady got into his car and tapped a tablet attached to the console for a few minutes. I took the opportunity to open the back door of Ashley's car so that she could jump in. It would take a while before she would be able to shift back. Until then, it was best she wasn't around to annoy Grady.

"Found it," Grady announced, and we went to look over his shoulder at the tablet.

"This is the only car that's being accessed in the suitable timeframe at the Marble Arch parking lot. The face isn't visible, but he's medium tall with a long, darkish hair. Fairly fit. A man in black. How original." This from a man in black. "The car looks to be a new Volkswagen Arteon. Nice … but I can't make out the number plate."

That was a disappointment.

"Is it an expensive car?" I asked, having never heard of such a car.

He shrugged. "I'd say it's in the upper price range for family cars, with some luxury features. A little under forty grand for the cheapest models."

"That would be yes, then," I said dryly. "So maybe we should add wealthy and unostentatious to our definition?"

"Could be a rental," Luca said. "He'd be a fool to arrive in his own car."

Grady tilted his head like a wolf and ran the footage again. "It's a foreign car. He enters from the left side."

He was right. "So a foreign mage?" I asked, and everyone nodded.

"If only we could figure out what he was looking for," Kane said with a sigh. He rubbed his face. "Let's wrap it up here. I'll set the alarm again and redo my wards." He nodded at Grady. "Thank you for arriving quickly. I hope I won't need your services again."

Grady nodded. "As do I. But if someone does break in, let's hope they're ordinary humans." With that, he closed the door of his car and drove away.

We only waited until Kane had finished his task before getting into ours and driving home. Bed was calling. Again.

I WAS BLEARY-EYED WHEN I shuffled into the kitchen for breakfast the next morning. I wasn't greeted by the usual smell of frying bacon but a baffled Giselle.

"I could have sworn I had two pounds of bacon here," she said, standing in front of the open fridge as if the breakfast meat would materialize if she kept staring long enough.

I blinked, but then my tired brain shifted into gear. "Ashley probably ate it last night. She had to shift."

It took a great deal of energy to shift into a wolf and back, and she tended to consume huge quantities of raw meat when in wolf form—cooked when in human. Giselle usually kept special meats for her during the full moon, but last night she'd had to make do with what she could find.

At least she hadn't had to go out to hunt for her food. That could've caused trouble.

"Ah, that would explain it," Giselle said philosophically, taking a carton of eggs out. "Only scrambled eggs this morning, then."

"Why did she have to shift?" Amber asked. "It was full moon only a few days ago."

I poured myself a cup of coffee and sat down. "There was a break-in at the antiques shop. She and Luca came with me to check the place."

I told them about our night, including the wolf security guy, but it was the description of the burglar that interested them most.

"I do hope you're right and it's not a mage from London," Amber said. "I'd hate to think we harbour thieves in our midst. But if it's a foreigner, he'll be more difficult to identify."

"Are you sure nothing was taken?" Giselle asked, placing a plate of eggs and toast in front of me.

"We'll have to do an inventory with Mrs Walsh today to be sure, but what could a mage possibly want with us?"

Giselle shrugged. "It doesn't have to be a magical item he was after. Maybe he's a career thief that uses his magic to steal. Maybe he was commissioned to steal a special piece of antique."

I wasn't sure that was any better.

"We had an uneventful night," Amber told me, pushing the notebook, which had been in their bedroom all night, across the table to me. "If the book glowed, it didn't wake us up."

I nodded, disappointed. "Pity. It would've been so much better if you'd witnessed it first-hand. I'd best take it with me again. Maybe Rupert will let us in today."

I wasn't holding my breath though.

Kane was already at the office, looking precise and neat like always, when I arrived at my usual time. I had to pause at the threshold to take him in, partly because his unusual presence so early threw me, partly because he looked so handsome and I needed a moment to recover.

We really needed to have a talk about the kiss. If it went well, I wouldn't have to pretend I didn't find him attractive.

Then again, if it didn't go well…

He was going through his desk drawers, and smiled when he spotted me at the door. "Just checking that nothing is missing here. How are you doing?"

"Tired, but not shaken anymore," I said, stepping into his office and heading for the kettle. No need for me to eschew the routines. "We'll do an inventory with Mrs Walsh in the shop. I'll be there if you need me."

It was a slow job to go through everything in the shop. I hadn't realised we had such a large inventory, most of it merely sitting there.

"We should organise an auction and cull this a bit," I said, annoyed, after crossing off yet another eighteenth-century gold pocket watch from the list.

"Londoners won't come for such small items," Mrs Walsh said with a sigh.

"Then we should attend an antiques fair somewhere outside London and sell all this there."

We got slightly side-tracked after that, as we started another list of the items we could take on tour. We hadn't, therefore, made much progress when Kane showed up at the shop around lunchtime.

"Can you manage without Phoebe the rest of the day?" he asked Mrs Walsh. "We need to run an errand."

We both straightened to give him questioning looks. "What errand?" I asked, and he smiled.

"Have you already forgotten about tracking the provenance of your mirror?" I kind of had, but I wouldn't admit it. "I arranged the meeting for this afternoon."

"Great! I'll wrap this up and fetch my things."

When he'd disappeared back upstairs, Mrs Walsh lifted her brows at me. "He didn't look happy about your meeting."

"That's because the meeting includes his ex-father-in-law."

Her eyes grew large, and she looked more sympathetic now. "That would certainly do it. I hope it's worth it."

"You and me both." In more ways than one.

Seven

THAMES DITTON WAS A MEDIEVAL village in the southwest of the Greater London area, on the south side of the Thames from Hampton Court Palace, the home of the Tudor kings. It took about an hour and a half to drive there through midday traffic, and Kane was unusually tense the whole drive.

I let him be. I wouldn't be happy if I had to meet the father of my ex a decade after the divorce either—especially since the reason for the divorce was because Danielle had gone to the dark side, so to speak.

Well, it wasn't even a euphemism.

"Are Danielle's parents ... you know, evil?" I finally hazarded. His grip on the steering wheel tightened.

"No." He sighed, and his tension eased. "It was difficult for them too. I don't know if they've kept in touch since."

This might be a truly awkward reunion, then.

"Did she cut them off or did they cut her?"

He shook his head. "I have no idea. Both, most likely. She did disappear for a long time."

She'd only reappeared in his life in August as part of a plot to take over the Mages' Council from him.

"Do the parents live in London?"

"Sutton." It was a medieval town within the greater London area, not far from where we were going.

"Then why are we meeting at the Mages' Council?"

London mages owned a council house in Thames Ditton, a brown brick Georgian in the middle of the village with a beautiful river view. It housed a large library, some offices, and a council room, spaces for spellwork, and a clubhouse in the basement. For a secret organisation, it was in a rather public place, but the country was full of secret societies, and no one paid them any attention.

Us, I should say. My stomach tightened when I remembered that I would have to enrol next week. I hadn't even practiced my spells.

"Edward's mother, Patricia Mercer, lives in the retirement home next to the council house."

That made more sense. The retirement home was converted from a large redbrick Queen Anne style manor that shared a car park with the council house. It had a vast landscaped garden by the river and expensive apartments for the wealthy, discerning elderly people.

Edward Mercer was already waiting for us at the car park when we arrived. He was a tall and thin man in his early sixties, with Danielle's downturned green eyes and dark brown hair, though his had some grey at the temples and was thinning a bit. He straightened when we exited our car, and his smile was warm when he greeted Kane. Kane had likely been the son-in-law of their dreams.

"Archibald. It's been far too long."

Kane shook his hand. "Edward. I guess I haven't had reason to contact you before."

"So why did you now?" Mr Mercer asked.

Magic by the Book

Kane indicated at me. "My assistant, Miss Thorpe, purchased a mirror that not only connects with your mother's family, but has a spell on it. She wants to know more about it."

Mr Mercer nodded at me. "Sounds interesting," he said politely. "May I see it?"

I dug out the mirror from my bag and gave it to him. Like with every mage, the moment he touched it, his brows shot up. "Definitely interesting. But I've never seen this before."

"It'd belonged to Justina Lewis since the late 1940s," I told him. "She'd only given it to a collector a couple of months before her death."

He looked surprised. "Why get rid of it after all this time?"

"She didn't have heirs. She may have sold everything to him."

"Justina was Mother's sister, but we weren't close. It had something to do with them selling the family business in the 80s, which Mother objected to. I think Aunt Justina donated everything she had to a charity."

He gave the mirror back to me. Then he shot Kane a hesitant look. "Have you ... seen Danielle since ... you know?"

Kane ran fingers through his hair, looking awkward. He couldn't very well tell her father that she'd returned to his life only to try to curse and kill him. I jumped to his aid.

"We've met her a couple of times in recent months. She's not a warlock yet and she's happy with a French mage called Laurent Dufort." He was a warlock, not a mage, but Mr Mercer didn't need to know that.

"She lives in France?"

"Yes," I stated, even though I knew she occasionally spent time in London too, and even had a house here. Laurent could create portals that allowed them to travel anywhere with only a step. And she'd lived here for the past two years, laying low, before messing with our lives. If she hadn't contacted her parents during that time, I didn't want to upset him by telling him about it.

"Good ... good." He was deep in his thoughts for a moment. "Not a warlock yet is ... good."

Not for a lack of trying she wasn't, but I wasn't going to tell him that either.

He gathered himself and straightened. "Well, Mother is waiting."

Mrs Mercer was an old and wrinkled version of Danielle, tall and dainty, if slightly stooped. Her green eyes were still sharp, and her hair in an elegant bob was completely white.

She met us in the common drawing room on the ground floor of the retirement home that faced the garden through French doors. It was a carefully restored and handsomely appointed room, with Chippendale and Hepplewhite furniture, though they were mostly modern copies. If it hadn't been for the lack of thresholds, doors wide enough for wheelchairs, and a retrofitted lift in the lobby, I could've imagined I was in a private home.

Tea had been set out for us, and a server in a maid's uniform poured before leaving discreetly. The residents certainly got their money's worth here.

After some polite conversation about the weather, Mrs Mercer asked to see the mirror. Her eyes lit up when I handed it to her. "I confess, I was sceptical when Edward told me about it, but it's definitely Justina's mirror. Where did you get it?"

"From the estate of an antiques collector named Richard Walters."

"Ah, Richard. I believe Justina and him grew close in their old age. I never met him, more's the pity, but she always spoke fondly of him."

I found that very moving. "Do you think it's possible she sold him other items before her death?"

"Oh no, she didn't sell this, she gave it to him. Otherwise the spell wouldn't work anymore."

I held my breath. "What does it do?"

"It's a ... blessing of sorts. Like Fairy Godmother's gifts in *Sleeping Beauty*. But instead of beauty and grace, or whatever it was they promised, this offers a family's love and connection to them."

"You need magic for that?"

She smiled, wistfully. "Grandfather Foster made two of these mirrors, one for my mother and one for her sister for their confirmation. He's the one who originally put the spell on them. Back then, it was more about keeping the girls from peril, mostly those involving men. After they married, the spells dissolved."

I nodded. I'd been a recipient of such a spell, though more vicious. It had made me repulsive to men. I wasn't surprised more of them existed.

"My aunt didn't have children, so she and Mother gifted their mirrors to Justina and me, at our confirmation. It was after the war, and the world was different. Their brother died in the war, his body never found, and they wanted to ensure we would always be connected with the family, no matter what."

"So they changed the spell?" Kane asked, as intrigued as I was.

"Yes. The same spell bound both mirrors. No matter where we were in the world, as long as we had the mirrors, we'd be connected by them. If something happened to either of us, the mirror would alert the other."

"Did it work?"

She sighed. "I don't know. It was never put to a test, and at any rate, phones were becoming more common, at least in London. It was easier to keep in touch with those—and Justina and I always did."

She looked briefly sad, remembering her recently passed sister. Clearly they hadn't been as estranged as Mr Mercer thought, or death had wiped the past upsets away.

"In due course, I gave my mirror to my daughter Annie and she later to her daughter Eliza. But Eliza isn't a mage, and she couldn't be told about the blessing, such as it was. And it didn't work for her anyway. She was a very troubled girl, had problems with drugs and the police. She sold the mirror for drug money. She's doing better now, but the damage was done."

It upset me more than it should. I hadn't even known there were two mirrors, but now that I did, I wanted to find the other. "So the other mirror can't be found using this one?" I placed a hand on the mirror, where it rested on the table.

Mrs Mercer made a noncommittal gesture. "The magic in this one is still active, so maybe it could."

She was right. The spell should've broken when I bought the mirror. That it hadn't, gave me hope.

"You didn't actually buy it," Kane reminded me when I said it aloud. "I took the mirrors on commission and gave that one to you."

"So the spell didn't break," I said, my heart jumping in delight.

"Then who is it blessing now?" Mr Mercer asked. "Aunt Justina is dead, and the man she gave it to is too. Did it transfer to Miss Thorpe?"

That was a lovely thought. Mrs Mercer smiled. "Possibly, though without its pair connecting you to its bearer, I don't know how it would work."

"Would it be possible to contact your granddaughter and ask if she remembers who she sold the mirror to?" I asked.

"You can certainly ask, but I doubt she remembers. It was twenty years ago."

She sent Edward to fetch her address book from her room, and he soon returned with it. It was an old, thick notebook, with a black wax cover that had worn through use. It held decades worth of addresses, but it opened at the right spot without searching.

There were several old addresses and phone numbers for Eliza, each carefully crossed out when a new one was added. She read the latest one aloud and I added it to my phone. Mine was a more practical method, but it would never have the sense of long life lived that her address book had.

When she was done, the audience was clearly over, but I had to bring up one more thing. "Would you like the mirror back?" I didn't want to part with it, but it had more value for her.

She patted my hand. "Thank you, but I don't need it anymore, and it won't bring my sister back. I hope it gives you as much happiness as it did to her."

If that wasn't the perfect blessing to leave with, nothing was.

"Do you want to contact Eliza right away?" Kane asked when we were driving back to London. The traffic was heavier than on our way out and we weren't going very fast.

I kind of did—the mirrors intrigued both the antiquarian and the mage in me—but we had a more pressing mystery to solve. "Now that I know the spell in the mirror is benign, we need to concentrate on the book. Let's take it to Rupert. Maybe he knows what it is."

His mouth tightened. "I still haven't been able to contact Mrs Hayling to ask how the book ended with us in the first place. She isn't answering her phone or emails, and hasn't called back. I'm starting to worry."

"Maybe I should call her neighbour and ask him to check on her," I suggested. Mrs Hayling hadn't looked like a woman who would have a sudden heart attack, even if she had been rather gaunt, but she was alone in a large house. Maybe she'd climbed on a chair to hang a painting and fallen. An image of her lying on the floor with a broken leg for days made me shudder.

I took out my phone and made a search for the neighbour's number. He answered almost immediately. I explained why I was calling, and he laughed good-naturedly.

"No need to worry, though it's nice of you. She's in Italy for two weeks. Asked me to keep an eye on the house. I doubt she'll answer calls even from her sons."

I thanked him and ending the call, told Kane the news. "What sort of time is this to go to Italy?" he huffed, making me smile.

"She's a recently divorced woman whose children are safely at boarding school. She's free to do whatever she wants. Where else would an art lover travel?"

He dipped his chin in acknowledgement. He usually spent his holidays in art and antiques destinations too. "I can't help thinking that she gave the book to you to get rid of it and fled so that we couldn't demand answers."

"That's one way to look at it…"

And probably the correct one. The book was unnerving. I'd want to be rid of it too—but not before I'd found all its secrets.

"The question is, why couldn't she give it to us openly? It's only occasionally odd. Rest of the time it looks like a perfectly normal workbook."

Kane pursed his lips, thinking. "There has to be something fishy about it that she feared I'd notice. But I have no idea what it could be."

"Maybe it's not the magic. Maybe it's stolen or something."

"Mrs Hayling didn't strike me as a woman who would steal a book and then pass it on to an unsuspecting outsider," he said dryly, giving me a brief glance before the traffic claimed his attention again when the lane suddenly cleared.

I racked my brain for a suitable explanation for Mrs Hayling's behaviour, though I'd pretty much exhausted my imagination already. "Maybe there's a curse on the book that comes into effect every ten years and she wanted to get rid of it before it happens."

His mouth quirked. "That I more readily believe…"

"We'd best hope then that the clock on the curse starts over whenever the book gets a new owner," I said with a grimace. "I've been cursed enough to last a lifetime."

"Maybe you should let me keep the book," he said, giving me a concerned look.

"And let you be cursed? I don't think so."

His smile was warm, and made my insides tingle. "I'm sure I'd be fine. But you're right. We'd best give it to the council and put a protection ward on it so that no one accidentally triggers the curse."

"If it's a curse. I want to find out what it does first. Perhaps it's the key to the greatest magic of all time."

"That would be something else. Pity no one can understand the language it's written in."

"Maybe it's for the best. Everyone would want their hands on it." I could imagine a dark mage or a warlock coming after the book. My experience with them so far didn't lend itself to a hope that they would ask nicely for it.

A corner of Kane's mouth curled with amusement. "Mrs Hayling wanted to get rid of it, so it probably doesn't make anyone all-powerful."

Relief washed over me. I wasn't entirely sure I could trust myself with unlimited power. I'd go to the dark side faster than Danielle.

"I barely know a couple of basic spells, so powerful magic is a little too much to aim at right now," I said. "And I don't know if I can cast even those well enough, but I'd better learn fast. My introduction to the council is already on Tuesday."

"You'll be great." He must have noticed my panic and disbelief, because his smile turned encouraging. "We can go over the spells together this weekend if you like."

I gave him a grateful smile. "I'd love that."

If nothing else, it would allow us to spend time together. And if I could get my adult act together, I might even bring up the kiss.

Yeah, right.

Eight

RUPERT'S DOOR WAS OPENED BY his ancient butler, Jones. He had a first name too, Bertram, but he'd become agitated when I'd asked if I could call him that, now that he was retired. According to him, it wouldn't be "right for him to presume." His words.

Mrs Turner had told me to leave it be. "He won't let me call him Bertram either. He's old school, and I don't think we should force him to change. It would upset him too much."

He wouldn't properly retire either, even though he was close to ninety, had trouble walking, and had recently been attacked by a dark mage, which had hospitalised him. He insisted on helping Mrs Turner, who came up with chores that would make him feel useful but wouldn't exhaust him. Opening the door usually wasn't one of them, because it took him forever to cross the hall.

"He polishes the silver, and crystals I've taken off chandeliers for cleaning. He can do it sitting down and I don't care if it takes him a whole day to polish a fork," Mrs Turner had told us. "And he gets to clean that empty room upstairs next to Rupert's study. I don't know why he thinks it needs so much cleaning, but if it makes him happy, he's welcome to it."

The room wasn't, in fact, empty. It was Rupert's workspace, with shelves lining the walls where he kept all the spell ingredients, magicked invisible when it wasn't in use. But Mrs Turner wasn't a mage, and she couldn't be revealed the room's true purpose, unlike Jones.

Jones' wrinkled face lit up when he recognised Kane. "Master Kane, welcome. Himself will be happy to see you."

Kane didn't question the statement that was more likely based on Jones' wishful thinking than reality. He only smiled and entered the large hall.

"I brought Miss Thorpe with me."

Jones beamed at me. "Welcome. Wonderful to see you, Miss."

"Thank you, Jones. I'm happy to see you in such a good health."

"Himself has been feeding me his potions," he said in a conspiratorial tone. My eyes grew large, thinking of magic potions that would bring back youth, but Kane shook his head behind Jones' back and mouthed "Iron supplements and vitamins" to me.

I was more disappointed than I should be.

"Mrs Turner has supper ready," Jones said, gesturing towards the hallway that led to the back of the house. "She's set the table for you as well."

It was a bit early for supper, but I was surprisingly hungry. The journey to London had taken so long that the afternoon tea was only a distant memory for my stomach.

The dining room was right by the entrance hall, next to the kitchen. It was a smallish room facing the narrow strip of a side garden and the neighbouring villa across it, with dark wainscotting and William Morris wallpaper—original Victorian, like so much in this house. The colours had faded, leaving the walls mostly dusty green, with pale ghosts of oak leaves.

A dark oak table seating ten took most of the space, with a crystal chandelier hanging above it. The spotless glimmer of the crystals revealed that Mrs Turner had advanced here in her task of making the house presentable. It had been in a rather bad condition after years of neglect when Jones had grown too old for handling the cleaning. Neither of the old men had considered changing the arrangement though, until Kane forced them to hire Mrs Turner.

The table was set for three, and Rupert was already seated at the head of the table, wearing his customary smoking jacket of faded red satin. He glowered at us when we entered. "Took you long enough. A fellow might have starved while waiting for you."

He could be anything from eighty to a hundred and ten, if Kane was to be believed, but he looked to be in his sixties. Only a few, faint grey streaks showed in his thick auburn hair, and if he hadn't been furrowing his brows, his wrinkles wouldn't have been visible.

"My apologies, Rupert," Kane said, not pointing out that we hadn't known we were expected to attend dinner. "We were visiting an old friend of yours at Thames Ditton and it took us longer than I expected to return."

His bushy brows shot up. "Oh?"

"Mrs Mercer," Kane told him, taking a seat on his right side. I sat on Rupert's left.

"Ah, Patricia…" A fond look softened Rupert's normally sharp eyes. "You know, if things had gone differently, she would've been Mrs Barnet. But that pesky northern upstart Charles Mercer had to cut in."

Kane stifled a smile. "Mercers are a very old mage family."

"But not in London."

A grave condemnation indeed. But it seemed to indicate he was nearer to ninety than a hundred, if he was the same age as Mrs Mercer.

Mrs Turner entered through the swinging door from the butler's pantry, pushing a service tray from which she lifted dishes onto the table. The scent made my mouth water and stomach growl.

"Eat your fill," she said, before exiting with the tray again.

Rupert began to lift the covers off the dishes, scrunching his nose at everything he saw. "I guess this will do, though it's not what I would've served for guests in the old days."

"Everything looks delicious," I assured him, and he shot me a withering look.

"She's no Mrs Lynn when it comes to culinary delights."

"Few people are up to Giselle's level in everyday home cooking. I'm sure this is lovely."

We filled our plates and dug in. The food was excellent, and it was all I could do to not wolf it down. Although … I'd seen wolves eat and they had very good table manners.

"Why were you visiting Patricia?" Rupert asked.

My mouth was full, so Kane answered him. "Phoebe acquired an antique compact mirror that used to belong to her sister, Justina."

"Ah, Justina … another one that got away."

Rupert was turning out to be quite a ladies' man.

Magic by the Book

"Did you ever marry?" I asked, curious, picking up my bag to take out the mirror. He shook his head.

"Magic has been my mistress, and it's been a demanding one. Maybe if I hadn't become an apprentice to my predecessor as an archmage, I could've devoted more time for a family."

He didn't sound like he regretted his decision, but my hand halted inside my bag, and I didn't dare to look at Kane. We were a long way from starting a family, but perhaps he regretted the kiss and wasn't willing to even consider a relationship, knowing he wouldn't have time for a romance as an archmage.

My hand shook a little as I gave the mirror to Rupert. His brows shot up when the magic zapped him. "Interesting..." He glanced at the butler's pantry, but the door and the service hatch between the rooms were closed. It had to be difficult for him to have a housekeeper who didn't know about magic, but it had been impossible to find one who did.

"I remember these mirrors. The girls were very proud of them. Their grandfather's handiwork. He was famous in his day, and mirrors like these were very coveted even without magic. What does the spell do?"

"It's a blessing that used to connect this mirror to Mrs Mercer's," I explained.

"Used to?"

"Well, we're hoping that a connection still exists, because Mrs Mercer's granddaughter sold the mirror and we're trying to locate it."

"The one that isn't a mage?" I nodded, and he sighed. "Annie should've given it to her son instead. He's a strong mage."

Kane furrowed his brows. "I'm not sure I'm familiar with him."

"You wouldn't be, though he's around Danielle's age," Rupert said with a brush of his hand that almost sent the mirror flying to the floor. "His father took him to Australia when he was little. Left Annie and Eliza here to manage by themselves."

Might explain why Eliza had been a troubled teen.

"I guess giving the mirror to her son wasn't an option for her, then."

"He did return to study in London, and I think he still lives here. What was his name…?" Rupert pressed his head down, deep in thought. "Elias. No, Ellis. But he's not Mercer. Annie took her old name back after divorce…" This time it took a bit longer, but I was still impressed that he could remember it. "Holt. Ellis Holt, that's the name."

Kane shook his head. "I don't recognise it. If he lives in London, he hasn't involved himself in council affairs."

"Danielle wasn't close with her cousins—or any family members—so she wouldn't have spoken of them, but it could be he's kept distance from the council because of her … defection." Rupert sighed. "Mind you, if she'd had a mirror like this, we'd probably have avoided the whole sorry event."

"It offers a blessing, not a miracle," Kane said dryly, making Rupert cackle.

"True. Also, I'm not sure it's a blessing either." He took the mirror again, studying it as if he could read the spell on it.

"What could it be, then?" I asked.

"I'll have to study it to know." He put the mirror down. "Is this why you wanted to see me?"

I shook my head. "I purchased old magic books while we were in Portsmouth, and we got one extra we didn't notice until we were back home. It's in a cipher language and it glows at night."

He straightened, excited. "Now that's an intriguing dilemma. May I see the book?"

I dug it out of my bag and placed it on the table next to his plate. He opened cover, read the title page—and went deathly pale.

"In my study. Now."

GOOD THING I'D ALREADY finished eating, or his sudden departure would've upset me. He stormed out of the dining room and to the stairs across the hall with more vigour than a man his age should. His strength had nothing to do with potions and everything to do with the longevity of archmages.

"We'll be in my study and are not to be disturbed," he announced to Jones, who bowed to Rupert's retreating back already halfway up the stairs.

"Very well, sir. Will you be taking tea there?"

"No time for tea."

Now *that* was properly ominous.

Rupert's study was on the top floor, facing the back garden that was still in glorious colours of the fall. He magicked the door closed and locked it the moment we entered, and with another wave of his hand made the empty-looking bookshelves that lined the room fill with books. It was the same spell Mrs Hayling had used for hiding her books, but unlike her it didn't tax Rupert at all.

"Where did you get this?" Rupert demanded, brandishing the book at us as he took a seat behind his large hardwood desk. It was filled with papers and books now that the spell didn't hide them, all in messy piles.

"We're not entirely sure," Kane said, looking grim. There were no empty chairs, all of them filled with books and papers, so he propped a shoulder against the closest shelf. "Mrs Hayling, a mage from Portsmouth, sold Phoebe six magic primers from the seventeenth and eighteenth centuries, and when we got home, this one was added to them."

"And now she's conveniently disappeared to Italy, and we can't ask her about it," I added.

Rupert shook his head, appalled. "This should not have been in the hands of a random mage."

"What is it?" Kane asked.

Rupert leaned back and crossed his arms over his chest. "The book itself is a perfectly ordinary workbook. Well, it's obviously old and unique and would interest a fellow in your line of business. Easy to sell to non-mage collectors because absolutely no one understands what it's about."

I went to his desk, infinitely curious. "Who wrote it?"

"A crackpot sixteenth century Dutch mage who called himself Contra-Josephus. Contra, as in *against*, though I don't know what he was opposing. The natural order of things, most likely, such as it was understood to be back then. He was an alchemist like so many fellows in those days, mages and humans alike. And like all of them, failed to find a formula for transmuting lead to gold. This book is supposedly his notes about it, but he wrote them in his made-up language so that no one could spy on him. After his death, people believed that he had managed the transmutation, and the book was incredibly sought-after.

A century later, it landed in the hands of an Italian warlock called Giovanni Battisti."

I translated that in my mind as John the Baptist, which was an odd name for a warlock, but his parents probably hadn't realised he'd turn evil. A misnomer if anything was.

He paused and stared at the book with distaste, but he wouldn't open it. "Battisti tried everything in his power to translate the book, and when that failed, summoned help."

"As in demons?" Kane asked, his jaw flexing as he swallowed. Demons often accompanied warlocks, and Kane had had a particularly nasty encounter with one sent by Laurent Dufort back when Danielle first reappeared in his life.

"Yes. One after another when they failed to help, each more powerful than the previous one. Until he summoned one so powerful he couldn't control it."

I stared at him, horrified. "What happened?"

"He managed to keep it inside the summoning circle, although it was a near thing. But he couldn't send it back. He needed to imprison it." He patted the book.

"Since the book was inside the circle with the demon, he made a prison out of it. No one knows the spell he used—likely something to do with warlock death magic—and it hasn't been tried since, as far as I know. All I know is that it worked, and the demon was captured inside the book."

Kane and I stepped back, horrified. "Is it still in there?" he asked.

"Is that why the book glows at night?" I shuddered at the thought. I'd had the book in my bedroom. Would the demon have escaped if I'd touched it when it glowed?

"I don't know," Rupert said. "Battisti hid the book in a secure vault somewhere, and there it should've remained. But that was three and a half centuries ago. Nothing remains secure for so long, and people have been actively searching for it."

"Why would they want the book?" I asked, appalled. He shrugged.

"Summoning demons is a difficult task, even the smallest ones, and you have to be a warlock. But with this, all one needs is to find a way to release it from the book. However, since there haven't been stories of a rampaging demon these past centuries, I'm fairly sure the demon is still in here."

"I'd like to be a hundred percent sure," Kane said dryly. Rupert nodded.

"There is a spell that allows us to peek in without breaking the prison."

Kane shook his head. "That sounds unnecessarily risky."

"You're going to be an archmage," Rupert said with a pointed look. "Risks like this are necessary and will be yours to take. Best you learn them while I'm still around."

Kane didn't look happy about it, but he nodded. I felt queasy. "What if the spell breaks the prison after all?"

"We need two circles, one for the spell and another around it to contain whatever comes out of the book," Kane stated.

Rupert smirked. "You'd best start drawing, then."

"May I help?" I asked Kane, who nodded.

"I need all the help I can get."

Under Rupert's careful supervision, we began to draw the circles on the floor of Rupert's summoning room with chalk, first the circle for the spell and then a large and complicated containment circle around it. I'd never drawn the circles before, but I was good at drawing, and I soon got the hang of the pattern I was creating. But it would've been easier to start with a basic pattern instead of an archmage-level one.

It took us an hour to finish. My back ached and my hand was shaking when it was finally done. Rupert went through everything one more time, before placing the book inside the inner circle.

Kane lit large candles on correct spots in the circle, and Rupert directed me to my place. Kane and I would feed energy to the containment circle.

"Maybe we should call Amber and Giselle to help," Kane said, studying the large pattern on the floor, a small crease between his brows. "I think this needs more energy than the three of us have to give."

Rupert brushed his concern aside. "The peeking spell doesn't need much. And the containment spell won't become active unless the demon tries to escape. We'll be fine."

With this, we began to gather energy into the containment circle. It was starting to become easier for me to chant and channel energy to the circle, though it still left me dizzy.

When the circle was full, Rupert nodded. Then he spoke a small incantation that sounded too simple for the task at hand.

Inside the inner circle, the book rose into the air and glowed blue again. I kept a worried eye on it, my heart so high in my throat I could barely swallow. I did not want to face a powerful demon.

With a thud, the book dropped on its spine and the covers opened against the floor. The pages began to flutter as if someone was skimming the book really fast, and the blue glow intensified. I bit my lip not to whimper aloud.

It stopped and the glow disappeared. I was about to sigh in relief, when a man rose out of the book.

Nine

I SHRIEKED. THE MAN SHRIEKED LOUDER, and flailing his hands, fell backwards, out of the inner circle.

Kane had him immobilised with a spell in an instant, and the man froze into a rather awkward position with his hands bent at the elbows like he was a crow trying to fly.

"Name yourself, demon!" Rupert boomed.

The man blanched, but he couldn't move. I'd seen the demon that had tortured Kane. It had looked like a perfectly normal man wearing tweed, and so did this one. He looked to be in his early fifties, with an average face and light brown, neatly cut hair. He was wearing jeans and a rugby jersey of all things odd.

"I'm not a demon," the man said, his voice rising into a squeak at the end. "I'm Andrew Hayling."

"What sort of name is that for a demon?" Rupert demanded, but I could only stare at the man, astonished.

"As in the ex-husband of Letitia Hayling?"

"Yes," he stated, then twisted his face. "Why can't I move? What is this place? Where am I?"

"We're in London," Kane told him.

"London?" the man who claimed to be Mr Hayling asked incredulously. "What happened? How did I get here?"

Kane and I glanced at each other, wondering what we should tell him. Mr Hayling wasn't a mage, and we couldn't reveal anything to him. Rupert was studying him like an interesting specimen.

"Were you in Portsmouth before?" I asked. Rupert shot me a baffled look.

"Do you know this man?"

"No. But we purchased the book from his wife there."

His eyes narrowed. "Interesting…" He studied Mr Hayling and the book that was still inside the spell circle, his head tilted. "It would seem that for some reason, Mr Hayling was caught inside the book. Question is, how and by whom…?"

"What do you mean, inside the book?" Mr Hayling squealed. He paled. "I … need to sit down."

Rupert nodded at Kane, who released the spell. Mr Hayling dropped on the floor, his legs unable to support him. He sat there, staring at nothing with empty eyes.

I felt bad for him, but I didn't know how to help. I'd only recently learned about magic myself, and it had taken a long time for me to accept it. Mr Hayling had to come to terms with that, as well as the fact that he'd been held captive.

"How long have you been inside the book?" I asked. He blinked at me.

"What day it is?" He looked around. "Why are the leaves yellow?"

"November fifth. Weren't they yellow before?"

He ran a hand down his face. "I can't remember. It's ... hazy." He shook his head. "It's as if it was summer just now, yet I seem to recall that Halloween was on us."

We left him gather his bearings and retreated to Rupert's study. "What should we do with him?" I asked in a low tone. "He's not a mage."

"He isn't?" Rupert asked, baffled. "Well, that certainly complicates things. But I absolutely need to know how he ended up in the book, and if the demon is still there. I say we ask him all the questions we can and then wipe his memory."

Kane furrowed his brows. "Our memory spells are notoriously unreliable."

"It's better than nothing," Rupert countered. "We can't have a human walking about telling stories of being held inside a book."

"Could we ask a vampire to do it?" I suggested.

Rupert's lips curled in distaste, but he nodded. "That would do the trick."

He and Kane headed back to Mr Hayling with a chair, and Kane helped Mr Hayling on it. I called Luca, asking him to come over immediately.

Rupert made a gesture with his hands and sat down in the air that had solidified into an invisible chair. Mr Hayling didn't even react, still stunned, but I was in awe.

"Mr Hayling, I'm Rupert Barnet, the archmage of London. You are in my house, and we believe you were transported here inside this book." He gestured at the tome on the floor. "Do you know how you ended up in it, and what was it like in there?"

Mr Hayling blinked a couple of times. "Is this a prank?"

Rupert's brows knitted, so I hastened to explain. "It may seem so. It certainly did to me only a short time ago. But magic is real, as are mages who are able to manipulate the elements." I pointed at Rupert, who was sitting in his invisible chair. "Your ex-wife is a mage too."

His brows rose, but not like he found it utterly unbelievable. "I've always suspected there's something odd about her. We were married for a long time. One picks up little things that don't seem to make any sense…"

"What's the last thing you remember?" Kane asked.

Mr Hayling pursed his lips, thinking. "Letitia and I are going through a divorce. It's been a long time coming, but I only moved out of the house last week and into a flat in Portsmouth." He shook his head, baffled. "No, that was in August…"

We nodded and he continued: "We don't have a prenup, so I anticipated the settlement negotiations to be difficult. She's the wealthy one, but she's been utterly reluctant to part with a penny."

Her house certainly had looked like she'd hoarded every one of them.

"And then, out of the blue, she showed up at my house with her precious Francis Bacon and told me I'd get it if I signed the divorce papers." He sneered. "It may be worth ten million, but that's only a fraction of what she's worth."

"So you didn't sign?" I asked, remembering that Mrs Hayling still had the Bacon.

"She promised to handle our boys' education too. That's almost a hundred grand a year for the two of them, and there are several years to go. So I agreed. I signed the papers she gave me and then turned to face her..." He frowned. "...and I was suddenly here."

"Was there anything between the two instances? Darkness? Emptiness?" Rupert asked.

"No. Yes..." He shook his head as if dislodging a memory. "It's so distant, like a dream, fading fast. But I ... I have a strong feeling I've lived my life as usual."

"What did you do with the Bacon?" I asked. If he believed he'd been living as usual, he would've acted on it. He frowned, trying to come up with an answer.

"I ... took it to Sotheby's to be evaluated?" He asked it as if he wasn't sure, then nodded resolutely. "I left it there. It's safer there than in my flat that doesn't have any security systems."

Kane and I glanced at each other. "We visited your wife a couple of days ago, and she had the painting on her wall," Kane told him, and he straightened, incensed.

"That's impossible. Sotheby's wouldn't have returned it to her. I have the papers to prove it's mine."

"Except, it never happened," I told him as gently as I could. "You signed the divorce papers and were somehow captured in this book, so your wife took the painting with her and went on with the divorce proceedings. I think you were supposed to be inside the book for the rest of eternity."

Mr Hayling paled. "She wouldn't do that to me."

Except she had. I turned to Kane. "She didn't seem like a strong mage to me. Could she have captured him?"

Kane nodded, his eyes narrowing. "More to the point, no one besides the warlock who originally captured the demon could cast the spell." He addressed Mr Hayling: "Did your wife arrive alone?"

Mr Hayling hesitated. "Before you asked, I would've said yes, but … I think there was a man."

"So we have an unknown mage to deal with," Rupert said, pursing his lips. "One who found the book and knows how the capturing spell works."

"Could he be the original warlock?"

"That would make more sense, though I don't know if even a warlock could live for centuries."

"Vampires can. Last week we defeated a vampire warlock," I told him. He nodded.

"I doubt the spell is anything a mage could cast." He leaned closer to Mr Hayling. "Tell me, was there a demon inside the book?"

"No," the man denied vehemently. He pressed his face into his hands for a moment, breathing deep. "It seems like a dream. But I went about my normal life, until I was here and then it was like only a blink of an eye between the moment I faced Letitia and here."

"Are you hungry?" I asked. His brows shot up.

"No, I just had…" His face crumbled. "No, that was in the dream…"

I addressed Rupert. "Do you think time stood still for him while inside the book?"

"I sincerely doubt the book could've kept him alive otherwise, even for a week."

"And the illusion of life going on is to keep the prisoner from going insane," Kane added. I shuddered.

"It's still a horrible prison."

"It was meant for a demon."

"And we still don't know if the demon is in there," Rupert said, annoyed.

Magic by the Book

"It must be, kept in suspended animation," Kane noted. "And what's worse, no time will have passed from its point of view if it ever gets out. It'll still be furious."

My stomach tightened. "We have to put this book in a safe place."

"Agreed," Kane said. "Meanwhile, what should we do with Mr Hayling?"

"I WANT TO GO HOME," Mr Hayling said. It would've been easiest, as he would be out of our hands, but I shook my head.

"In case you failed to notice, your wife pulled the world's greatest corpseless murder. She might try to kill you again if you show up out of the blue."

His cheeks flushed with anger. "I can't let her get away with it!"

Kane pursed his lips. "He's right. She must answer for this."

"Let's call the police," Mr Hayling stated. Kane cocked a brow.

"And tell them what? That you were locked inside a book for a week?"

Mr Hayling deflated. "Then what can I do?"

"Your wife is currently in Italy anyway, so we have time to make plans." I was relatively certain she intended to come back. Her sons were here after all. "And I'm sorry, but we'll have to wipe your memory of all this."

"You can't do that!" Mr Hayling protested, but was cut off by Luca's arrival.

He took one look at the floor and whistled. "You've been pulling some upper-level shit here."

Rupert glowered at him. "I'm the archmage. Everything I do is upper-level *shit*."

The two were almost the same age, with Luca the older, yet you'd never know it by that exchange.

"So, what do you need me for?"

I gestured at Mr Hayling and introduced him. "He came out of the glowing book. Apparently his wife, or a warlock working for her, imprisoned him inside it. He's lost maybe a week, and has been given a crash-course on the magical side of life."

Luca's brows shot up, his eyes large. "I see…" But he didn't look like he meant it.

"Is there a way to take a peek inside his mind and see who imprisoned him?" Kane asked. Luca scratched the back of his head, thinking.

"I can try, but I might not find anything."

He went to Mr Hayling, who was staring at him suspiciously. Luca didn't ask permission, but wiggled his fingers and the man's eyes glazed over, his mind taken over by Luca. "Let's see…"

He placed fingers on Mr Hayling's temples and closed his eyes. A deep furrow appeared between his brows as he concentrated, and the power of his presence grew stronger. For the first time, I could truly sense his age.

"His last real memory should be of signing divorce papers," Kane told him. "It should have made a strong emotional impact."

"Yes, I can sense it. But there are these other memories after it."

"They're not real. They're created by the book," I told him, and his brows shot up.

"You're right. No scent or taste memories."

"You can detect those?" I asked, curious.

"Those are often very strong memories. But dreams don't create them. And emotions are the strongest." He stared inside Mr Hayling's mind, his eyes closed.

"Signing the divorce papers is definitely a strong memory. And there are scents too. A perfume, likely his wife's as it's so familiar to him, and another scent..." His voice trailed off as he furrowed his brows. "Could be a man."

"Do you see a face?" Kane asked.

"Mr Hayling turns around, and there's a book, open, like being offered to him. His attention is on it. It's held by a man wearing a tan summer suit. I can see his wristwatch. It interested Mr Hayling more than the book. He's lifting his gaze—but he was captured before he saw the face."

We sighed in disappointment. "What about earlier?" I asked. "Did he enter the house with Mrs Hayling?"

Luca took another peek, but shook his head. "Mrs Hayling came in alone. There's some kind of audio memory of her opening the door while Mr Hayling is reading the divorce papers, but he didn't turn to look."

He let go of Mr Hayling's head and opened his eyes. "Should I wipe his memories?"

Rupert nodded. "We can't let him remember us or being in the book."

"But we need to give him something in return," Kane said. "He's lost a week that needs to be explained."

I tensed as a thought occurred: "He's been away from the real world for that long. People would've missed him, unless Mrs Hayling has given them some sort of cover story. She's the first person the police would suspect when he disappeared."

Others nodded, agreeing. I took out my phone and placed a call to Mrs Hayling's neighbour. "Mrs Hayling still isn't home," he said before I'd asked anything, sounding like he was smiling.

"That's fine. I'm trying to reach Mr Hayling. Do you happen to have his contact information?"

"Ah…" He paused awkwardly. "Andrew had some sort of mental breakdown and Letitia had to put him into a sanatorium to rest. He hasn't come home yet."

I blinked a few times to wrap my mind around his news. Then I cleared my throat and thanked him. "I'll have to wait for Mrs Hayling to return, then."

"If it's urgent, you can call Andrew's gallery in Portsmouth. His partner is handling everything while he's gone."

I ended the call and faced the others. "Apparently Mr Hayling is recovering from a mental breakdown in a sanatorium somewhere."

Kane's brows shot up. "That's convenient. No one asks where he is or wants to visit."

"But now we can't exactly take him home, can we," I pointed out. "People will want to know how he is and how was his time in there."

Luca sneered. "Take it from someone who's been alive for quite a long time. No one wants to bring up a mental episode. They'll pretend nothing's happened."

Rupert harrumphed. "You can't take him home. There's a warlock around who knows he's supposed to be in the book. What if he comes after him, fearing he'll recognise him?"

That threw us. "Where do you suggest we take him, then?"

"I don't care, as long as it's not here."

"We need a safe house," Kane said. "But it can't be the council house, because Mr Hayling isn't a mage. Besides, there aren't any sleeping quarters there."

"And he still needs his memory altered to give him some explanation of where he's been that makes sense and is compatible with reality," Luca said. "I'm good with wiping the memories, but if he needs a complex memory alteration, I'll need help."

"You mean ... Hunt?" I asked, shuddering. Morgan Hunt was the most powerful vampire in London, and their unelected leader. Luca and I had spent the previous week helping him to find a murderer, barely escaping with our lives. I'd hoped I'd seen the last of him.

"Yes. And he might have a safe house too."

I rubbed my face, thinking. "We need a story that would explain to Mr Hayling why he needs to be in a safe house."

"One that's close enough to reality that the memory sticks," Luca said.

"He's been abducted," I stated. "He signed the divorce papers, and she and her accomplice sedated him, which is the last thing he remembers, and kept him locked up somewhere, sedated. You won't even need to alter those dream memories. And now he's been rescued, but he needs to stay in a safe-house until the police have captured his wife—currently in Italy—and her accomplice."

Luca nodded, impressed. "Neat story that requires minimum memory alteration. But I'd still be happier if Hunt did it. And we'll need his safe house anyway."

I grimaced. "What are the odds that he would help us without demanding something in return?"

Luca rolled his eyes. "Really good," he said, his voice oozing sarcasm.

"Whatever you promise him, it can't have anything to do with the book," Kane stated. "In fact, it would be best if you didn't even mention the book."

"I'd best remove all his memories of today first," Luca said, turning to Mr Hayling again. When it was done, Rupert stood up.

"Excellent. Now, go away." He made to march away, but Kane halted him.

"What about the book?"

"I don't think any demons will come crawling out of it," Rupert said, waving his hand dismissively. "Take it away."

Shaking his head exasperated, Kane picked up the book. "I'd best take it to the council house."

I nodded at Rupert. "Thank you for your help. Should I clean the floor before we leave?"

He stared at the chalk lines that had begun to fade now that we'd walked all over them. Then he made a gesture with his hand and the floor was clean. A smug look on his face, he left the room, leaving us to follow in dismayed silence.

Ten

WE PARTED WAYS OUTSIDE RUPERT'S house. Kane took the book with him, but decided he wouldn't go to the council house until the next day. "I've been driving enough for today. It'll fit the small safe in my home and I'll put heavy wards on it."

Luca and I manoeuvred Mr Hayling, still under Luca's thrall, into the passenger seat of Amber's small Nissan that Luca had driven here. I climbed in the back seat and Luca sat behind the wheel. Then he just sat there, without starting the engine.

"I really don't want to involve Hunt."

I sighed. "Me either, but what else can we do?"

"How about the wolves? They're bound to have safe houses."

I pursed my lips, giving it a thought. Their safe houses were more likely meant for keeping wolves in during the full moon, but the moon was waning now, and they would be empty. "But why would they help?"

"Maybe Ashley could ask nicely," he suggested, and we both laughed. Then he shook his head. "But I'll still need Hunt for the memory alteration."

"Do you want me to call him?" It was the last thing I wanted to do, but I didn't want Luca to be in Hunt's clutches again. Or deeper in his clutches than he already was.

"No, I'll do it," he said, but didn't move until I poked him on the shoulder. Utterly reluctantly, he pulled out his phone and placed the call. His jaw tightened when the phone connected, and he had to swallow before he could speak.

"Do you by any chance know a vampire who is exceptionally good at creating false memories?"

I was baffled by the question; I'd thought he would ask Hunt directly. But he knew what he was doing, because after a brief conversation he put the phone away and started the car.

"We'll meet him at the club."

Hunt owned several, but I knew instantly which one he meant. It was a gay club in Soho, where less than two weeks ago we'd discovered the dead body of a vampire's victim. Hunt had accused Luca, leaving us no choice but to find the real killer. Successfully, I might add, though not easily.

I filled Luca in on everything about the current mystery as he drove us to the club. The early evening traffic was heavy, so we had time. He was full of questions. "Where did Mrs Hayling get the book, if it's been missing all these centuries?"

"Maybe her accomplice found it, or maybe he's Giovanni Battisti, the original warlock. Where Mrs Hayling found him is another question entirely." Italy, maybe, considering Battisti was Italian and she was currently there.

"Maybe he's her new man," he suggested. "If she divorced Hayling for not being a mage and sold all the magic books because her children aren't either, then maybe she really feels the need to connect with that side of her."

"Could be, but it's a big leap to dating a warlock. I didn't even know there were so many of them around."

He tilted his head in grim acknowledgement. "But why did she give the book to you, if it belongs to the warlock?"

I inhaled sharply, not having come to think of it. It couldn't mean anything good. "I bet the warlock didn't simply give the book to her. What if she stole it from him and left it with us so that he can't find it?"

"But why?"

I spread my arms, searching for answers. "Maybe he threatened to release Mr Hayling?"

"What if he comes after you?"

My heart stopped. "I think he already did. Why else would a mage have broken into the antiques shop?"

He gave me a stunned look over his shoulder, almost ramming the car into the one in front of us, only his vampire reflexes saving us when my horrified screech alerted him. He spoke when he had the car under control again.

"We have another warlock after us…"

With shaking hands, I dug out my phone to warn Kane. He wouldn't answer, and my panic kept rising until I remembered that he couldn't be home yet and wouldn't answer while he was driving. So I wrote him a hasty message, my fingers so dry that the touch screen wouldn't register my attempts and I ended up poking the device with more force than should've been necessary.

I held the phone tight against my chest for the rest of the drive, hoping Kane would call before we met Hunt, but he didn't. "What if the warlock was waiting for him at his home?"

Luca's jaw tightened, but he gave me a reassuring look through the rear-view mirror. "There's no reason to assume he would know where Kane lives. And Kane can't even be home yet, not with this traffic, when he has a longer drive than us."

I wasn't entirely convinced, but we were at the club already, and it wouldn't be prudent to keep Hunt waiting while we went to check on Kane. Luca drove down a narrow alley to the side door of the club, and gave Mr Hayling a command to exit the car and follow us. He moved like a zombie, slow, with jerking steps, but he obeyed Luca.

We entered through the side door that was opened by Ronnie, Ashley's brother, a larger and more muscled version of her who worked as a bouncer. His black brows shot up when he saw the mesmerised man.

"What are you two up to now?"

I resented the implication that we were habitually *up to* something, but he'd met us during the murder investigation, so he knew us only as amateur sleuths.

"We're trying to save him from a warlock and a vicious ex-wife. Do you think we could stash him in one of your safe houses until we have everything sorted out?" I gave him a hopeful look.

"I don't think our safe places are suitable for humans. You'll have to ask the boss."

I grimaced. "That's what I feared."

With a grin, he led us down the hallway to Hunt's office, a small room crammed full of old furniture. It wasn't his main place of business, but we hadn't merited an audience in a more important setting. I didn't mind.

Magic by the Book

Hunt was sitting behind the desk, looking bored as he read something on his phone, ignoring us. He was a tall man with a lean body that looked great in a form-fitting suit. His face was narrow and classically defined, with a Roman nose—handsome, but not overly so. His wavy, dark auburn hair was combed back from his face and reached to the collar of his jacket. And despite looking like a modern businessman in his late thirties, he was over two and a half centuries old, as I'd recently discovered when I'd poked into his past.

He didn't seem frightening—until you felt the power he emanated even when relaxed. Then he became terrifying. My legs began to shake, and I desperately wished I was elsewhere. Would it really be so bad if Mr Hayling told the whole world about mages?

Hunt cocked a bemused brow, and the power eased a little. "I must say, I was half thinking you weren't serious."

"Oh, we're deadly serious," I said, and then wished I hadn't spoken. He would certainly demand a higher price now.

"Let's hear it, then."

My stomach tightened. I didn't want to tell him anything, least of all the truth, but I couldn't lie either, because he could most likely detect it somehow. And he would not take it well. "It's complicated…"

"Then uncomplicate it."

I would have to stick as close to the truth as possible. "This is Mr Hayling, from Portsmouth, a human, but his wife is a mage. They're going through a divorce, and she didn't want to part with her considerable fortune, so she … had him imprisoned."

Hunt pulled back and regarded me down his nose. "How?"

"With magic. I don't know how. Not even Rupert could figure it out. It's a warlock thing, most likely."

It was the truth, so Hunt nodded. "How did you free him, then?"

"By accident. She'd imprisoned him in a piece of antique she gave us, likely hoping we would sell it to an unsuspecting customer so she would be rid of him for good. But the item felt odd, so we took it to Rupert—and Mr Hayling came out."

Both of Hunt's brows shot up. "Just like that?"

"Well, there was a spell involved," I said with a brush of my hand, as if that part wasn't important. "Anyway, since he's human, we had Luca erase his memory of the magic, but it turned out he's been missing for a week. Everyone believes he's recovering from a mental breakdown. We thought we'd give him memories to match, but that wouldn't help us bring his wife to justice."

"And you care about that?"

"Of course," I said indignantly. "From both a mundane and a magical point of view. You can't have people around who can imprison people inside objects."

"Can't you?"

I knew he'd find it an opportunity. "No, you can't. We don't know the spell for one, and it would be a horrible thing to do."

His lip curled into a sneer. "So what kind of memory do you want him to have?"

"One that is as close to the truth as possible, without magical elements. That his wife sedated him with the help of her accomplice, and he's been kept sedated ever since. He was then rescued by private security and whisked to a safe house until his abductors are captured."

"That's a neat little story," he drawled.

I shrugged, though it took an effort to pretend nonchalance. "It's close enough to the truth that it might stick."

"Where exactly did you think to keep Mr Hayling until then?"

"We ... were hoping that you'd know of a safe house where he could be kept?"

"Were you now...?"

He rose sinuously and rounded the desk. I took a step back, wanting more distance between us, even though he'd never physically threatened me. He didn't have to.

He gestured for Luca to seat Mr Hayling on the guest chair and release the enthrallment. A fraction later, he'd taken over the poor man's mind.

I couldn't help feeling for the guy. If it hadn't been for a merest chance, my mind would've been wiped too when I accidentally learned about magic. To have it done to you without consent just felt ... rude.

But vampires had never concerned themselves with consent in anything. "I can see you already erased his knowledge of magic," Hunt said with a pointed look at Luca. He didn't need to keep his eyes closed to see inside Mr Hayling's mind.

"I'm not entirely useless," Luca said, though that wasn't what Hunt had meant. "Look for the moment when he signs the divorce papers."

"There are memories after that point too."

"They're ... fake," I said, and the sharp gaze was directed at me, making me step back.

"Fake?"

I swallowed. "Dreams?"

"The magical prison created false memories for him," Luca explained, coming to my aid. "They don't have any scent or taste traces, and barely any emotions."

"I see…" Hunt was quiet as he concentrated inside Mr Hayling's mind. "And I can see that you've carefully removed the image of the item he was imprisoned in."

I shot a grateful smile at Luca, who looked smug. Too soon. Hunt removed his hands from Mr Hayling's head and faced us.

"Shall we negotiate my price now."

My heart sank, even though I'd known to expect it. "What do you want?"

"Dufort's contact information."

"Absolutely not!" The denial was out before I could consider it. Even if I'd had his information, which I didn't, nothing good would come of putting a powerful vampire together with a warlock.

His brow rose, slowly. "No?"

Suddenly there wasn't enough air in the room. I tucked my scarf but I couldn't back up. "Choose something else."

The air returned and I pulled a deep gulp. He was studying me with cold amusement that I didn't share. "Fine. I want the prison."

Clearly he'd baited me with the first request. "I don't have it."

"But you can get it to me."

I glanced at Luca, who shook his head minutely behind Hunt's back. I bit the inside of my lip to be able to answer. "I can't."

"What good are you to me, then?"

I had no idea. "Please, ask for something that doesn't potentially lead to the destruction of the world."

"When you're as old as me, destruction is pretty much the only thing that amuses anymore…"

I hoped he was joking. He was too powerful to feel that way.

He considered, tapping his lip with a slender finger. "Fine. I want you to be my date to a City function this Sunday."

Air whooshed out of my lungs, and it had nothing to do with his power. I could only stare at him as a slow sneer spread on his face.

"I believe I hit the jackpot. Could it be the little assistant is spoken for? There was that passionate kiss on Saturday…"

He'd seen it? I don't know why it dismayed me so much, other than it gave him fodder to tease me.

Luca inhaled. "Kane kissed you? Why didn't you tell me?"

"It was a spur of a moment thing," I said, desperately. "To celebrate that we're alive…"

"That's not how it looked like to me," Hunt said. "But I take it the good boss hasn't taken it further?"

I cleared my throat, trying to gather myself like an adult. But he'd hit a sore spot and it wasn't easy to admit. "It was only a kiss." And it couldn't be more, because I'd been a chicken and hadn't brought it up with Kane.

"Good. It's settled, then. It's a charity auction. That should interest you. I'll send a car to pick you up at six."

I hadn't agreed to anything, but it was the best of bad options. Didn't mean I'd let him walk all over me.

"To be clear, even if there's nothing going on between Kane and me, there definitely won't be anything with you.

The car picks me up and takes me home, alone, the moment the event ends, if not sooner, and if you try anything funny, we'll learn whether vampires can regrow appendages."

"Define funny." But he must've seen on my face that I meant it because he smiled and bowed. "I'll be a perfect gentleman."

I had no idea what he gained from this deal, but it was infinitely better than providing him with a powerful artefact, so I nodded. A tingle of magic made my skin tighten as he sealed the deal. I wouldn't get out of this one.

"Now to your end of the bargain." I nodded at Mr Hayling, who was still immobile in the chair.

"What was the story again?"

We went through the abduction and sedation story. Then he placed hands on both sides of Mr Hayling's head and concentrated. The pressure in the room began to rise, but I didn't dare to move or complain. Who knew what would happen to poor Mr Hayling's brain if Hunt lost his concentration.

The pressure eased and I could breathe again. Hunt let go of Mr Hayling. "I'll release him now, so be ready to take his mind again," he said to Luca. "Only release him in the safe house. I've planted some chaotic and hazy memories of his rescue."

"Where did you come up with those?" I asked, curious. He shrugged.

"Movies."

As long as it worked.

"Now it's only the matter of finding a safe house," Luca said.

Magic by the Book

"I have something…" Hunt took out a phone and made a call. He didn't negotiate or make a request, so whoever was at the other end was on his payroll. "The company doing my security will look after him. Their guy will come and pick him up."

With that, our audience was over. We weren't willing to prolong it, so Luca gave Mr Hayling a command to get up and follow, and we exited the office. I resisted the need to lean against the door for support when it closed behind us, but my legs were shaky.

"That went well…"

Luca gave me a concerned look. "What will you tell Kane about the date?"

A brief surge of annoyance made me straighten. "If he doesn't want me to go out with other men, he should've talked about the kiss. We've had all week."

But his question made me remember that Kane hadn't answered his phone. I dug out mine, but there weren't messages or missed calls from him. I was starting to be genuinely worried.

"The moment we have Mr Hayling in a safe house, we'll go see him," I said to Luca.

Ronnie opened the alley door at the other end of the hallway and peeked in. "Your ride is here." He didn't sound happy about it.

Curious, we crossed to the door and exited. A large black car was parked behind Amber's Nissan. It had a familiar logo on the side.

"It appears Kane and Hunt use the same security firm," I noted.

"And the same guy," Luca said, nodding at the driver's seat, where Marcus Grady, the silver-haired werewolf, was sitting, looking as annoyed to see us as we were him.

Or it could be Ronnie that irked him.

He exited the car and opened the back door. "Get him in before he's detected."

I doubted the warlock had followed us here, but since the point of a safe house was that no one knew you were there, we obeyed. Ronnie stood by the door, tall and tense, and I could practically feel him growling the whole time.

Grady closed the back door and made to open the driver's, but instead he pivoted to face the mouth of the alley, his lip pulling into a snarl.

I was about to wet myself in fear when a familiar voice greeted us. "What the fuck is going on here?"

Eleven

ASHLEY STALKED DOWN THE ALLEY to us, her black jeans and windbreaker having hidden her in the shadows for those of us with ordinary noses—me—until she was within reach of the light above the door. She stopped a few yards from the car and Grady, her arms tense and shoulders hunched as if ready to ram him. He stood his ground, fists on his hips, growling.

I glanced at Ronnie, alarmed. "Can't you do something?"

He was tense, his gaze never leaving the grandstanding pair. "She can handle herself."

"Doesn't mean she has to," I said, miffed, and before I could reconsider the sense of my actions, I edged past Grady and greeted Ashley. Putting myself between two growling werewolves wasn't the smartest move I'd ever made, but they probably wouldn't attack me.

Probably.

"Hey, Ashley. I thought you'd be at work." Her schedules were odd, and shifts were usually twenty-four hours at a time.

"Have a couple of hours off, will return to work by midnight," she said, her attention on Grady. Mine was too. It was unnerving to stand in front of him, the low rumble in his chest making my neck hairs stand up. "Came to ask my brother if he wanted to go for a bite, only to witness this. What the fuck?"

Her upset made me wince. "It's a long story. Hunt promised us Grady's help. He's taking us to a safe house."

"We have safe houses."

"It's for a human."

She finally moved her attention to me. "What?"

"We need to get going," Grady said behind me. "You can brief her when you get back."

"I'm not letting my friends go anywhere with you alone, Grady."

She didn't wait for a permission but walked to the front passenger door. I sprang into action. Sharing the car with two irate werewolves wasn't my idea of a good time, but it would be infinitely worse if the two were seated side by side.

"I'll take the front seat."

She gave me a slow look but didn't argue, and followed Luca into the back seat. Only when Grady took his seat next to me did it occur to me that this wasn't exactly the best place to be either. Close up, he was almost as frightening as Hunt, but in a more visceral way. He was larger and angrier, and while I sort of trusted Hunt to control himself, I wasn't sure Grady could, or wanted to.

But the only other option was Luca, if we didn't want to move Mr Hayling to the front. A vampire wouldn't be any happier next to Grady, so here I was.

Grady twisted his torso to look out through the rear windscreen as he reversed the car out of the alley, giving me a close view of the contemptuous snarl he gave Ashley. But it was more for form's sake, and he calmed down after he turned to face the street.

"So what are we doing?" Ashley demanded.

It was my turn to face the back seat. "This is Mr Hayling, a human. We're saving him from a warlock."

Grady was instantly alert, which didn't make him any more fun to sit next to.

"How did he piss off a warlock?" Ashley asked.

"It's Mr Hayling's ex-wife's doing. She's a mage. The warlock could be her lover, but he could also simply be someone she paid to lock her husband inside a magic item, which she then gave to us." I didn't want to reveal details in front of Grady, in case he blabbed to Hunt. "The warlock is likely after the item."

"Hunt altered his memories and arranged for a safe house," Luca added.

"In exchange for what?" Ashley understood Hunt well. I grimaced.

"I have to be his date on Sunday."

She pulled back. "What about Kane?"

"That's what I said," Luca exclaimed. "Did you know they kissed?"

Did they all assume there was something going on with me and Kane? I blushed, and it didn't help that Grady shot me an amused glance, as if he could smell my embarrassment. Ashley looked offended.

"And you didn't tell us?"

"There was nothing to tell." I sighed. "I haven't told Kane about the date yet, because he won't answer his phone. The moment we're done with Mr Hayling, I want to go check on him."

"We'll come with you," Ashley promised. "It wouldn't do for another warlock to send a demon after him."

I shuddered, remembering that the book contained a demon too. What if the warlock released it? Or Kane accidentally did it himself?

"This one will be infinitely worse than the previous one you fought with."

Grady gave me an incredulous stare. "You've fought demons?"

"I haven't. She has." I pointed at Ashley, who sneered at him, the look full of smugness. He tilted his head slightly, reluctantly impressed.

Grady drove us sixteen kilometres to Wembley in Northwest London, right next to Wembley Stadium. A brand-new luxury estate of several high-rises with landscaped yards between them stood by the stadium, but not so high you could see into the stadium from the top floors, so you got all the noise and throngs and none of the fun.

Residents' car park was underneath the complex. Grady drove us in. It was a huge space that covered the entire area of the estate, and it was half full of ordinary and more expensive cars. He drove all the way to the other end and pulled over by a lift.

We exited the car and Luca gave Mr Hayling a command to enter the lift. Hayling obeyed in his zombie way, but when it was time for Ashley to enter, she balked.

"I'll stay at the car."

Grady smirked, but didn't say anything as he pressed the button that closed the door on her angry face. It was tense enough in there with one werewolf. Two would've made the small space suffocating.

We rode to the fifteenth floor. I spent the time googling the estate, and learned that a two-bedroom flat here cost over two and a half thousand quid to rent. Not in my price range, even if it came with a concierge and a gym. It wouldn't come with Giselle's cooking.

Hunt had money though, or Grady's security company did. He let us into an open kitchen and living room with a view towards the gardens. The walls and kitchen cabinets were white, and the furniture was from IKEA, but everything looked elegant and new.

A man younger than Grady with russet hair instead of silver, and wearing the same uniform, was waiting by the kitchen isle. He stood to attention when we entered, only to sneer when he smelled Luca. "We're harbouring vampires now?"

So another werewolf. Maybe the company only employed them.

Grady shook his head. "No. Human."

That didn't seem to be any better, judging by the other wolf's disgusted look. Grady ignored him and walked us to the back of the flat and opened a door to a bedroom. It wasn't large, and most of it was taken by a double bed with a red bedspread. A TV was mounted on the wall.

"He can stay here. Bathroom's here." He opened the door across the hall. "There's someone here at all times, providing food and keeping an eye on him."

I nodded. "Thank you. But remember that he's been through a traumatic experience, even if he won't properly remember it, and some of the memories are false. He knows nothing about magic or your kind, so no growling and intimidating him."

He smirked. "We'll try our best."

Luca directed Mr Hayling into the room and sat him on the bed. Then he released the enthrallment. "Mr Hayling? You're safe now."

The man startled, looking around wildly, before calming down a bit. "Thank you, thank you so much. I don't know how to thank you. Was ... anyone hurt?"

Clearly the false memory had taken.

"No, but I'm afraid we didn't catch the people who were holding you. So we've brought you to a safe house until we do. This is Mr Grady. He and his people will look after you and keep you safe."

Tears sprang to Mr Hayling's eyes. "Thank you. I don't know what possessed Letitia…" He pulled straight, alarmed. "I have to call my sons."

"You don't need to do that," Luca said with a tone that held a little bit of calming suggestion. "Your wife has told them you're recovering from a mental breakdown, and it would be best if they don't learn otherwise, so that they won't alert your wife to your release."

"Yes, of course…"

With some more assurances that he was safe and looked after, we retreated to the common area. I gave Grady my phone number and he promised they'd call if anything alarming happened.

"I doubt the warlock comes looking for him here."

The other security bloke straightened. "We're protecting him against a warlock? Nice…"

Grady cuffed him on the back of the head. "You won't stand a chance against a warlock, so watch out."

"I can handle anything."

"There might be a demon in play too," I said, then inhaled sharply when I remembered: "Kane!"

ASHLEY WAS WAITING by the car, leaning against the bonnet, hands crossed over her chest. She straightened when we exited the lift with Grady. "You couldn't leave him there?"

Grady sneered. "You thought to walk back?"

"Sixteen kilometres may be too much for you, *alpha*, but I can handle it just fine."

Luca and I glanced at each other and bit our lips not to laugh at their bickering. I climbed in the back seat with him. I couldn't face another ride next to Grady, so I threw Ashley to the wolves—or a wolf, as it were.

"The alarms at Mr Kane's home haven't gone off," Grady said when he drove us out of the car park. "Do you still want to go and check?"

I nodded, though he couldn't see it. "The warlock could've attacked him before he got indoors, or disabled the alarm."

"Let's go check, then. But if dealing with warlocks and demons will be a regular thing, I think we'll have to renegotiate our contract with Mr Kane."

"Scared, are you?" Ashley taunted him, but he didn't take the bait, making him the more mature of them.

"So what's with the hostility between you two?" Two outraged faces turned to stare at me from the front seat and I lifted my hands up. "Just asking. Is it a pack thing or did you used to date or something?"

"No!" they said simultaneously, with such force that it was almost physical. Luca kicked my leg, urging me to shut up, but I clearly had a death wish, because I couldn't leave it be.

"No for the pack thing or dating? Because this kind of hostility usually stems from one cheating on the other. I know I cursed my ex the first chance I got." It had been an accident, but I wasn't sorry it had happened.

"It's a pack thing," Ashley growled, and Grady shot me a questioning look over his shoulder.

"Cursed? Really?"

"Yes. And he deserved it."

He dipped his chin, impressed. Then he glanced at Ashley before concentrating on traffic again. "Dating between the packs is allowed, even encouraged to avoid inbreeding. But our packs have been rivals for centuries. There's no socialising, and definitely no dating between us. Hatred comes naturally."

And it was tangible. "Pity. Ashley would eat a weaker man than you alive."

"Phoebe!" she said, outraged. Grady snorted a laugh.

"That's the trouble with strong wolf females."

"Oh, so you want a nice submissive who keeps your home tidy and raises your cubs," Ashley drawled. He shrugged.

"Something like that…"

"You'd be bored in a month," she declared. She crossed her arms and leaned against the door, putting as much distance between them as possible. But at least they'd stopped growling, so I took that as a win for me.

My tension began to rise as we neared Belgravia, a luxury area of Regency terraces in Central London where Kane lived in one of the mews. Would we find him injured—or worse? Or would he be perfectly fine, having gone to a dinner with his phone on mute?

Grady drove us straight into the court between the mews and to Kane's two-storey, two-car garage house, indicating he'd been there before. I rushed out of the car before he had the engine cut off, and was already ringing Kane's doorbell before my friends had followed.

"Nothing smells threatening," Ashley said, and I belatedly realised I should've been more alert.

"Or of the mage who broke into the shop," Luca added. But I stood tense until I heard the sound of Kane descending the stairs.

He opened the door and straightened, baffled, when he saw our odd group. He was wearing black sweatpants and a white T-shirt, and his hair was damp after showering. Tears of relief sprang to my eyes, seeing he was fine.

"Why didn't you answer your phone?" I demanded. He gave me an alarmed look, and then grimaced, chagrined.

"I'm so sorry, Phoebe. I got your message and drove straight to the council house after all. I only now returned home."

I punched him in the shoulder, a bit more forcefully than I intended. "And you didn't think to call me?"

His bewilderment melted and he reached a hand towards me, a bit hesitantly. I didn't wait for a better invitation but stepped into him, wrapped my arms around him and buried my face in his chest. Behind me, I heard my companions clear their throats and step back.

"We'll be going," Luca said, but I didn't turn to look.

Kane pulled both of us over the threshold and closed the door. He wrapped his arms around me and held as tightly as I did. "I'm really sorry, Phoebe," he murmured in my hair. I kept my face buried in his chest. He smelled wonderful, and being held by him made my tension melt away. "It's been so long that anyone's been worried for me that I didn't come to think you would."

I pulled my upper body back to look at him, but I wouldn't let go of him. "After all we've been through? I was absolutely certain the warlock had attacked you."

His mouth quirked. "Took you over two hours to come to rescue me."

"Yeah…" That didn't look good. "We didn't want to keep Hunt waiting."

He laughed aloud at that. I grinned too, wiping my cheeks. He brushed a tear with the back of his hand too, an inscrutable look in his eyes as he studied me. "Phoebe…"

I held my breath, searching his face, hoping he would say more, do more, but he didn't. Instead, he released me and turned to climb the stairs.

"Come up. You can tell me all about it."

A combined kitchen and living room opened at the top, the windows facing the courtyard. His bedroom was towards the back, with a bathroom in between. He'd furnished the place in mid-century modern style, Danish design from the 50s mostly, with cherrywood and off-white upholstering and some red accent pieces here and there. Art and bookshelves covered the walls.

I liked his style, but then again I'd always thought he carried interesting pieces in the shop too.

He gestured at the sofa and I took a seat. "Do you want something to drink? Tea? Whisky?"

Tea would mean he'd disappear behind the isle that separated the room from the kitchen, and I didn't want him to go. "Whisky sounds fine."

He smiled as he turned to the side table that held a carafe and two tumblers, and poured us small measures. "It'll put some colour in your cheeks."

"I'm not that upset anymore."

He handed a glass to me, more serious. "I shouldn't have upset you in the first place." He sat next to me with his own glass, closer than he usually did, but didn't drink. I didn't touch mine either.

"I've been a coward, postponing the conversation we should've had already on Monday," he said, staring at the golden liquid in his glass. He glanced at me from the corner of his eye. "I'm sorry."

"For kissing me or not talking about it?"

His mouth quirked. "The latter. I don't regret the kiss." He faced me. "Do you?"

I shook my head, suddenly unable to speak as my heart was beating too fast. He put his glass on the coffee table in front of us and took mine away too. Then he turned to study me, holding my hands. His blue eyes were serious and warm, and hesitant, and ... I couldn't name the emotion there, but it took my breath away.

"I've been attracted to you since you first came to work for me," he said, making my heart stop, only for it to continue its frantic beat faster than before. "But I didn't intend to act on it. I'm your boss for one, and I thought you were an ordinary human. I couldn't get involved. So I've kept my distance as best as I could."

I blinked. "Is that why you've been so ... proper?"

"I'd like to think myself as gentlemanly," he said, teasing. "Part of it is who I am. But the closed door and not taking you on antique acquisition trips has been deliberate."

That was a relief to hear. He hadn't kept me away because he didn't trust my skills or ability to learn.

He ran a thumb up and down the back of my hand, absently, as if he hadn't noticed he was doing it. Shivers coursed through me from the contact. "But things have changed, and I find myself hoping that you might be as attracted to me as I am to you."

He studied me from under his brows, a question in his eyes. I could only nod again, then cleared my throat to say it aloud.

"Yes. Very attracted."

His smile was instant and blinding. "Good." He leaned down and kissed me, and I kissed him back. It was everything I'd hoped for, and over too soon, as he pulled back and gave me a questioning look. "I hope you mean you're interested in a relationship?"

I smiled. "Yes. Though I would've settled for a quick tumble in the sack too."

"Oh, there won't be anything quick about it…" The heated flash in his eyes warmed my body all over. And then he threw cold water on me. "But not tonight."

My shoulders slumped in disappointment, and he grinned, bringing out the dimple. "I think we need to learn to know each other first, to have a proper relationship. We've never really talked about who we are."

I could see his point. Phoebe at home was a different person than Phoebe at work, and I was sure he was too. So I nodded and he smiled. "How about I take you to a dinner? I'm busy on Saturday, but how about Sunday?"

The mere prospect made me smile brightly. I opened my mouth to say I'd love nothing more, when I suddenly remembered. I stared at him, upset.

"I can't."

Twelve

KANE PULLED BACK, BAFFLED. "You can't?"

We really should've had this conversation on Monday. Then I wouldn't have hesitated to decline Hunt's demand. I inhaled and plunged in.

"I have a prior engagement, and you're not going to like it."

His brows shot up. "Oh?"

"I promised Hunt I'd be his date for a City charity function," I told him with a grimace. His face assumed the polite mask I was so familiar with.

"Well, you were certainly free to do so."

His politeness may have been genuine, or hiding deeper emotions, but I didn't want him to think I'd agreed to go with Hunt because I wanted to.

"I'm not interested in him." The mere thought made me shudder. "It was the payment he demanded for helping with Mr Hayling. It was either that or give him the book, and I judged this a lesser evil."

He dipped his chin, and his stiff demeanour melted a little. "I can definitely see that…" He sighed and shook his head. "The timing is unfortunate, but I can't really make any demands and order you to cancel."

Part of me wished he would, for form's sake if for nothing else, but he was right.

"Especially since he sealed it with magic."

He rolled his eyes. "Of course he did. And I'm partly to blame for your predicament too. Did he at least come through with Hayling?"

"Yes. He also arranged a safe house. Grady took us there. That's why it took so long for us to come and save you."

He smiled. "I wondered why he was with you."

"Are you ... upset?"

He took my hand again. "Disappointed that our date will be postponed, but it has waited for two years already. A little longer won't matter."

I sighed and made a face, and he grinned. "Do you want me to throw a jealous fit? I'm not very good at those, but I can try. The sentiment will be genuine even if the execution is lacking."

"Just kiss me."

So he did.

We came out for air sometime later. His damp hair was mussed from my fingers sinking into it, making him look deliciously dishevelled. My lips were swollen, and I'd climbed on his lap at some point, straddling his legs. The hard length under me indicated he was more than ready to move to the bedroom, but he didn't suggest it. So I did.

He grimaced, breathless. "It's been a while since I've been in this situation, and I don't have any condoms in the house."

I didn't have any either. "Damn..." I groaned, more than a little frustrated. Having him so close, his delicious body free to touch, had pushed me close to the edge already.

"I'm sorry. Give me a moment to recover and I'll drive you home," he said.

"That's okay, I can take a cab."

But he wouldn't hear of it. He pulled on jeans, and I followed him out to his Jag. We spent the drive talking about all the things we'd never done before. I learned that both his parents were mages, they lived in Oxford where they held academic posts, and that he was an only child. We had that in common. I also learned that he'd dated only sporadically since his divorce a decade ago.

"It's difficult to be more than casual with women when I can't reveal my true self."

So one-night stands, then. I didn't hold it against him, but I did feel a pang of jealousy.

"Do you want to do this openly or keep it a secret for now?" he asked as he pulled over outside the magic shop. I gave it a thought. Part of me wanted to keep him to myself and not share him with anyone. But I shook my head.

"Ashley and Luca will smell you on me the moment I enter. There's no point hiding things with those two around."

He smiled, pleased. "Good. And we'll have to tell Mrs Walsh too."

"That worries me more. What if she doesn't approve?"

He cupped my cheek. "I think she'll be happy for us."

I hoped he was right.

We kissed some more, but then I had to reluctantly exit the car. He waited until I'd opened the door to the shop before driving away. I watched him go and then turned to face the shop—only to shriek.

The entire household was gathered in the middle of the shop, watching me expectantly. "Took you long enough," Ashley groused. "I almost had to leave for work before you came home."

"Well?" Giselle demanded, her eyes twinkling. They'd probably been watching us make out in the car, but I found I didn't care. I blushed and smiled happily.

"All is very well indeed," Amber said, her tone warm.

"Tell us everything," Luca demanded.

"Absolutely not." I crossed the shop and they followed me.

"You don't smell of sex," Ashley declared. I gave her a horrified look.

"Will you tell it to the whole world if I one day do?"

She shrugged. "Nothing to be ashamed of."

"Well, I'd like you to keep it to yourself, thank you."

"Suit yourself. I have to go to work anyway." She exited the shop through the back door with a wave of her hand.

Giselle had saved me dinner and she warmed it up while I told them of my evening. "And then I almost ruined it with the Hunt thing," I finished.

Luca had already told them about the deal with Hunt, so they nodded. "Can't be helped. He sealed it with magic," Giselle said, full of sympathy. "Archibald will understand."

"He did. Doesn't mean he was happy about it."

Amber pursed her lips. "If you ask me, you got off cheap with Hunt."

I thought so too. "The safe house alone has to be expensive. I bet he'll up the price later."

"He'll likely come after me next," Luca said glumly. "I'm surprised he didn't make any demands outright."

Magic by the Book

That soured our mood a bit, but not so much that I wouldn't have been giddy while I prepared for bed. I didn't know if Kane was the one for me, but I hadn't been this excited about a man before. I was happy I had a chance to find where it would lead.

I couldn't sleep, I was too full of feverish energy. I jumped out of the bed, and after pacing the room for a moment, paused in front of the bookshelf to find a book that would help me calm down or divert my mind for long enough to get tired.

My gaze landed on the magic books I'd purchased from Mrs Hayling. I hadn't had a chance to study them yet. What if they held unpleasant surprises too?

Suddenly uneasy, I took out the lot and carried them to the bed, where I piled pillows to prop my back and pulled the duvet over my legs to be warm and comfortable. Grizelda materialised from under the bed and settled over my feet.

The books smelled old, but not dusty or mouldy, and were soft to touch. Nothing zinged or zapped my fingers. The contents were what I remembered. There were a lot of margin comments from mages of the past too, and those held my interest longest. It was fascinating to think that so many different mages had owned these books, studied with them, and contributed to their commentary. The moment I had time, I'd read them with proper thought.

I didn't try any of the spells. I wasn't in a suitable frame of mind to concentrate even on the easy ones. Moreover, reading how a spell was cast strained my brain in a completely different level than when Amber explained how it was done. But I made a note of a couple of interesting ones to ask her about. Maybe they'd be something I could practice for my council presentation.

That wiped what sleepiness I'd managed to gain. What if I failed and wouldn't be allowed in? I couldn't expect Kane and Amber to do me any favours and enrol me behind the backs of the rest of the council.

My tension annoyed Grizelda, who stood up and stretched, before finding a new spot to sleep. I picked up the next book in the pile and began to go through the pages without really seeing what was on them.

It took me a moment to realise it wasn't a spell book at all. It was about lives of notable mages and warlocks of Europe written in the early eighteenth century, all males, unsurprisingly. Rupert had had a similar book, with brief lives and even pictures of some of them, engravings based on painted portraits. Maybe mages hadn't been as great a secret in the past as today.

Watching the pictures of the mages of the past and reading about their lives was oddly soothing. I even found Contra-Josephus—his real name was Josephus Cuijper—but there wasn't a picture of him. The author seemed to believe that he had truly managed to transmute lead to gold and praised him accordingly.

And then, towards the end of the book, I found another familiar name.

LUCA WAS IN THE SHOP when I rushed there in my robe and slippers. It was kept open until midnight most days, and occasionally even later, so I'd known I'd find him there.

"Look at this!" I thrust the book at him. He took it and gave the page a curious look.

"Who's Giovanni Battisti?"

"The warlock who created the prison out of the book," I declared triumphantly, as if I'd managed a great feat finding him. Was that how Mrs Hayling had found him too? "And look here, it says he hadn't died by the time the book was written, even though he was allegedly over a hundred and twenty already."

"Is he a vampire?" He seemed more interested now.

"I don't know. But I think warlocks can live longer than ordinary mages too."

"You think he found the philosopher's stone?"

"I don't know. I think this book would tell if he'd learned to transmute lead to gold."

"It also supposedly helps one to live longer."

Right. "Never mind how. What if he is still alive? Here's his picture."

It was an engraving of a man in his thirties in an elegant, split-sleeved satin doublet and a floppy lace collar that covered his shoulders. His dark hair was long and wavy, and he sported a Vandyke beard and moustache that told the portrait was painted sometime in the seventeenth century, as they went out of fashion soon after. He looked very Italian to me, but not very sinister or warlock-like.

Luca studied the picture with his head tilted. "Have you seen him before?"

"Not that I recall. Was he in Mr Hayling's memory?"

"Impossible to tell, as he never looked at the mage's face."

My shoulders slumped in disappointment. "We'll have to keep an eye out for him."

The bell above the door chimed as a customer entered. I turned to greet them, and inhaled sharply.

"That's the man who asked about the book at the shop," I muttered to Luca as silently as I could, knowing he could hear me. I hadn't given the odd customer a thought since that day, but now I was sure he was the one behind the break-in.

But to my disappointment, Luca shook his head. "Doesn't smell like the mage who broke in."

He didn't look like the man in the engraving either, or young enough for the mad run the burglar had made, plus his hair was short. He studied the shop with polite interest, before crossing the floor to us. His brows rose slightly when he spotted me, but I think it was for my Minions tank top and boxer shorts underneath the pink robe, not because he recognised me from the antique shop. Without any makeup, my long cinnamon hair down, I didn't look like the efficient assistant I tried to present at work.

He addressed Luca. "Good evening. I'm looking for a book on alchemy, and this looks like a place that might have one."

"Not very popular, those," Luca said. He rounded the counter to the nearest bookshelf and pulled out a book. "This is the only one we have."

The man frowned. "It's not what I'm looking for. I want an old book. From the sixteenth century."

He had to be after Contra-Josephus's book, and it couldn't be a coincidence he was here right when we'd acquired it. But if he wasn't the mage who had broken into Kane's shop, who was he?

"We haven't got anything that old," Luca said with an apologetic shrug. "But if you give me your contact information, I'll let you know if something like it surfaces."

Magic by the Book

The client's brows furrowed. "That's not what I want to hear."

"That's all I have to offer, I'm afraid," Luca said, unperturbed. Most people didn't scare him, as he could control their minds if he wanted to. The man didn't realise Luca was a vampire, which made me wonder if he was even a mage. "We mostly sell herbal teas and such."

"If I could look at the back?"

Luca curled his lip in amusement. "As if an antique book we know nothing about would mysteriously materialise there."

"What's that, then?" the man asked, pointing at the book I was holding.

I showed it to him, still open at the page with Battisti's picture on it. "It's an eighteenth-century biography."

He didn't react to the face at all, and I stifled my disappointment. Either he wasn't connected with the mage who had used the book against Mr Hayling, or the mage wasn't Battisti.

"I'm not interested in that." He turned abruptly and crossed the shop to the door. "I'll be back."

The moment the door closed after him, we hurried to peer out of the window. He entered a car idling by the curb. I couldn't get a good look at the driver, but the car wasn't the one the burglar had left in on Wednesday. It pulled off and Luca headed out of the door.

"I'll go after them. Close the shop." With that, he sped after the car unnaturally fast, keeping in the shadows.

I locked the door and turned the closed sign over. I dimmed the lights in the shop and was in the process of taking the day's sales report from the till when he returned.

"I lost them at the Angel," he said, barely winded, even though he'd run three kilometres at a car speed.

"They're headed north?" I inhaled. "That route leads straight to Rupert's."

His eyes grew large. "Fuck. You don't think they're going there at this hour?"

"If they found this place, they may have followed us to him too. I'd rather not take chances."

"I'll take Amber's car and go check." He made to rush up the stairs, but I halted him.

"I'll come with you."

"In your nightwear?"

I glanced down at my clothes. "Give me a moment to run upstairs and put on my clothes."

"Too slow. You can wear mine."

He disappeared to the back room and down the stairs to his lair, and returned with a grey tracksuit before I'd even removed the robe. "Pull these over your nightclothes."

He was about my height, so the bottoms fit, even if they were a little snug around the, well, bottom. The top was too large, but it didn't matter. As I dressed, he made another dash and fetched my shoes and coat from the foyer a floor up along with the car keys. Only moments later, we were in Amber's car and driving towards Rupert's house.

"You don't think they'll break into Rupert's, do you?" I asked, my stomach tightening.

"This was your idea," he said. "But I'd like to see them try. I bet the house is warded to the rafters."

"It didn't stop Julius Blackhart and his minions."

Blackhart was a dark mage vying to become a warlock, and we'd barely survived the encounter.

He grimaced. "Let's hope these men are less skilful and more scrupulous."

"If one of them is a warlock, I'd say they're better at magic and even more evil."

There was no traffic, and we soon reached Rupert's neighbourhood. Luca drove by his house, but it was dark, and there was no sign of the car Luca had followed. Everything was quiet. No one was even walking a dog in Highbury Fields, the large recreational park across the street from Rupert's.

He pulled over onto an empty spot someway up the street and we exited the car. Keeping under the trees lining the park where the light from streetlamps didn't reach, we headed back on foot. Outside Rupert's house, we hid behind a hedge growing by the park to study the house without being detected.

Well, Luca did the studying. My eyesight wasn't good enough in the dark, even with a streetlamp right outside Rupert's gate offering help.

"The topiary is too dense, and the wind's the wrong way. I can't get a scent," he said, frustrated. "We have to get closer."

We dashed across the street to the front yard of the house next to Rupert's and peeked over the low brick fence that separated them. I could see even less, now that the houses blocked the light from the street, but Luca perked.

"I think I see movement in the back yard."

He made to climb over the fence, but I stopped him. "What if they attack?"

"We can handle them."

"I don't know any attack spells," I hissed.

"Didn't you just learn the levitation spell?"

I'd barely managed to lift a pen off a table, but maybe I'd manage to trip the intruder with it. So I nodded, and began to concentrate as we climbed over the fence.

Luca hurried towards the back garden. I tried to keep up in the dark whilst reaching for the spark inside me. I wasn't entirely sure I'd be able to cast the spell, but I had it ready for a good try when we rounded the corner, only to ground to a halt.

A person was standing in the middle of the garden, studying the house with hands on their hips. Darkness hid their face, but the form and size indicated a man much taller and younger than Rupert or Jones.

I didn't hesitate, but cast the spell as the man noticed us. Startling, he took a step closer just as my spell hit him, but instead of lifting him up like I'd hoped, it only made him lose his balance.

I couldn't let him regain it.

Closing the short distance as fast as I could, I rammed into him shoulder first. Unbalanced by the spell, he dropped on his back with a yelp, and I landed heavily on his chest. Straddling it, I was about to punch him with what little strength I had when Luca grabbed my arm. He was laughing so hard he was wheezing.

"That's not an intruder," he managed to say.

"What?"

I turned to look at the man underneath me. He wasn't struggling. He was smiling.

"I see you've found a good use for the levitation spell, Phoebe."

Thirteen

I STARED AT MY BOSS'S—AND boyfriend's!—amused face, stunned and a bit embarrassed for attacking him. "What are you doing here?" I scrambled up and offered him a hand. He took it, though he didn't need it for getting up.

Luca was still laughing. The bastard could've stopped me before I reached Kane. He certainly had the speed for it.

Kane smiled as he dusted wet leaves that had clung to him from his clothes . "The same as you, I'd venture."

"But ... how?"

He wrapped an arm around me and gave me a brief hug. He didn't seem to hold my tackle against me.

"I couldn't sleep for some reason," he said, eyes twinkling at me. "So I went for a jog. I don't know why I decided to run here, but as I reached the house I felt my wards being tampered with, so I came to check."

"You've put your own wards around the house?" I asked. I wasn't surprised that he'd jogged eight kilometres through Central London in the middle of the night. The wards shouldn't have surprised me either. Rupert was getting old for such a straining task.

"I did after Blackhart's attack. So what drew you here?"

We told him about the client and following the car. He furrowed his brows. "I don't like that so many people are after the book."

"Maybe the client is with the mage who broke into the shop," Luca pointed out. "I'll only have to get a good scent."

"Are they still here?" I asked, glancing around, as if I could see in the dark.

Kane shook his head. "I don't know, but no one's trying to take down the wards anymore."

"I'll go check," Luca said, disappearing into the darkness. Kane and I walked back to the street hand in hand. I hadn't even notice him take it, and it made my heart beat faster like a schoolgirl with her first crush. For a man who'd always been so proper with his conduct, he showed affection with ease.

We paused under the trees across the street. I glanced around, but we were alone. If the mage was still here, he was on the other side of the house.

"I'm sorry I tackled you."

He grinned. "No harm done. The lawn was soft. And it's not every day a hot woman lands on me."

"Better not be…"

His grin turned teasing. "We need to work on your levitation spell a bit though. You should've been able to lift me with it."

"I can't even lift a pen properly," I said miserably. "I'll fail the council presentation."

He pulled me into a hug, his arms around me, and cheek pressed on my head. "It's not a serious event. They simply want to know you're a real mage and not a trickster."

I hoped he was right.

Luca took some time to return. "There definitely had been two people sniffing around the house. I followed the scent, but they got into a car before I reached them."

"Was one of them the mage who broke into the antiques shop?"

"No."

Bugger. "It would be so much simpler if we had only one mage to deal with."

"I don't think the mage here is very good," Kane said. "The one who broke into the shop got through my wards easily. This one didn't."

"That's something, at least," I sighed.

"Pity we can't find out who he is," Kane said, but Luca grinned.

"Oh, but we can. I memorised the number from his plate when I chased them earlier." He dug out a phone from his pocket and started a search.

I shook my head, exasperated for his illegal software. But I didn't say anything, as his apps came in handy.

It didn't take long. "The car's owner is Christopher Holt."

"Why does it sound familiar?" I asked, but couldn't place the name. "Google it." I would've done it myself, but I didn't have my phone. I felt naked without.

Luca made the search and shook his head. "Nothing."

"That's not odd at all…" I said dryly.

"Maybe he's old," Luca suggested. "Or a vampire. I try not to leave traces of myself."

"So he could be Battisti."

He rolled his eyes. "He doesn't have to be *that* old. Besides, the client didn't react to the picture of him."

"He didn't react to me either, and we'd met."

"I don't think he looked at your face," he said dryly. Kane pulled back, dismayed, so Luca hastened to add, "It was her Minions nightshirt that drew his attention."

Kane's mouth curved into a wry smile. "Maybe I'll get to see it one day too…"

I shook my head. "I can assure you, when the time comes I won't be wearing it." But I pulled down the zipper of my windbreaker and lifted the hem of Luca's sweatshirt to give him a good look at the top underneath. "Here."

He grinned. "That is an excellent nightshirt."

I rolled my eyes, but couldn't help being pleased as I zipped the jacket again. He glanced around.

"I don't think they're here. It's past one in the morning. I think we'd best head home."

LUCA DIDN'T SHOW UP for breakfast, so I got to regale Amber and Giselle with the tale of our adventure. I left out the part where I tackled Kane, both because it was embarrassing and because I didn't want to reveal to Amber that I couldn't cast the levitation spell properly. Luca would tell them all about it later anyway.

Amber shook her head, worried. "I don't like that there's more than one mage after the book. And I don't know who Christopher Holt is."

"Maybe he's the client who visited the shop and not the driver. He's not a mage."

"I don't like the idea that a mage would team up with a human for nefarious purposes," she said, her face grim.

Magic by the Book

"If this Holt is a mage, he could be from the south too," Giselle suggested. "It would be too much of a coincidence if random mages suddenly came after the book."

"I'll ask around." Amber said. "Meanwhile, I'd best ask Archibald to up the wards around the council house with me. The last thing we need is the mage trying to break in there."

"Or a warlock," I added as I finished my breakfast and got up. "An ordinary mage wouldn't know the prison spell."

"Do you think it's Battisti himself?" Giselle asked, worried. I shook my head.

"Probably not. But until I know for sure, I'll keep my eyes out for him."

Except in the Tube, that was, because I mostly dozed off the whole ride, though I did remember to switch lanes at the correct station this time. I began to hum with energy as my destination neared, and there was a bounce in my step as I approached the shop. I even dropped by the café across the court to buy blueberry muffins.

I did my morning tasks in record time, and then struggled to calm down while I waited for Kane to arrive. It was excitement and heat coursing through me today, a far cry from Monday.

Since it had worked for me then, I took a pen and tried to levitate it. I managed it better than before, and I began to feel hopeful that I might survive the presentation on Tuesday.

The door opened downstairs, and Kane practically ran up the stairs. I faced the door and he paused on the threshold, a bit out of breath but with a beautiful smile on his face.

"Hi."

I smiled. "Hi."

He crossed the floor in a few strides, and I stood up as he reached me and pulled me into a kiss. "I've wanted to do that every morning since you've been here."

"I wish you had…"

He gave me another kiss, brief this time. "I didn't quite anticipate that our regular work might suffer for this."

"Good thing we don't have an auction coming."

He perked. "True. Maybe we can devote the day for our mysteries."

"Nothing much we can do about the people after the book, but I'll call Eliza Mercer and ask who she sold her mirror to."

"That's almost work related."

"And Amber wants to know if the wards around the council house need upping."

He turned serious. "They might. I'll call her right away."

I followed him to his office with the muffins and poured us tea. I figured I could stay and have a cup with him now. He smiled, pleased.

"I absolutely craved a muffin this morning."

"Ah, so it was tea and muffins that made you hurry up the stairs…"

We had tea side by side on the sofa. Some kissing was involved, but not much, and we agreed to try to keep things professional at work. Then he took his phone to call Amber, and I returned to my desk to call Eliza Mercer. To my pleasure, she remembered the mirror well.

"Of course I remember it. Odd, old-fashioned thing that I had no use for back then, but which Mom insisted

I needed." Since she wasn't a mage, it must have seemed strange to her.

"Do you remember who you sold it to?" I held my breath.

"To my brother. He was very interested in it for some reason. Maybe he wanted something to connect with Mom's side of the family, having moved back to England to study at the LSE."

"Do you think he'd still have it?"

"He might. You'll have to ask him yourself though. I'll text you the number."

A couple of minutes after ending the call, my phone beeped with the promised information, so I called him right away. He didn't answer, but that wasn't unusual; he was probably busy at work. So I sent him a message instead.

I didn't have to wait long before the phone rang. "This is Ellis Holt." There was a faint Australian accent in his voice, and I remembered that he and his father had moved there when he was little. "You called about a mirror?"

"Yes, I did." Then the name registered, and I blurted, "Are you by any chance related to Christopher Holt?"

There was a deep sigh at the other end of the line. "What has he done now?"

I was acutely embarrassed. "I'm sorry. I'm not sure he's done anything. The name just rang a bell."

"Trust me, if you suspect him, he did it." He sounded fed-up. "My father is a grifter. If there's money to be made easily, he'll try it."

Huh. "Is he by any chance interested in transmuting lead into gold?"

He laughed. "No, but he'll find some poor fool who is and make the most of it."

I tried to come up a way to bring up magic over the phone. I vaguely recalled Rupert say that Ellis Holt was a mage, but without knowing for sure this would be a difficult conversation.

"About the mirror I mentioned, is there by any chance anything … special about it?"

"Ah, we can speak openly. Good. Makes this easier."

I was relieved too. "So the spell on the mirror hasn't broken?"

"Why would it be?"

"Your grandmother said that if the mirrors were sold it would break the spell."

"Well, I didn't exactly buy it from Eliza." He paused for a beat. "She had some … personal trouble and needed money. So I gave her the money. I know I shouldn't have, it only went to drugs, but…" He drifted away. "Anyway, she gave the mirror to me as a thank you."

"And do you still have it?"

"No, I'm sorry. My cousin was interested in it, and since I wanted to get to know her after living almost two decades in Australia with no contact with Mom's side of the family, I gave it to her."

That was disappointing. "Could I get her name and number to ask about it?" I closed my eyes, hoping for the best, but I wasn't surprised by the answer.

"Danielle Mercer."

Bugger.

"I'm afraid I can't give you her contact information," he continued. "She's … disappeared."

I sighed, trying to get over my disappointment. "That's okay. I have it."

"You do?" He sounded astounded.

"Yes. She's my boss's ex-wife." I was amazed how easy it was to say, though I couldn't quite declare Kane my boyfriend yet.

"Oh." He cleared his throat. "Is she well?"

I cursed the woman for cutting her family off so completely. "Well enough. She's shagging a French warlock and it's a bit of a tempestuous relationship, but they seemed happy the last time I saw them."

"You've seen her?" Did I imagine it or was there hope in his voice?

"Last week even. She hasn't contacted her parents either, so I think she wants to keep her distance."

He sighed. "I can't say I blame her. We didn't take it well when she chose to become a warlock. Unforgivable things were said."

Kane had divorced her, so he didn't exactly take it well either. But since becoming a warlock required killing someone, I didn't question their choice.

"About my father, then," he changed the topic in a brisk tone. "Has he tried to swindle you?"

"No. He's looking for an old book on alchemy, or a friend of his is. We're trying to identify them. We got your father's name from his car's number plate."

"Dad doesn't do legwork, so whoever is with him is the mark."

I sighed. "I can't imagine what sort of a con he could be pulling with the book. And they were casing a house last night, believing the book is there."

"That's ... a lot of extra work," he said, baffled.

"Maybe the mark is pushing him?"

"Could be. He'll play along as long as it's useful for him."

I tapped my lips with a finger, thinking. "Is your father a strong mage?"

"Not particularly. He's not good at grifting either, so we moved a lot when I was a kid. Australia is large, so there was always a new town to move in. I hoped he'd stay there, but he moved here a couple of years ago."

"He lives in London? Could I get an address?"

"No, Portsmouth." He sighed. "Though I guess he's here now."

So that was the connection. "Do you have a photo of him? We'd like to keep an eye on him."

He promised to send it. "And if you need my help in handling him, give me a call."

"I will. And maybe you could warn him? We believe there's a warlock after the book too."

"Of course there is…" he said with a disgusted drawl. "I'll do my best."

We ended the call, and I went to tell Kane what I'd learned. He looked surprised. "I don't remember Danielle having a magical compact mirror. Otherwise we could've started with her immediately."

That was disappointing. "Maybe she's given it away?"

"Could be. Do you want me to call her?"

I gave it a thought and shook my head. "I don't need to get the pair that badly. It's enough to know it exists and the spell is still intact."

"You could try to contact her with the mirror," he suggested with a smile. I shuddered.

"I'll pass."

"In that case, I think it's time we go have a chat with Helen."

Mrs Walsh was neither surprised nor offended about our news, to my relief. "Took you two long enough," she said with a meaningful look. "I was starting to think I'd need to meddle."

Kane and I smiled at each other and then at her. "It's not easy when one is the boss of the other at work."

The rest of the day wasn't quite as productive as the morning had been, but we managed to behave professionally. It helped that I spent most of it with Mrs Walsh in the shop, continuing the project of sorting out the items we could take on tour.

Kane waited for me when it was time to head home, and we walked hand in hand to his car. For once I didn't mind the heavy traffic, as it gave us time confined in his car. "Giselle would love to have you for dinner," I said when we neared the House of Magic.

"And what about you?" he teased me.

"I could skip the dinner..."

He groaned and closed his eyes, so it was good we'd stopped at traffic lights. "Couldn't you say that earlier?"

My heart jumped, for excitement and for disappointment too. "Truthfully? I kind of wanted to show you off."

"They have met me before."

"Not as my boyfriend."

Giselle greeted us like she was my mother meeting my boyfriend for the first time, excited and flustered, and a little suspicious too, in case he turned out to be bad for me.

I was amazed how much it warmed my heart. My mother would make a fuss too, if I ever got to introduce Kane to my parents, but she'd be more concerned about what his parents did and his station in life than my well-being.

Dad would love him.

Everyone was present at dinner, so I told them what I'd learned about Christopher Holt. "What's his angle, then?" Luca asked when I was finished. "How will he profit?"

"And how did he learn about the book?" Amber added. I could only spread my arms.

"His son didn't know. But the elder Holt lives in Portsmouth. Maybe he knows Mrs Hayling, or the warlock, learned about the book from them, and thought it was a good opportunity for a grift."

"So he's not after the book personally?" Giselle asked.

"Well, he's not the client who visited the shops," I said, showing the photo of Christopher Holt. He was in his mid-sixties, with thinning hair combed back and a debonair air that somehow showed in the photo too.

"I'm not an expert on grifts, but I've seen one or two in my life," Luca said. "Usually the one pulling the con tries to make the profit scheme seem as easy and painless for the mark as possible, not make them do the legwork."

"Maybe Mr Holt fears that the mages in London will recognise him," Kane suggested. "Just because we don't know him doesn't mean the older generation mages wouldn't."

We hadn't come up with better explanations by the time dinner ended. It was Friday night, and I didn't have to worry about getting up in the morning. So I took Kane by the hand and led him to the stairs up, ignoring the jeers behind us.

"Quit it. I'm not a teenager anymore. I'm allowed to have a boy in my room."

"Don't be loud. I have sensitive hearing you know," Ashley shouted after us.

"If that didn't kill the mood..." I muttered as we climbed the stairs.

"We did decide to take things slow," Kane reminded me. "A werewolf chaperone will guarantee that. And it's not that I don't want you, but it's been so long since I've been in a relationship that I'm quite excited about the deeper side too."

All my relationships so far had been thin on personal, so his approach made ours instantly feel more mature. And we did give it a try. Lying side by side on my bed, facing each other, we talked about all the little things for hours. Neither one of us was tired, and neither suggested calling it a night.

The house quieted around us as we progressed from words to kissing. Kissing led to touching, which heated things up fast, and we were soon pulling our clothes off. I was busy feeling his abs under his shirt while he reached behind me to the clasp of my bra. He was about to open it when the alarm went off downstairs.

Fourteen

BREATHING HEAVILY, WE STARED at each other, bewildered, as we tried to comprehend what the sound was. It wasn't until Ashley rushed out of her room that we acted. Kane pushed up, tugging his shirt back into his trousers to my disappointment.

"I think we'd best go see what's happening."

I wanted to say that Ashley and Luca could handle everything without us, but curiosity won. I pulled my clothes hastily back on and we headed downstairs. Amber and Giselle rushed out of their room as we went past their floor, tying their robes.

The alarm was still beeping when we reached the shop and switched on the lights. The shop was empty and there was no sign of an intruder, or Ashley and Luca.

Amber went to the alarm box and managed to stop the beeping, but the red light wouldn't stop its furious blinking.

"It's like the system at our shop," Kane said. "The security company needs to switch it off."

Giselle opened the back door to look if anyone was in the back yard, just as the car from the security company drove in. Grady's. I wasn't surprised to see Grady himself exit the car. Apparently he handled all the alarms personally.

Wordlessly, he came in and entered the code that switched off the alarm, before facing our group that was standing there in various states of dishevel. He lifted his silver brows.

"So what's it this time, mage, warlock, or a demon?"

"We don't know yet," Amber told him.

He took a sniff, his eyes sharpening. "Smells human. Are Ashley and Luca giving a chase?"

We looked at each other. "Possibly?"

"Well, the intruder can't have gone far. It's been five minutes since the alarm went off, and those two can outrun anyone."

That was a high praise, coming from him.

He'd barely finished the sentence when Ashley returned, barefooted and dressed in the boxer briefs and sports bra she usually slept in. She held a limp man over her shoulder in a fireman's carry, but I couldn't say whether he was docile for fear or because he was unconscious.

She strode across the back yard in unhurried steps, snarled at Grady for form's sake, and carried her catch into the shop. She dropped him down, steadying him when his legs wouldn't hold. He looked terrified—and I recognised him instantly.

"That's the man asking after the book," I said, only a little surprised. "Was he alone?"

Ashley sneered. "The other fled in a car, ditching this one. Luca is giving a chase."

Giselle fetched a chair for the man and he dropped down, his eyes shooting around the room. We formed a wall around him, two huge werewolves, two middle-aged women in their nightgowns, and Kane and I, our clothes slightly askew.

"Who are you people?" he asked, bewildered.

"We're the ones asking the questions," Grady growled. The man looked like he'd pass out for sudden fear, a primal part in him recognising the predator Grady was, so I cleared my throat to calm things down and addressed him.

"What's your name?"

He focused on me, looking relieved. "Eric ... Eric Newman. You were at the shop last night, weren't you?"

"Yes, and we told you we don't have the book, so why did you try to break in?"

He looked offended, as if it was my fault they'd done it. "We didn't believe you."

"Why would we lie about it?" I asked, baffled.

"Because it's a valuable book."

I spread my arms, gesturing at the shop. "If we had a valuable book, do you really think we'd keep it out here where anyone can walk in and steal it?"

"That's why I wanted to see the back room," he stated, as if it made sense. I pinched the bridge of my nose. I didn't have headaches often, but I was getting one now.

"Why do you want the book?" Kane asked. Mr Newman looked at him down his nose, quite a feat considering he was sitting.

"Because it tells one how to transmute lead into gold."

Kane blinked, stunned. "And you believe it?"

"My sources are reliable." He sounded absolutely serious. "I've been researching it for years. It's a book written by a Dutch alchemist in the sixteenth century, and all sources agree that he managed the transmutation."

At least he was looking for the book we actually had and not some random book on alchemy. "And yet no one has managed it since?"

Mr Newman huffed. "He wrote the book in clever cipher."

"So how would you know it tells how to do it when no one can understand what he's written?"

He gave me a pitying look. "That's how I know. Of course he wouldn't have written it in a language that anyone can read."

It was difficult to argue with that logic.

"And what about your accomplice? Christopher Holt," Kane said. "How is he involved?"

Mr Newman didn't find it odd we knew his companion's name. He settled more comfortably in the chair, and assumed an air of an academic lecturer. "The book disappeared for centuries, but I managed to locate it to Portsmouth."

Kane's throat flexed, as if he was trying not to laugh. "How did it end up there?"

"It had been in my companion's family the whole time, only they didn't know what it was. They'd moved to Australia in the late nineteenth century, and now that he'd moved back to England, he had the book with him."

I blinked. "Then why are you looking for the book here?"

"Someone stole the book from him before he could show it to me," he said, looking angry. "We traced it here."

Kane studied him, incredulous. "So you've never seen the book and only have a random person's word that it exists, yet you're willing to steal it on his say so."

"I wouldn't have stolen it," Mr Newman protested. "I merely wanted to confirm it was here. Then we could've come and claim his rightful property."

"Or he sent you here alone because it's not his book," I countered. The man looked uncomprehending.

"Why would he lie about it?"

I sighed. "Because he's a conman, and it's a valuable book that you want. He's doing it for money."

He huffed and all but rolled his eyes. "There's no money in this for him."

That pretty much aligned with our notion of the matter, but it didn't make things any clearer. "Then what does he want?"

"Absolutely nothing."

Right...

"I mean, he'll sell the book to me once we find it."

"So there is money for him in this," Amber said dryly. "I'm only surprised he didn't sell it to you outright and disappear, leaving you without the book."

That would have made more sense.

"Why would he lie about owning the book?" Mr Newman demanded.

"Because he's a con artist," we said in unison, exasperated.

"So it doesn't exist?" He looked like he would cry, and I took pity on him.

"The book exists. But it's not here, and it doesn't belong to Mr Holt."

"Where is it, then? And who owns it?"

"It's in a safe place," Kane said. "And we don't know who owns it. But Holt might know. We need to talk to him."

Luca entered through the back door, looking cross. "He got away. Tracking cars is annoyingly difficult. They all smell the same."

"Mine didn't," Ashley said smugly, pointing at Mr Newman. Luca leaned down to face the man.

"Where did your companion go?"

Mr Newman pulled back. "Are you calling the police?"

We looked at Amber, who shook her head. "Nothing's been stolen. So no."

"Then I think he went back to our hotel. But I don't understand why you would need him if you're not going to arrest us."

"We only want to talk to him," Kane assured him. He gestured at Luca, who put the man under his thrall.

"What do you want me to do with him?" Luca asked. We looked at each other.

"He doesn't know about magic," Kane said, "so there's no need to wipe his mind."

"But he'll keep coming after the book, and that'll put him against the warlock," I pointed out.

After a brief negotiation, Luca removed all traces of the book, Mr Holt, and their time in London, and planted a suggestion that he should go home first thing the next morning. Amber and Giselle stayed home while the rest of us filed into Grady's car with Mr Newman, and drove to his hotel.

It was a small place on a side street between Paddington Station and Hyde Park. At this time of night, the front door was locked, but the keycard to Mr Newman's room opened it. We took him to his room, Luca gave him a command to forget us, and released his enthrallment as the door closed.

"Will he be all right?" I asked, worried.

"I'm not as good as Hunt when it comes to altering memories, but I can manage a small job like this," Luca assured me. "Now, Holt is in room twelve."

It was at the other end of the hallway. We paused outside the door and Grady made to knock, when the door was pulled open. Christopher Holt stood behind it, a suitcase in his hand.

GRADY TILTED HIS HEAD like a wolf and sneered. "Going somewhere?"

Mr Holt took a startled step back, his eyes large and fixed on Grady. Unlike his companion, he knew exactly what stood in front of him. He deflated a little and stepped aside.

"You might as well come in. Did you catch Eric?"

"Yes."

Holt studied us as we filed into the room. His brows shot up. "Two weres? And a vampire too? If I'd known the book would be that difficult to get, I'd never left home."

Grady stayed at the door, leaning against it, and Ashley propped her shoulder against the nearest wall, arms crossed over her chest. She'd dressed up before we left the house, but she would've been equally impressive in her underwear.

Kane gestured for Mr Holt to take a seat on the only chair in the small room. We remained standing, staring down at him.

"Wonderfully intimidating," Mr Holt said dryly.

"Not your first time being intimidated, I presume?" I said, and he lifted his brows.

"What makes you say that?"

"We talked to your son."

"Ah." He was silent for a beat. "He has nothing to do with this."

"We know. We're more interested in how you're involved, and who else is."

He leaned back in his chair. "What's in it for me?"

Luca leaned down and looked him straight in the eyes. "Freedom. With your mind intact."

"I guess that's the winning offer. What do you want to know?"

"Who owns the book and who else knows about it?" Kane asked. Holt sighed and crossed his hands behind his neck, as if preparing to tell a long story.

"I moved to Portsmouth a while back and have been making acquaintances with local mages. Getting the lay of the land, so to speak."

"To find easy pickings?" Luca suggested, and he shrugged.

"It's what I do. There was this rich mage woman who looked most promising. I got to know her and was invited to some do at her house. Cased the place. It was full of art, but that's difficult to move, and at any rate I'm not into stealing stuff. But then I found a bunch of old books on magic."

"Just like that?" I asked. He sneered.

"As if I don't know how to remove a spell hiding things. Anyway, there was an interesting book among them, written in an odd language, and very old. I couldn't immediately see the profit, but I made a note of it. Mostly I thought to blackmail the woman for cheating on her husband, which I learned about at that party too."

"But you didn't?"

Magic by the Book

"The couple separated soon after the party anyway, so there was no point. Then I found Eric in a chat group for old books and had to move fast. Rich pickings if anyone was. Totally barmy, believes in transmutation. He was looking for a book on alchemy he was sure was the real thing. I said I had it."

"And he believed you?"

He shrugged, dropping his hands and pushing them into his trouser pockets. "He was convinced of his superior research skills, having found me in that chat group. Anyway, I remembered Mrs Hayling's book. I decided it was mystical enough to suit Eric's fancy and went to liberate her from it. Only the book wasn't there anymore." He glowered at us.

"So you didn't know for sure it was the book he was looking for?" Kane asked. Mr Holt startled.

"Is it?"

"Yes."

He stared at us, mouth hanging open. "Then how did Mrs Hayling have it? Because the way Eric spoke of it, it's supposed to be impossible to find."

"That's what we'd like to know too," Kane said. "So how did you end up in London?"

"Mrs Hayling wasn't home. I talked to the neighbour, who was very chatty. He told me about the visitors that had been stranded by the storm. I told Mr Newman that I knew who had stolen my book and we came after you."

"Were you merely guessing, or did you know we have it?"

"You have it?" he asked, outraged. "Then why didn't you admit to it?"

Kane leaned down. "Because, Mr Holt, it's a very dangerous book in the wrong hands. And what's more, other mages are looking for it too."

"The one Mrs Hayling was cheating on her husband with?"

We glanced at each other. "We have no idea, but if you could give us a name?"

"I don't know it, but he was this Italian fellow."

I inhaled. "Battisti."

"It doesn't have to be him," Luca said. "It could be a descendant of his, or someone unrelated who simply knows the spell and had access to the book."

"And if Battisti is alive, why would he give the book to Mrs Hayling and not demand it back?" Kane asked.

"And how did she make him cast the spell to capture her husband?" Luca added.

"Money?" Ashley suggested. We turned to Mr Holt, but he lifted his hands.

"Don't look at me. I don't know anything about spells. I only wanted to sell the book to Eric."

Kane shook his head, disgusted. "Well, we've altered his desires. He's not interested in alchemy anymore and is going home. You should do the same."

"The least you could do is pay a fellow for information," Mr Holt grumbled. Ashley and Grady growled, and he recoiled. "All right, all right, no need to bite my head off. I'm going."

He got up and took his suitcase, and we followed him out of the hotel. There was no one at the reception desk, and I was pretty sure he was leaving without paying for his room, but he'd likely organised for Mr Newman to pay.

That might not go well now that Mr Newman didn't remember Mr Holt anymore.

We watched him get into his car and drive away. Only then did we relax. "Now what?" I asked.

"It's getting late. We should go home," Kane said.

"Will this be the end of break-ins to your properties?" Grady asked. Kane shook his head.

"Holt and Newman didn't break into my shop. That was a different mage."

"So is that mage the one who captured Mr Hayling, or someone else?" Luca asked.

"And we still don't know why Mrs Hayling gave the book to us in the first place," I said.

"Too many mysteries for one night," Kane said. "Let's just go home."

We were filing back into the car when Grady's phone began to beep. He dug it out and read the display. His brows furrowed.

"Someone's breaking into the Mages' Council."

We froze for a beat and then scrambled to our seats. "Floor it," Ashley ordered, and for once Grady didn't snarl in return.

There was no traffic at that time of night. Grady used all shortcuts he could find, and drove faster than the speed limit, but it still took us forty minutes to get to the council house. The place was dark and quiet when he pulled over outside the front door and we got out of the car.

"Luca, with me," Ashley commanded, and the pair went to round the large building, sniffing for clues. Grady looked like he wanted to go with them, but he needed to switch off the alarm that we could see blinking through the glass pane of the closed door.

He made to step to the door, only to ram into an invisible wall. He shook his head, baffled. Kane looked grim.

"My wards have activated."

"What sort of wards are they?" I asked. "The alarm wouldn't have gone off if they hadn't got in."

"It's the kind that allows people to get in and out normally. It wouldn't do to have the entire council blocked out of their own building. It only activates if the alarm goes off and closes you in."

"Clever," I said approvingly. "But won't removing these wards release the burglar?"

"These aren't the only wards holding them."

He gestured with his hands for a moment, and I felt the wards come down. Grady entered the building and switched off the alarm. He took a sniff.

"Not the same person who broke into your shop."

"How many mages are there after the book anyway?" I asked, exasperated. Grady shrugged.

"Well, this one wasn't good enough to disable the alarm first—or the wards."

"That tells us something, at least…" Kane muttered grimly. We followed him through the building to a small room on the ground floor and he switched on the lights.

My mouth dropped open.

Standing in front of a safe that hadn't been opened, held by wards, was Mrs Hayling.

Fifteen

SHE FACED US CALMLY, A SMALL SMIRK twisting her lips. "I guess you've caught me." She was dressed in black leggings and a black raincoat, with black leather gloves. The only thing missing was a beret and she could've auditioned for a French spy movie.

Kane nodded, studying her. He didn't look angry, he looked puzzled. "The question is, why were you here to be caught in the first place?"

"Isn't it obvious? I want my book back."

I stared at her, amazed. "Couldn't you simply have asked? We tried to call you when we found the book, but you didn't answer. You would've got the book back the next day."

"It's not your book. You have no right to keep it here."

"But is it your book?" Kane asked.

She sighed, disgusted. "Could you release me before we continue this conversation?"

Kane glanced at Grady, who shrugged. "I can catch her if needed." Even in human form, he was a powerful, intimidating figure. Mrs Hayling crossed her arms defiantly.

"I'm not going anywhere."

Grady leaned forward. "That's right."

Even I was intimidated now.

Kane gestured at the air in front of him and the wards became visible, a wall of complicated, colourful sigils that formed a half circle in front of the safe, closing Mrs Hayling in.

"This will take a while, so you might as well start talking." He began to work on his wards, so I focused on Mrs Hayling, giving her a questioning look.

"Why did you give us the book in the first place?"

"It was by mistake," she stated. "It was on the same shelf, and I added it to your purchases."

I rolled my eyes. She was lying, but I decided to leave it be for now. "And you couldn't ask for it back because…?"

"I wasn't home. I went to Italy and only realised the book was gone when I came home this morning."

"And decided it had to be here and came to steal it instead of contacting us?"

She only shrugged.

I stepped aside to give Kane room to work, his hands moving gracefully like a harpist's as he picked the threads of the wards, and then faced her again. "Let's pretend for a moment that I believe you. Where did you get the book?"

"It's been in my family for ages."

"A book that disappeared in Italy in the seventeenth century somehow ended up in Portsmouth?"

"It was salvaged from a shipwreck after the Spanish Armada," she stated, as if we were too stupid to know about the important event in British history.

"The same Spanish Armada that happened a century before the book was lost?"

Magic by the Book

She pressed her mouth tight. "Well, some other shipwreck, then."

I closed my eyes and stifled a sigh. "Would it make you lie less if we told you we know exactly what the book is and what you did with it?"

She remained silent. I rubbed my eyes with the heels of my hands. It was getting late, and I hadn't slept much the previous night either.

"Fine. Let's talk about the mage you've been working with. Who is he and why is he after the book?" I lifted my hands when she looked like she would deny it. "We know that you're having an affair with an Italian mage. We know what happened with your husband. What we don't know is where the book came from, who the mage is, and if he's dangerous."

"Yes, poor Andrew had a nervous breakdown," she said with an almost convincing sigh. "I don't know what he has to do with any of this."

Kane paused in his task and gave her a hard look. "If you keep up this pretence, I'll leave the wards up until your archmage can come and handle your judgement."

"Exactly what am I being judged for?"

"For capturing your husband inside the book!" I said, getting angry.

"He's in an institution."

"No he is not, and never was. He came out of the book and told us you put him in there."

Her jaw flexed. "It wasn't me. You can't prove it."

"We had a vampire go through your husband's memories when we released him from the book. We know exactly what happened. We have him now."

Her face hardened. "He's not a mage. The archmage will never believe him."

"He doesn't have to talk to the archmage. He'll go to the police."

She snorted. "They'll never believe him when I've told everyone he was committed."

"He's not the only one whose mind can be altered," I drawled. "We only need to plant evidence in the mind of a detective for them to come after you."

"And how's that better than what I've done?"

I shrugged. "As long as you pay for it."

"I pay?" she demanded. "Do you know how much I've suffered as his wife? How boring he is?"

"Abuse of magic is a bit more serious accusation than a boring husband."

She brushed with her hand, dismissing my argument. "Well, we don't have an archmage in Portsmouth, so no one can judge me."

"We have rules for those occasions," Kane said. "The archmage of London will handle it. And since Rupert was present when your husband came out of the book, he doesn't even need convincing."

"You released him?"

Hadn't she been listening? "Yes. And in case you thought to go after him, he's currently in a safe location, watched over by werewolves."

Grady bared his teeth and she paled. "You're lying. He's not a mage. You wouldn't bring werewolves to him."

"All he knows is that he's being watched over by a private security firm because his wife tried to abduct and kill him." I rubbed my face again. "Just tell us who the mage is who cast the spell."

"I did."

Magic by the Book

I shook my head, exasperated. "You're not good enough a mage to cast it. And we know there was a man present who did. Give us a name."

"Why, so you can punish him too?"

Duh. "Is there a reason why he shouldn't be? He captured a man inside a book with magic. For all we know, you intended to keep him there forever."

She crossed her arms and studied Kane, who was deftly dismantling the wards. There was a flash in her eyes, hatred maybe, or envy.

"You're right. I'm not a strong mage. But my lover is. And yes, Camillo's Italian, though I don't know what that has to do with anything. We've been together for years. I would visit him in Italy, or he would come to England. We'd meet in London."

She rolled her shoulders and faced me. "I wanted a divorce, but Andrew wouldn't hear of it. Months we fought about it. I was getting desperate. Camillo and I even contemplated killing him, but that couldn't have gone well. And then Camillo learned about the book and the spell."

"Where?"

"His family is old and has strong mages. They have contacts. They knew of this ... warlock who provided the book and the spell."

"Just like that?" I couldn't believe the warlock would've let the book go.

"I can pay well. And it worked perfectly until you came and the book ended up with you."

"Why was it with you still? Didn't the warlock want the book back?" He'd managed to keep the book hidden for centuries until now.

She pursed her lips together. "Fine, if you must know, Camillo had second thoughts and wanted to release my husband. I couldn't have that. I had to take the book where he couldn't find it. I needed to move it fast and hope it wouldn't be found soon."

"So you sent it with us?" She nodded. "What changed your mind, then?"

Her face hardened. "Things turned nasty when I arrived in Italy. Camillo wasn't there, even though he'd travelled ahead of me. The warlock was threatening his family, and he was looking for the book. Luckily, he had no idea who had it, so I had to come and find it before he did."

"Does the warlock now know where the book is?"

She shrugged. "I have no idea what he knows or where he is. All I know is that if I don't get the book, he'll kill Camillo."

I had a feeling she wasn't telling us everything, but she'd lied so much during the conversation that it was difficult to imagine what it would be. Before I could probe, Kane made a triumphant sound.

"The wards are down."

"Can I go now?" Mrs Hayling asked, as if we hadn't made it clear that she was a captive. It took a special kind of person to believe they were above the law.

Grady growled. "No."

"You must face Rupert and the council," Kane reminded her. "But we have a more comfortable place to hold you than this."

Where that would be, I had no idea, because we couldn't take her to the safehouse where her husband was.

He gestured for us to exit the room before him. I went first, then Grady next to Mrs Hayling, and Kane kept the rear.

"What's keeping Ashley and Luca?" I wondered aloud what I hadn't noticed before. It wasn't that large a building to round. Had they encountered someone or run into trouble? We reached the entrance hall—only to abruptly halt.

My friends were standing in the middle of the floor, immobile. They were trying to shout a warning but couldn't move their mouths.

A man stepped out from behind them. He was about Luca's height, with very Italian features, and black hair combed back. Before I could react, he gestured with his hands and I suddenly couldn't move my legs. Darkness fell.

Kane acted immediately. He threw an energy ball to where the man had been, but it didn't hit anything. He created light, but it didn't permeate the darkness. Noises indicated two people running.

It seemed to take forever, but was maybe only a minute, before the darkness receded, and we could move again. The man and Mrs Hayling were gone.

RELEASED FROM THE SPELL, Luca, Ashley, and Grady rushed out of the door, but no one was there. A sound of a car driving away echoed off the buildings on the nearby street.

Luca ran after them, and Ashley began to pull off her shirt in order to shift, but Grady barked at her: "Into the car."

Amazingly enough, she obeyed. Soon they were gone too, leaving Kane and me standing there looking after them, dismayed and angry.

"That went well."

Kane pulled me into a hug and kissed my temple. "Are you all right?"

"Yes." I leaned against him, weary. "A bit embarrassed that I didn't come to think of an ambush—or couldn't react to it fast enough."

"It takes years to learn combative magic, and even then one seldom needs to use it." He paused, his lips pursing. "I haven't done this many magic battles in my life than I have these past months."

"Well, you're good at it," I said, leaning back and smiling at him. He pressed his lips on mine for a brief kiss.

"I need to improve my aim though…" He released me and rubbed his face to banish tiredness. On top of the late hour, he'd spent a lot of energy taking down the wards, and battle magic was especially draining. "I take it that was the lover and not the warlock?"

I wrapped my arms around my torso, feeling cold without him warming me. "I have no idea, but I doubt the warlock would've left without the book. Or bothered with Mrs Hayling."

He dipped his chin, considering my words. "Camillo, then. Let's go put the wards back on, in case they come back."

"If Mrs Hayling was acting alone, how did Camillo know to come here?" I asked when I followed him back to the room where the safe was. Kane shrugged.

"It took us forty minutes to reach the council house. Mrs Hayling had plenty of time to call him while she was held by the wards."

"Or he was waiting nearby for us to release her. I knew she was lying about something," I said, annoyed. "He was in England the whole time."

"I thought she was lying about everything. Very cold-hearted woman." He paused outside the safe and shook his shoulders, gathering strength. I felt bad that he had to create wards again after spending so much energy already.

"Do you think it was Camillo who broke into our shop?"

He considered it. "It's possible, though that mage would've been able to free Mrs Hayling. And there's still the warlock to consider."

The rest of our group returned from their chase, looking cross. "They got away. I'll check the traffic cameras for where they went, but I'm not hopeful," Luca said, slightly out of breath for his mad dash, which told me he must have run fast indeed this time. "Who was he?"

"Mrs Hayling's lover, Camillo," I told him. "Was he the mage who broke into the shop?"

"No. Wrong smell and a different car," Grady said. "And short hair too. Which means there's one more person after the book."

"The warlock who owns it," I said with a shudder. "How did Camillo get you anyway?"

"From behind," Ashley growled. "We'd gone through the perimeter and there were no hostile scents, so we came in and he froze us. Fucked if I know where he came from."

"But you're not physically harmed?"

"No, only our pride," Luca said with a grin.

Kane faced us. "I don't think we can leave the book here after all. If the warlock is keeping an eye on them, he might come here, and he will get through my wards. I'd best take the book home where I can be ready to defend it."

"Shouldn't you give the book back if it's his?" Grady asked. He was emanating wild, angry energy that kept the hairs on my arms standing up.

To my surprise, Kane nodded. "Technically, we have no right to it. But if he knows how to lock people inside it, it's too dangerous to give back."

"Is the spell specific to the book?" I asked, only now coming to think of it. He gave me a startled look.

"I don't know. But if it's not, why would he want it back so badly he's threatening Camillo's family?"

"Because he's an evil warlock?"

"There is that…"

With a brush of his hand, he undid the wards he'd cast so far. Then he went to the safe, entered a long code from memory, and opened the door. I wasn't entirely surprised that the safe mostly contained books.

He picked the correct one, closed and locked the safe, and then faced us. "Let's go home."

"Won't you redo the wards?"

"No, they were for this book anyway, and I don't have the energy."

I wrapped an arm around his and we followed the others out. This time Grady went first, sniffing. At the front door, he sent Ashley and Luca to check the perimeter once more, before allowing us to go to the car.

My shoulders finally relaxed once we were on the move. It had been a long and eventful night. But it wasn't over yet. We drove to Kane's house, where Grady and Ashley made sure no one was waiting for us again, before allowing Kane in.

"You can go home now," Kane assured us when we looked like we'd follow him in. "I'll come for breakfast tomorrow."

He leaned down to kiss me, and I arched up for it, ignoring the *oohs* and *ahhs* Luca and Ashley made.

The kiss ended all too soon. I studied his face, concerned. I didn't want to go home and leave him to face a warlock attack when he was already drained, but our relationship hadn't exactly progressed far enough for me to casually suggest I stay the night—even if it was only to keep him company.

He smiled at me and brushed my cheek. "I'll be fine. No one will come here."

"They'd better not." A demon had attacked him in his home before. The image of him tied to the coffee table in his living room flashed in my mind, and for once it wasn't his near naked body I concentrated on.

He walked me to the car, closed the door behind me, and watched us drive away. I only turned to face the street when I couldn't see him anymore. Grady must've sensed my upset, because he gave me an assuring look through the rear-view mirror.

"I'll send someone to keep an eye on the house."

Relief brought tears to my eyes. "Thank you. You've been extremely helpful."

He grinned. "We haven't had this much excitement in a long time."

"We could do with a bit less…" I sighed.

"Or less often," Luca added. "I don't mind the action."

"At least this one doesn't seem as bad as the crazy vampire warlock," Ashley stated, and we hollered in protest.

"Don't jinx it!"

She gave us a puzzled look from the front seat. "What? It wasn't a jinx. Phoebe's not cursed anymore."

Grady laughed. "You've really had odd adventures."

"Odd is one word for it…" I muttered.

"What do you want me to do with our guest?" he then asked.

I glanced at Luca, who shrugged. "His wife and her lover got away, so you'd best keep an eye on him still."

"Maybe you should leak his location in the hope that they come after him," Grady suggested. "We wouldn't be taken by surprise again, and could capture them."

The idea had merit, but we decided against it anyway. With our luck, it wouldn't be Mrs Hayling. It would be the warlock. And I wasn't sure we could defeat him.

Sixteen

I WASN'T ENTIRELY AWAKE THE NEXT morning when I dragged myself to breakfast. I'd had two long nights in a row, and I hadn't slept well when I'd finally crawled into bed.

Giselle was already at the stove. She shot me a concerned look. "You were away late last night. What happened?"

"What didn't?" I said with a sigh that turned into a yawn. "The pertinent bit is that Mrs Hayling broke into the council house, only to be captured by Kane's wards."

"So you got her now?"

"No." It irked me as much as the previous night. "Her Italian lover, *Camillo*..." I put as much derision on the name as I could. "...showed up and managed to snatch her away."

Ashley emerged from the hallway and growled, as irked as I was. "The fucker surprised Luca and me."

The rest of our group arrived before Giselle had finished making breakfast. Kane had come by car, judging by the jeans and a cable knit cardigan he was wearing over a white T-shirt instead of jogging clothes. We told Amber and Giselle everything that had happened the previous night.

"I think we need to regroup and start over," Kane said. Amber nodded.

"Let's go through all the players once more."

Everyone looked at me, so I started listing them, holding a finger for each name. "We have the owner of the book, who wants it back. Presumably an Italian warlock. Mrs Hayling wasn't exactly forthcoming with truth, but since the book was owned by an Italian warlock before, I'd say that's a safe assumption. And since we don't have a better identification, I'll call him Giovanni Battisti."

Everyone nodded. "How likely is it that he's the original Battisti?" Amber asked.

"There's really no knowing how long warlocks can live," Kane said. "And that was before we knew vampires can become warlocks too."

"Too bloody long, if you ask me," Ashley grumbled.

My grip tightened around the finger I was holding. "I think we're safer assuming that he's the original Battisti. Which means he'll be more powerful than any other person we've encountered before."

"Do you think he's hostile?" Giselle asked worriedly. I'd sort of taken it as self-evident, but now I hesitated.

"He hasn't done anything violent yet. Even the break-in at the shop was neat."

"We don't know it was Battisti," Luca reminded us. "He hasn't done any follow-ups to it. I mean, if Holt and Newman could find here, why wouldn't Battisti have."

He had a point. "Maybe he decided to let others find the book for him?"

"Maybe he's been here during the day and his scent was mixed with other customers, so you didn't notice him," Amber said to Luca.

Magic by the Book

"I have his portrait in a book. I'll show it to all of you later," I promised.

Kane tapped the table with an absentminded finger as he considered the possibilities. "I really don't think there would be an unknown player in the mix. How would they know that the book is in England after all these centuries? Mrs Hayling wouldn't tell because she was using it for criminal purposes, and Mr Newman wouldn't tell because he desperately wanted to find the book before anyone else did."

"So Battisti it is," Amber concluded. "We have to hope he tries to get the book peacefully."

Luca looked dubious. "Wouldn't he have asked for it nicely if he wanted a peaceful solution?"

That silenced us for a beat. Then Giselle shook herself and rose. "Who wants more tea?"

Once we'd filled our cups, I continued the rundown. "We have Mrs Hayling and Camillo. She claimed they were working separately, but based on events last night, I'd say they're together. And since Battisti is threatening Camillo's family, I'd say they're pretty desperate to get the book back."

Everyone nodded. "Mrs Hayling isn't a strong mage, but Camillo is," Kane said. "Together they can cause quite a bit of harm."

"I think we should avoid confrontation at any cost," Amber declared. "Couldn't we simply give the book back to Battisti and be done with it?"

Kane nodded. "That would be the most prudent option. However, I don't like how Battisti has suddenly decided to lend the book willy-nilly to any mage with a grudge so that they can capture people inside it. We can't control the actions of a powerful warlock, but we can control the book."

"Provided people stop coming after it," I sighed. He gave my shoulder a consoling squeeze.

"Maybe we can negotiate a deal with him."

That was optimistic of him. "Maybe we could pay him? Mrs Hayling said she paid a lot for the use of the book. Maybe Battisti has run out of money after all these centuries."

I doubted even our combined funds would be enough, even though Kane was well-to-do, but for this I'd gladly ask my parents for money.

Kane narrowed his eyes, considering. "That would explain why he's suddenly lending the book away."

"I guess he hasn't learned to transmute lead into gold, then," Luca said with a grin. I smiled too.

"Or hasn't figured out the language the book's written in."

"So why does he want it back so desperately, then?" Giselle asked. "If it's valuable to him still, he wouldn't let it go with random people."

"It does have a demon inside. Who knows what he could do with one," Ashley noted, but unlike me, she seemed to find the thought exhilarating.

Kane furrowed his brows as he gave it a thought. "What if it contains more than one demon? Or human. What if this wasn't the first time Battisti has lent out the book, or captured people inside it himself?"

We stared at him with our eyes large. Then Amber slapped the table, making us jump. "That settles it, then. We can't give the book back to him."

"Should we try to release the people?" Giselle asked, but Kane shook his head.

"We released Mr Hayling by accident. I don't want the next accident to be the demon."

I took a sip of my tea, thinking of all the poor people that might be trapped inside the book. Battisti had let go of the book too easily for that not to be the case.

"Maybe we could ask him to release the people," I suggested, but was met with sarcastic faces.

"Because evil people are reasonable," Luca said, and Ashley nodded.

"If he's been taking money to capture people, there are any number of fuckers out there who'll do anything to keep those captives inside."

"So there could be even more mages coming after us?" Giselle asked, horrified. I didn't like the thought either.

"We should destroy the book," Amber stated. "Just burn it. We can't help the possible captives since we don't know the release spell, or don't know how to release only the people and not the demon. And at any rate, they could've been inside for centuries. But we can't let Battisti use the book anymore."

The mere thought of destroying a unique artefact like the book horrified me, even though I could understand the reason for it. Kane's mouth pressed into a grim line.

"I agree with you, but I don't think we should do it. Battisti's retaliation might be more than we're able to handle."

"And burning the book might release the captives too," Luca pointed out. "Even if it's only the demon inside, it'll be too much for us to handle."

"This would all be easier if we could talk with Battisti," I sighed. "We could ask if the demon or other people are inside. Do you think Camillo would have his contact information?"

Kane nodded. "He might, but we don't know who Camillo is."

That was a problem. We sat stymied in silence. Then Luca lifted a hand like in a schoolroom.

"We should ask Mr Hayling."

"Why would he know about Battisti?" I asked, amazed.

"Not about Battisti. Camillo. There's no way he didn't know his wife was having an affair all these years. At the very least, he's known that she travels to see him. Maybe she's told he's a business contact or something, but he'll know where Camillo is from and what his last name is. Then we can ask his family about Battisti."

Kane nodded. "It's a longshot, but the only one we have."

"I can even take a peek inside his mind, in case that'll reveal details Mr Hayling can't remember," Luca promised.

Energised with a plan, no matter how weak, we ended the breakfast. I went to dress up while Kane contacted Grady to arrange a meeting with Mr Hayling.

Ashley followed me upstairs. "I need to go to work, otherwise I'd come with you. You can't trust those wolves."

"Grady's been nice so far."

"He's biding his time to bite you, mark my words."

"I rather think it's you he wants to bite," I said with a sassy grin, and then quickly locked myself into the bathroom when my taunt caused her to mock attack me, leaving her to growl behind the door.

I wasn't worried about Grady. At the end of the day, I'd rather face him than the unknown warlock who might do something worse than bite.

I could only hope it wasn't to lock us all inside the book. Because even Rupert wouldn't be able to release us.

GRADY WAS WAITING for us outside the underground garage of the estate in Wembley to let us in. Kane drove the Jag to a visitor's space, and we got out.

"You didn't bring the she-wolf this time?" Grady asked, eyeing our small group. Only Luca had accompanied Kane and me. The day was overcast enough for him to be out and about at that hour, though he'd pulled a hood tightly over his head and was wearing sunglasses.

"Disappointed?" I teased him, because it had gone so well with Ashley earlier. To my surprise, he flashed me a genuine grin that I wished Ashley had been there to witness. She'd surely change her mind about him then. Then again, maybe he was this relaxed only because she wasn't here.

"Absolutely. Nothing gets a man's blood coursing like a hostile woman."

"Must be a werewolf thing," I muttered as I followed him to the lift. He heard me though, and his smile deepened.

"You should try it with your man."

I shot him a startled look and then glanced at Kane, who looked amused. "You're not my subordinate outside work, you know."

It stunned me to silence. I hadn't paid attention to how I interacted with him now that we were together, but

I did tend to look up to him like my boss and be polite and agreeable. That wasn't a good relationship dynamic.

"It's really difficult to change the habit."

He put an arm around my shoulders as we filed out of the lift. "We'll get there."

One more reason to postpone getting intimate. I wanted to be myself with him, not an employee with her boss.

There was a guard wolf right inside the door when we entered, a different one than when we were here before, but equally scary. He glared at us, but didn't try to stop us.

Mr Hayling was in the living room watching a movie, but he immediately paused it when he spotted us, and rose. He was wearing fresh clothes, so someone had gone shopping for him. He looked a little weary, but otherwise in good health.

"Have you caught my abductors?" he asked as we crossed the floor to him. He gave Kane a confused look. "Have we met?"

Kane almost nodded, before remembering that Luca had wiped Mr Hayling's memory of everything that had happened at Rupert's—although not well enough, if a memory of Kane had surfaced.

"I'm Archibald Kane and I'm investigating your case," Kane said, sounding like a detective in charge. He offered his hand and Mr Hayling shook it. "Could I ask a few questions?"

"Absolutely. Nothing else to do but watch TV."

We took seats on the brand-new furniture that still smelled of manufacturing chemicals. Luca sneezed and I almost followed suit. The wolves had to find the smell insufferable.

Magic by the Book

Kane sat next to Mr Hayling and took out his phone. "Do you recognise this man?"

Grady had given him a screengrab of the surveillance footage from the council house. It was from the lobby when Camillo had come in to wait for Luca and Ashley, and in black and white, but the quality was good.

Mr Hayling sat straighter. "Yes, of course. It's Mr Lippi. Or *Signor* Lippi, as he's Italian."

"And how do you know him?" Kane asked.

"Art circles. He's a gallerist like I am, from Florence."

"Do you do a lot of business with him?"

He nodded. "Quite a lot, actually. He has excellent sources of old Italian art by lesser-known artists that he sells all over the world. I have clients that really want genuine old art but can't pay the prices of the big names."

He didn't sound like a man who knew his wife was having an affair with Signor Lippi, and I for one didn't want to break it to him. Kane clearly didn't either, because he nodded.

"Do you have his contact information? We need to talk with him."

Mr Hayling shot him a suspicious look. "Why?"

Kane bit his lip, trying to come up with a diplomatic explanation. "We believe your ex-wife is in Italy, and we're trying to locate people who might know her whereabouts."

The mention of his ex-wife deflated him. "Right, um…" He patted his pockets. "I don't have my phone."

That was a setback. "Do you remember the name and address of Mr Lippi's gallery?" I asked, and he smiled.

"Yes, it's Galleria Lippi in Florence, on Via dei Renai, across the street from Museo Stefani Bardini."

Kane and I nodded simultaneously, both familiar with the art museum of a private collector. I'd visited there a few times, and apparently so had Kane. It made me ridiculously pleased to have the shared experience, even if we hadn't been there together.

"I know the place. We'll find it. Thank you for your time."

Kane rose and so did Mr Hayling. If he found it odd that a London detective would be familiar with a Florentine art gallery, he didn't show it.

"So you haven't found Letitia yet? How long do I have to be here?"

Kane spread his arms. "I wish I knew. But for now, this is the safest place for you."

Luca mesmerised Mr Hayling and gave us a questioning look. "Do you want me to plant a suggestion that would make him want to be here?"

"It's best we don't tamper with his mind more than we have to," Kane told him. "He's a grown man. He can handle being confined in here for a few more days."

"We'll keep him entertained," Grady assured us. "And he won't do anything rash."

The wolf guarding the door flashed his teeth in a manner that suggested Mr Hayling wouldn't do anything rash *twice*. But since we had no other place to keep Mr Hayling safe, Luca released the compulsion, Kane thanked the slightly confused man, and we left with Grady.

"Should we up the security?" Grady asked when we were on our way down to the car park.

"Your guess is better than ours," Kane said. "But currently everyone is busy trying to find the book, so no one should be coming after Mr Hayling."

Grady nodded. "Good to know, but I was more concerned about your security. Is the book still in your house?"

"Yes. My best wards are holding it secure."

"No one followed us yesterday, and my men said no one came sniffing around your house either, so it should be safe for you, for now."

I tried not to read ominous meaning into his "for now."

I googled Galleria Lippi while we drove back to Clerkenwell. It was easy to find, and had a good website in English too. I'd studied Italian—what art lover hasn't?—but it wasn't my strongest language.

The owner and personnel page listed two Signor Lippis, Senior and Junior, both called Camillo. Since I didn't know which one I was trying to reach, I selected Senior.

"*Pronto Galleria Lippi,*" a man answered faster than I'd anticipated, before I'd figured out what to say and how to say it in Italian. He sounded rather old, so he was likely the father of the Camillo I was trying to reach.

I gathered what Italian I could muster and introduced myself. "I'm not sure I reached the right Signor Lippi?"

"If you're calling from England, then it's my son you should contact," he said, switching to English that was better than my Italian. "He handles the clients there."

"Will he answer at the number listed for the other Signor Lippi?"

The man hesitated. "Is this about art? Maybe I can answer your questions."

"It's actually about the owner of a sixteenth-century book on alchemy."

He inhaled sharply. "You don't want to get involved with him."

"Believe me, that's what I'm trying to avoid. But I need a name and a way to inform him that I have the book."

"You have it? Then give it to my son."

It was my turn to hesitate. "Do you know what your son has done with the book?" He didn't answer, so I continued: "I can't let your son have it, and if he comes for it, the local ... *authority* on such matters will deal with him." I couldn't say archmage since I didn't know for sure that Signor Lippi Senior was a mage. "Can you let him know?"

"We are much better equipped to dealing with the owner of the book. Just hand it back."

"The owner is already in London. Tell me his name so that I can be better prepared." Again the silence. "Is it Giovanni Battisti?"

"*Sì.*"

My stomach tightened painfully. "The original?"

"*Sì*. And he's powerful beyond belief."

I could imagine plenty powerful. "We'll be ready for him."

"No one is ready for him. Be careful." He ended the call.

I stared at the phone. "That wasn't as useful as I had hoped. But we know now that the warlock is Battisti. The original."

"Shit," Luca said from the back seat.

Kane's hold tightened around the steering wheel. "I don't know how we'll be able to handle him without him annihilating all of us."

Cheerful thought. "We'll have to make it as impossible as we can for him to attack us."

"And how do you propose we do that?"

"Give me a moment…" I spent the rest of the hour-long drive mulling it over, and I found the answer as we reached home.

"We'll do it in a public place!"

Kane and Luca didn't look convinced. "Wouldn't that simply give him more victims?"

It might, but I knew I was right. "A warlock hasn't lived centuries by massacring people left and right. He'll play nice."

"But we'll likely have to give the book to him," Luca pointed out.

That was a problem. "Maybe that's the only peaceful outcome. We could ask him not to capture people inside it anymore."

"That'll work," Luca said, oozing sarcasm. I agreed, but it was the only option we had.

"So where do you suggest we arrange the meeting?" Kane asked.

I had the answer ready. "At the charity auction tomorrow."

Seventeen

I HAD AN UPHILL STRUGGLE CONVINCING the household that the auction was the best place for arranging a meeting with Battisti. "Think about it," I tried to explain as we sat around the kitchen table again, for lunch Giselle had prepared while we were away: vegetable soup made with homegrown ingredients, and freshly baked bread. Yum.

"It's a high-profile event with enough people around that he shouldn't try anything funny, yet contained enough that there won't be much collateral damage if he nevertheless does."

"But there will be too many people who might witness magic being wielded," Amber pointed out as she filled her soup bowl. "Wiping the memories of them all is near impossible."

"But it can be done?"

"It might take quite a few vampires."

We turned to Luca, who shrugged. "I don't know all that many of us, but I guess it could be done." Vampires were secretive as it was, and they'd shunned Luca for decades for not draining and killing his blood donors, a logic only vampires could understand.

"How would we even lure Battisti there?" Kane asked.

"With the book," I said. "We'll put it in the auction."

"Then what's to stop him simply walking in and out with it?"

"I'm not entirely sure that's a bad option," I confessed, as I accepted the ladle from Amber to fill my bowl. "He'd be gone for good. But we'll put good security measures and wards around it."

"What about the auction? We'll have to let humans bid for the book, and one of them might win it," Giselle pointed out. I nodded.

"That's a genuine concern, but I don't think people will bid very hard on an obscure old book, even for charity. Besides, we'll wipe their memories anyway."

"Hunt would pay good money for it," Luca said gloomily. Kane nodded, his mouth pressed in a grim line as he swallowed a spoonful of soup.

"He can't be allowed to get his hands on it."

"Then we'll make sure he doesn't," I said with more confidence than I felt.

"Because we've been good at making him do what we want before?" Luca asked sardonically. My stomach tightened, threatening to turn the excellent soup sour, but I wasn't about to give up.

"We'll have to make it worth his while not to go after the book."

"We could say that he's no match for the warlock," Amber suggested, but Luca shook his head.

"We don't know that he isn't. And for a vampire like Hunt, it's more like an invitation to try his mettle against a worthy opponent. Opportunities like that are priceless when one is as old as him."

For a moment, I entertained the notion that we'd lure the two to the same place and let them have at it. Problem solved.

"Maybe we should include Hunt in our planning, then?" I suggested instead. I received horrified looks in return. Only Giselle agreed.

"You'll have to tell him anyway, otherwise he'll think you're a lousy date, running after a warlock in the middle of an important event."

"I hadn't exactly planned to be a model date either…"

"No need to antagonise him unnecessarily."

She was right. "What should we do, then?"

Kane ran his fingers through his hair with an impatient tug. "I'll ask around who's handling the auction and contact them first. If we can't even get the book on the catalogue, there's no point in continuing with this plan."

He knew all the players, and it didn't take him long to get the name of the auctioneer. The call to him was brief and not what we hoped. "Outsiders aren't allowed to put items in the auction," Kane told us. "Only those with an invitation."

I gave him a pointed look. "Well, we know who's invited…"

The reluctant looks around me told that they weren't any happier with involving Hunt than before. I wasn't sure I was.

"This is the best opportunity we have," Amber finally said, pushing her empty soup bowl aside. "If we don't announce today that the book is in the auction, there's no knowing who comes after it tonight. I'd like to be the one to set the time and place for once."

Kane inhaled resolutely and nodded. "I'll call Morgan."

"Maybe we should go see him without a warning," Luca suggested. "He'll have less time for scheming or refusing us."

"Do you think it's wise to surprise a vampire?" I asked, and he shook his head.

"No. But let's do it anyway."

HUNT LIVED IN A LUXURY high-rise of insanely priced, huge flats by Hyde Park, with top-notch security to keep the children of oligarchs and oil sheiks safe when they came for their regular shopping sprees in London. The guard at the lobby looked like he knew how to kill a man with his little finger, and he wouldn't let anyone pass without an invitation from a resident. Which we didn't have.

We had Luca though.

"This place would do well to have vampire guards instead of human," he said smugly when we were riding up to Hunt's floor after he had mesmerised the guard to let us pass. "Or at least someone who can resist us."

"I'm sure Morgan will seriously consider it after today," Kane said dryly, making my stomach tighten in dread of what Hunt would do if he was furious with us.

Who was I kidding, there was no "if" about it.

The lift let us out in a small, marbled lobby with a door on each side, each flat taking half a floor. Hunt's door was on the left, and it didn't have a doorbell. You didn't need one when security usually let you know you had visitors. Kane hesitated briefly and then gave the door three firm knocks that echoed inside the flat.

"Maybe he's not home," I suggested hopefully when nothing happened, only to jump back surprised when the door opened abruptly.

Hunt stood at the doorway, glowering at us. His auburn hair was mussed up, and he was dressed in an embroidered brocade robe and deep red silk pyjamas with the top open, revealing a smooth, muscled chest, looking like a decadent eighteenth-century aristocrat come to life.

Which he was.

I hadn't imagined we would surprise him at his leisure—I couldn't imagine him ever being at his leisure—and I felt acutely bad. He wasn't happy either. His angry power filled the small space, and I leaned closer to Kane, hoping his shield would help me too, my brain too addled to create a shield of my own, one of the few spells I knew how to cast well.

"This had better be good," he hissed.

Kane nodded, seemingly unaffected by Hunt's anger. "Yes. May we come in?"

For a moment it looked like Hunt would throw us out. Then he pivoted and sauntered deeper into the flat, the robe flouncing around his legs. Hesitantly, we followed. The door banged closed behind us without any of us touching it, making me even more reluctant to be there.

But this had been my idea, so I inhaled to fortify myself and crossed the marble foyer to a lowered lounge area in the middle of his flat—just in time to see a barely dressed form of a woman disappear down a hallway on the other side. A brunch was set on the dining table on the dais that faced the atrium in the middle of the highrise.

We were so dead...

Hunt threw himself on one of the comfortable seats around a large gas fireplace, his long legs stretched out and arms spread on the backrest, by all appearances perfectly relaxed. But his anger was still rubbing against my skin, making shivers of fear run down my spine.

"We are so sorry to barge in on you like this," I managed to say through a mouth so dry that my tongue stuck to the roof. We were standing on the steps that led down to the lounge, neatly in a line like the supplicants we were. "But we need your help."

He cocked a dark auburn brow. "And you thought interrupting my morning would ensure it?"

I didn't point out that it was well past midday already. He'd clearly had a late night and was making the most of his Saturday with his girlfriend.

I also didn't ask why he needed me as his date when he already had a girlfriend. Because she couldn't be a one-night stand. One didn't offer lavish brunches for those.

Or maybe vampires did. Maybe she was his blood donor and needed to be replenished afterwards, because Hunt didn't kill his donors either.

That thought did not help with my fear.

"We're a bit pressed for time and didn't want you to find excuses to not see us."

"It wouldn't have been an excuse…" He gestured impatiently with his hand. "Sit down, for fuck's sake."

We hurried to obey, though Kane managed to look like he'd meant to do so anyway.

"We would like you to place an item on auction at the charity event tomorrow," Kane said without preamble.

"Would you now?" Hunt drawled. "And what kind of item would it be?"

"A desired one."

Magic by the Book

"Not by humans, I presume?"

"No."

Kane's curt answer made Hunt huff. "I'm going to need a little more than that." I glanced towards the bedrooms where the woman had disappeared to, and he sneered and made a gesture with his hand that I recognised as a spell—the kind that vampires cast. "She won't hear us."

Kane considered him for a moment and then nodded. "It's the magical prison."

Hunt's eyes flashed. Literally. That wasn't good. "And who'll come after it?"

"The owner."

Hunt tilted his head and regarded us one by one. "I don't think we can handle this with minimum information."

Kane turned to me and nodded, indicating it was my story to tell. I wet my lips, considering how much to tell. "Almost four centuries ago, a warlock named Giovanni Battisti imprisoned a powerful demon inside a book on alchemy. For all we know, the demon is still inside. The warlock definitely is still alive."

Hunt's brows shot up. "Is he a vampire?"

"We don't know. We presume warlocks can live forever too."

"Hmmm…" was all he said.

"For some inexplicable reason, Battisti lent the book to two mages along with the spell that can capture people inside it. Instead of returning the book to him, they gave it to us. We accidently released the person who was captured."

"The human who is currently residing in the safehouse."

I nodded even though it hadn't been a question. "The mages and Battisti are in London, and they want the book back."

"Why don't you give it to them, then?"

"For ethical and moral reasons?" But he only gave me a slow look, so I continued. "We're giving the book back to Battisti. We're not happy about it, but we can't fight him forever. However, we'd like to do it in a way that prevents him from harming us."

"Hence the auction?"

"Yes."

"Do you expect him to bid for his own book?"

I hadn't thought about it, but I shrugged. "Whatever works. But we believe he'll simply snatch the book and be on his way."

"Simple as that?"

"I doubt any of this will be simple," Kane said dryly. "But if it comes to that, we'll try not to oppose him."

"Can you get the demon out of the book?"

My stomach fell. Trust him to ask about it. "No. Nor would we want to. It was captured in the first place because Battisti wasn't powerful enough to control it, and he was already powerful enough to summon it."

"That was four centuries ago," Hunt pointed out. "Who knows how powerful he is now."

"That's what we're afraid of."

"The demon might be more powerful now too," Luca said. "It can't be released."

Hunt sat in silence for a moment. "What is it that you want me to do?"

"Only invited guests can place items on the auction," Kane said. "We'd like you to place the book."

"I already have a painting there."

Kane shrugged. "Then change it. It happens all the time."

"And why would I do that?" Hunt drawled.

"Because you're a nice person?" I said before I managed to curb my tongue. Both his brows shot up.

"If you believe that, a change in our relationship is in order."

Me and my stupid mouth.

"It's not like you're motivated by money." Which we didn't have.

He shrugged one shoulder. "You'd be surprised..."

"You'd have a chance to get acquainted with a powerful warlock," Luca suggested.

"That's more tempting."

"You might get to fight him too," I said.

"But we want to avoid that," Kane added hastily. "We especially want to avoid him releasing the demon among the guests. Or summoning any demons."

"He doesn't have to summon one right there to have it at his beck and call," Hunt said. "But it has been a long time since I fought a demon, so I wouldn't mind that option."

"The reason we want to handle this at the auction is to prevent him from getting violent," Kane said. "So if you want to fight him, you'll have to lure him away from people."

"How exactly do you anticipate this to go?"

We glanced at each other. "We really have no idea," I said. "We don't even know if the items to be auctioned are on display during the dinner or not."

"They are. But do you really need the auction? If you place it in the catalogue and put it on display tonight with a minimum of security, the warlock might fetch it already."

Kane gave him a pointed look. "Or someone else might get to it first."

"There is always that possibility," Hunt said with a small shrug. Kane shook his head, exasperated.

"The book is highly sought after. For all we know, half the European warlocks will show up if there are no security measures."

"They might show up nonetheless. And they might do it during the auction."

My stomach tightened painfully. Warlocks could create portals that allowed them to travel huge distances in the blink of an eye. It was entirely possible all of them would show up.

"We'd best make sure that doesn't happen, then." The last thing we needed was a horde of warlocks interrupting dessert.

Hunt leaned abruptly forwards, startling me. "I'll do it, with these conditions: Luca comes to work for me for six months, job description to be decided. Phoebe will have two more dates with me, in more private settings, and, Archibald, you will not prevent me if I have a chance to take the book."

We glanced at each other in dismay. "I won't do anything criminal," Luca stated.

"Fine."

"I'm dating Kane now," I said, sitting closer to him. Hunt's lip curled.

"I know."

The look in his eyes indicated he didn't so much want me as he wanted to annoy Kane. Judging by the tightening of Kane's jaw, it worked.

"Owning the book won't do you any good," he only said. He could've at least tried to defend me, for what good it would've done. "And might keep the warlock breathing down your neck for centuries."

"He can try…"

"He might win," Luca said, but Hunt only shrugged.

"I've lived long enough."

Oddly enough, the thought that he might die dismayed me. I kept the emotion to myself though.

"Do we have a deal?"

I glanced at Kane, who gave me a serious look. "You don't have to say yes," he said. I nodded and turned to Hunt.

"The dates will not include any kind of bodily contact, mind alteration, or blood donations."

He flicked his head to the direction of the bedroom. "I don't need you for blood or sex."

"So it's to piss off Kane, then."

The first genuine smile during this meeting spread on his face. "That's a bonus."

I inhaled deeply. "Fine."

Kane nodded too. "We agree. Now, will you call the auctioneer?"

Eighteen

ONCE HUNT COMMITTED TO THE plan, he really committed. He had clout enough to simply inform the organisers of the charity event that he not only wished to change the lot he'd donated, he'd be bringing his own security to watch over it. No vampire tricks needed.

The charity auction was held at the Guildhall, the seat of the City of London government, the square mile where London originated from and still a self-governing entity. The current building was from the fifteenth century, but the place had served a similar function since the Roman era. Ruins of an amphitheatre had been found underneath the current building in the 80s, and there had been a Guildhall on the site since the twelfth century.

The large, rectangular sandstone building, located northeast of the St Paul's, looked like a one-nave gothic basilica on the outside, complete with small spires at the corners. It had suffered some damage during the Great Fire of London in 1666, and the Blitz in 1940, and had been repaired. The great hall at the heart of the building had been restored in the 50s, and not entirely to its original form, but with its gothic, ornamental sandstone walls, high, vaulted ceiling, and stained-glass windows, I could imagine it looked much like it used to.

The space was large like a cathedral too, and even with round tables already brought in for the dinner the next day, it didn't feel cramped. A quick calculation of the tables, each of which seated ten, revealed that three hundred guests would attend the event. It was only half of the room's dinner capacity, but it was still too many potential casualties.

At one end, was a low, room-wide stage that was perfect for the auction. The lots would be on display there so that the guests could look at them before the dinner. Currently, though, the cases were empty.

"We hadn't thought to put anything on display until a little before the doors open tomorrow," Simon Zhang, the auctioneer, said. He was a Chinese transplant in his sixties who had lived in London for so long that he'd adopted a Western name. He'd handled a couple of auctions in our gallery too, so we knew him well. He was great with the audience, entertaining but with a firm hand on the gavel, which always brought excellent results.

"Until then, everything's kept in the vault here. Not that any of the lots are terribly valuable, but one doesn't want to upset the donators."

"You don't expect the auction to bring much?" Kane asked, and Simon shrugged.

"It depends on how charitable the guests are feeling. It's for famine relief, so maybe they'll feel guilty having stuffed their guts at a lavish dinner. But most of the money comes from the five-thousand-pound dinner tickets."

I paled and couldn't help glancing at Hunt, who gave me a mock bow. "Yes, I paid that much to bring you here."

"I guess I'd best look grateful, then..."

"And eat your stomach's fill," Luca added with a grin.

"I doubt it's an open buffet," Kane said wryly, his eyes twinkling. I took it to mean he wasn't upset that I would be Hunt's date. Handling Battisti without casualties was the main concern.

He turned to Simon. "We don't need all the items here yet, only the one we're placing in the auction so that we can put heavy security on it."

"Wouldn't it be better to keep it in the safe?" Simon asked.

"There'll be less damage if whoever comes after it doesn't have to break into it."

Simon lifted a well-groomed black brow. He was always impeccably coiffed and dressed, with fun details in his outfit, like a red handkerchief with white polka dots in the breast pocket of his jacket today. "It's that valuable? Who'll come after it?"

"The owner."

He pulled back, dismayed. "I'm not auctioning stolen items. What exactly are you foisting on me, Archibald?"

"Would you believe if I told you it's a dangerous magical artifact that belongs to a powerful, vindictive warlock?" A small smile hovered around Kane's mouth, as if he were kidding, but his eyes were serious. Simon considered him with his head tilted.

"I've seen weirder things in China, but I never would've thought you'd be involved in such matters."

"Well, I am."

Simon nodded. "We'd best do this your way, then. But I want to watch."

Grady arrived with a group of werewolves who even in human form looked tight and lethal enough to secure the crown jewels, let alone a small book. They emptied the room and the adjoining kitchen, much to the annoyance of the waiting staff who were busy setting the tables and preparing all the food that could be done today.

"Come back tomorrow," Hunt told them, lacing the words with enough vampire suggestion that they left without more complaints. I hoped they would have enough time to prepare everything tomorrow, but they couldn't be here overnight, in case Battisti showed up.

The men and women working for Grady went through the huge building to make sure it was empty. When they were done, Kane placed the book on its appointed place on the stage, opening it to a random page so that it would look interesting to potential bidders.

"Phoebe, can you help me draw a containment circle around it? The same we used at Rupert's."

Under the watchful eyes of Hunt, Luca, and a bemused Simon, who would have his mind altered later, no doubt, we drew the circle with chalk around the display case, making it large enough that the potential thief couldn't reach the book across it. Once it was done, Kane began to weave complicated wards around it.

"These will hopefully hold Battisti inside, should he get through," he told me. "Though he might be powerful enough to either portal out or bring down the wards."

"Pity we don't know the stun wards that protected the crypt at Highgate cemetery," I said with a shudder, remembering how they'd incapacitated Kane so badly I'd needed Laurent Dufort, Danielle's warlock boyfriend, to revive him.

"I don't think we'll need such drastic measures," Kane said with a tight voice, his energy and concentration taken by the wards. "Moreover, they took too many people to unravel."

Once he was done, he studied his work with a critical eye, and then turned to Hunt. He gestured at the book. "Go ahead, do your worst."

"I'm to be your guinea pig?" Hunt asked, amused.

"I'm more worried about you getting your hands on that book than Battisti," Kane said.

Hunt rolled his eyes. "What do you think I can do with it? I can't read it, I can't release the demon, and even if I knew the spell to capture people inside it, I wouldn't be able to cast it. Vampire magic isn't compatible with mages'."

"Yet you want it anyway."

Hunt shrugged his shoulder minutely. "True."

He rounded the display case, giving it a wide berth as he studied the wards Kane had put up around it. Then he concentrated and I could feel his power flaring. He gestured with his hands—and stepped through the wards.

He shot Kane a smug smile. Kane nodded calmly in return. "Now step out."

Hunt obeyed, only to hit an invisible barrier. "What the hell?" He looked almost comically baffled. He banged the wards, then began to unravel them. But no matter how hard he tried, what magic he threw against the wards held him; he was stuck.

"Get me out of here, Archibald." He looked angry, but his power was contained by the wards, and for once didn't affect me.

It was Kane's turn to look smug as he released Hunt with a wave of his hand. "I made some improvements," he explained when I mentioned that the lock-up wards at the council house had taken him eons to pull down. "We won't have much time tomorrow, should Battisti come for the book. We only want to keep him for long enough to strike a deal with him that he won't use the book against people anymore."

Simon had watched all this without a word. Now he nodded. "Western magic is very different from Chinese."

"You're familiar with Chinese magic?" Kane asked, surprised. I'd also assumed Simon had merely meant that he'd seen strange things in his time, but the older man nodded.

"Yes, but I'm not a practitioner. My mother was though. She was a *wu*, a sort of…" He gestured with his hand, searching for translation. "…sorceress, I guess, or shamaness. We have many sorts of practitioners. They used to be an integral part of society, but first Confucius and then communism tried to rationalise them away. But you can't stop them from being born."

"We call ourselves mages," I told him, intrigued by his account. Thanks to Amber's thorough lessons, I knew that there were different magical traditions around the world, but we hadn't covered any details.

"We keep it a secret unless the child shows signs of having inherited the skill," Kane told Simon, who shook his head.

"Pity. Much is lost that way." He gestured at the book. "So what's going to happen here?"

Since he didn't need to have his mind wiped, we told him. He looked stunned. "This will be the strangest auction I've ever held, won't it?"

Magic by the Book

Kane gave him a tight smile. "Just don't do anything rash if Battisti shows up."

"And keep people clear of the display case," Luca added. "We don't want them to become trapped."

Simon frowned. "That might be difficult."

"They won't get through the wards," Kane assured them. He fixed the wards he'd taken down for Hunt and then sighed.

"We're as prepared as we can be. At any rate, I have a dinner meeting with my parents, so I must go. We'll have to hope Battisti doesn't come tonight."

"We'll be ready for him," Grady promised, gesturing at his people, who bared their teeth like wolves.

Luca and I assured Kane that we'd get home fine—it wasn't far—so he kissed me, all too quickly, and left with Hunt, who had arrived with us. We headed home too.

Luca put away his phone he'd been working on the whole time. "I've placed info on every vampire and mage site I can think of where Battisti might see that the book is here."

I'd sent messages to Camillo and Mrs Hayling, telling them to stay away but to relay the info to Battisti should he show up.

"Now we can only wait."

WAITING TURNED OUT TO be the most difficult part. I slept poorly, expecting Battisti to show up either here or at the antiques shop, but nothing happened. Giselle and Amber looked like they hadn't slept much either. Luca never slept at night. Only Ashley, who had been at work, had had an uneventful night with no major alarms and had managed to get a full night's sleep at the station.

When Kane arrived for breakfast looking well-rested but serious, he said the night had been quiet at the Guildhall too.

"I hope this doesn't mean Battisti hasn't got the message," I said, worried.

Kane shrugged a shoulder. "If that happens, we'll come up with another plan."

"Maybe we could mail the book to him?"

He laughed. "That would work."

We went through the evening's plan one more time. We would all attend the event. Kane would assist Simon with the auction, which gave him a reason to be on the stage the whole time. Luca and Ashley would join Grady's people, a fact that rubbed Ashley's fur the wrong way, but she promised to behave.

"Keep him far enough from me and we'll do fine."

Amber and Giselle would be part of the wait staff. Hunt had had to use his suggestion skills on the manager to achieve that, after the woman had flat-out refused to hire outsiders on such short notice.

Knowing that the room would be filled with people I could rely on eased my nerves, but I still had trouble forcing my breakfast down.

"Would you like to practice spells for your presentation?" Kane asked after breakfast. I couldn't bring myself to worry about it like I'd done before, as I might not survive tonight, but I nodded. It would be something to while the day away. And I always liked when he taught me.

We climbed to the attic and settled on the wooden floor. "We should bring pillows here to sit on," I grumbled, making him grin, which in turn made my heart jump.

"I think it's supposed to teach you how to concentrate even when you're uncomfortable." He paused, and his mood changed to apologetic as he looked me in the eyes, studying me with concern.

"I hope you weren't upset that I didn't ask you to join us for dinner with my parents yesterday. I honestly only came to think of it when we sat down and they asked what was new in my life. I told them about you though."

Acute panic and embarrassment washed over me. It made our dating seem more official that he'd told his parents. "No, of course I wasn't. We haven't even managed a proper date yet. We're far from meeting the parents."

His smile was relieved and a bit teasing. "It'll likely happen sooner rather than later. They're eager to meet you."

His assurances distracted me so thoroughly that I stopped obsessing over the auction. My ability to concentrate on the magic vanished too, and I had to try several times before I managed to levitate a feather. Luckily, I didn't burn it this time, because the stench of a burning feather was awful.

Eventually, I managed to cast the four required spells reliably several times in a row to his satisfaction. It gave me some desired self-confidence. I might get through the presentation after all.

Practicing spells was draining, and Kane let me go before I was completely exhausted. He left home and I took a short nap to recover, before it was time to start preparing for the evening.

Giselle did my hair. She'd been a hairdresser before she trained to become a cook, and she created a large, elegant knot on the nape of my neck. She even managed to soften the effect of the blunt fringe.

I did my own makeup, which took longer than it should because my hand kept shaking with nerves. I had to sit down and prop my elbow against my writing desk to finish drawing my eyes.

I dressed in the only gown I had that was good enough for the occasion, a dark blue Dior I'd purchased for my cousin's engagement party. Well, Mother had paid for it. It was a silk cocktail dress with a flouncing pleated hem which reached my mid-calf and continued diagonally up the fitted strapless top. I added a black silk wrap around my shoulders to ward off the chill of the November night.

For jewellery, I wore my grandmother's pearl drop earrings and a black velvet choker with a cameo on it that I'd borrowed from Giselle. Shoes caused a bit of a problem. Not that I didn't have suitable ones; I had beautiful high-heeled silver sandals that worked perfectly with the dress. But I wouldn't be able to run in them, should the need arise—and I was pretty sure that arise it would.

In the end, vanity won though, and I wore the sandals. They matched the evening clutch I wanted to use, and I really didn't have running shoes that would go well with the dress. I could only hope I lived to regret the decision.

The clutch was just large enough for my phone, lipstick, and the compact mirror. I didn't really need the mirror, but I hoped it would bring me good luck. I didn't need the phone either—I doubted I'd take photos, and I wasn't so rude I'd check my social media during the dinner—but I simply couldn't leave home without. No room for house keys, so I had to hope one of my housemates would be around to see me home.

Magic by the Book

By the time I was finished with my attire, the house had emptied, everyone having left for the Guildhall to prepare for their appointed tasks. Only Grizelda was keeping me company, though her idea of company was sleeping on my bed and then disappearing somewhere in the large house.

I was restless, nervous, and worried. I tried to watch TV as I waited for Hunt's car to arrive, but nothing interested me, and I kept obsessively changing the channel. Every creak of the floor and car passing on the street below made me jump. I kept expecting someone to break into the shop at any moment. I paced the living room floor, or watched the cars driving by, my stomach tightening every time one slowed down by the shop.

When my phone suddenly rang, it startled me so badly I almost flung the clutch across the room. I fished the phone out with shaking hands, and stared at the display with its "no caller ID" text. Hoping for a telemarketer that would distract me, I connected the call.

"I have received your message," a male voice said with perfect English that held no trace of accent that I could place. I'd never heard the voice before, but I knew it had to be Battisti. He was centuries old; he probably spoke all the languages of the world perfectly by now. The voice was low and somehow threatening, but it could be my nerves projecting. "I will meet you at your chosen location. But I have taken precautions."

My entire body froze. "What precautions?"

"Surely you don't expect me to reveal them?" He was amused now, but the threat level seemed to increase. "*Arrivederci.*"

The call ended, and I stared at the phone, dismayed, swallowing the sudden nausea. The plan was working. No choice but to go forward with it.

"Are you ready to go?"

The second fright in less than five minutes made me shriek. My legs gave out under me, and I dropped on the stuffed sofa, slowly pressing my head between my knees as I fought to calm my heart.

"How the bloody hell did you get in?" I demanded of Hunt. "And weren't you supposed to send the driver?"

"I'm a vampire. Locks don't really pose a problem for me," he answered, speaking right next to me. I hadn't even heard him move across the floor. A hand landed between my shoulder blades, bare in the corset top of the gown. It was cool at first, and then warmth began to spread from it. As it did, calmness took over.

"I thought we agreed no mind alterations," I managed to say, but I didn't really put heat into it. I needed to be calm.

"This is more a body alteration." He removed the hand and offered it to me. I took it and he helped me up. My legs held and my breathing was calm.

Hunt looked expensive and elegant in his form-fitting dinner jacket and crisp white shirt, his hair newly cut and face cleanly shaven. A picture-perfect man of power and money. He gave me a critical once over and nodded.

"You'll do."

"Hey!"

I'd put effort into my appearance, the least he could do was acknowledge it. He smiled.

"And now you have colour on your cheeks too."

Bastard.

Nineteen

THE EFFECTS OF HUNT'S CALMING spell soon wore off and I was tense and silent the short ride to the Guildhall in his chauffeured Bentley. Cars queued slowly down a short accessway to the red carpet across the courtyard, dropping off the guests one by one. Each time we drove a car's length forward, the knot in my stomach tightened.

A small cluster of photographers was waiting near the main door, adding to my tension. I hadn't realised this was the kind of event that would be featured on the society pages of evening papers. I'd never attended one, and I wasn't sure I wanted to do so now—not with Hunt at any case.

When it was our time to exit the car, Hunt got out first and then held a hand to me, politely helping me. I let him, mostly because I wasn't sure I'd manage a graceful exit otherwise, and I didn't want to plant on my face in front of the press. He even checked quickly that my skirt hadn't hiked to my waist or something else embarrassing before stepping aside.

"I bet this is easier than helping women with pannier dresses and high wigs out of carriages," I muttered. A delighted grin spread on his face, making the cameras flash. Great.

"That was its own kind of operation, but we had groomsmen and ladies' maids for that. An aristocrat in my position didn't have to bother with being polite to women."

At least he'd learned since. Sort of.

"You could've warned me about the cameras," I said as he offered me his arm. I placed a hand on it, keeping a bit more distance between us than needed. I didn't want the whole town—or at least my family—to think I was dating Hunt.

"You'll do fine."

Calmly, as if the cameras didn't bother him at all, he led me down the red carpet. I tried to smile, or at least not to look like pre-death rigor mortis had settled on my face, but my hold on Hunt's arm tightened, the only thing that prevented me from bolting.

I only relaxed when we entered the foyer of the Guildhall and the heavy oak door closed behind us. "If I never have to do that again, it'll be too soon."

"If everything goes well, it was the scariest part of the night," he consoled me, but it had the opposite effect. I pivoted to him, all nerves again.

"I forgot to tell you. Battisti called right before your surprise appearance." It had managed to wipe the call off my mind completely. "He'll be here tonight, and he has taken precautions."

His face turned grim, even as he nodded politely to his acquaintances milling in the foyer, making last minute checks on their looks before moving to the steps upstairs.

"I don't like the sound of that."

Magic by the Book

"You don't think he's summoned a demon to help him?" I hissed in a low tone, but he heard me even over the din of a hundred or so people.

"I more fear he's taken hostages."

His dire prediction caused me to trip, but luckily I was still holding his arm and didn't fall.

"There's nothing we can do about it right now," Hunt said, steadying me. "Let's pretend we're here to have a good time."

"And to raise money for starving children."

"That too," he added with a mocking smile.

We joined the slow progression upstairs. At the top, a waiter was offering glasses of champagne from a tray, and I managed to grab one without upending the whole thing with my shaking hands. I took a sip to wet my mouth whilst trying to locate my friends over the rim, but there were too many people crammed in the small space to spot them, the guests halting at the door to the great hall, causing a block.

I recognised some faces from the news, politicians, councilmen and celebrities, but most of the guests were businesspeople leading companies I'd likely never even heard of. There were no trophy girlfriends, and even most of the celebrities were over forty. Hunt was among the youngest men here.

Well, he *looked* like he was younger than most.

"Have you ever calculated how many of these events you've attended in your lifetime?" I asked him as we made our slow way to the great hall, and received a horrified look in return.

"Why would I do that?"

"Fun? Education?"

"There's nothing fun in knowing how old one truly is."

Despite his words, Hunt was in his element, greeting acquaintances approaching him left and right until we were finally through the door. And then it was my time to pause and block the door, in awe.

The great hall had been transformed since the previous day. The tables were beautifully set with enough crystal and silverware for five courses, and each table had a tall, baroque silver candelabra with live candles as a centrepiece. Red and purple floodlights were set on the floor by the walls, the beams aimed up to highlight the reliefs, adding to the gothic atmosphere.

The stage had changed too. The lots on auction were in a row of display cases on pedestals and illuminated by spotlights. People were slowly walking past them to take a closer look, though it didn't seem they were terribly interested in them.

I spotted Kane at the opposite edge of the stage and my heart jumped in delight. He looked like he always did, neat and precise in his dinner jacket, but more vigilant than normal. Behind him, partially hidden in shadows, were Luca and Ashley, both dressed in dark suits like the rest of the security.

They were safe at least.

"We need to get word to others that Battisti is definitely coming," I said to Hunt, who nodded and led me onto the stage.

There was no hurrying the procession past the lots, no matter how impatient I was, so I settled to give them a good look. Despite my tight nerves, the antique dealer in me took over and I studied everything with a critical eye.

I wasn't impressed, and I didn't wonder Simon wasn't hopeful for the result.

There was a miniature oil landscape from the early eighteenth century by an unknown artist. We sold those in our shop for around a thousand pounds, maybe a little more depending on the condition, and the starting price had been set for two hundred today. If it fetched more than two thousand, I'd be surprised.

There was a pretty Qing Dynasty vase Simon had authenticated to the mid-nineteenth century, but those had been produced on an industrial scale and imported to England by the shipload. We didn't often sell Chinese antique in our shop, but a similar vase we'd had was sold for less than a thousand pounds.

Other lots were similar, though not everything was art or antique, like a luxury Caribbean cruise for two that claimed to be worth ten thousand pounds, and a Louis Vuitton handbag. The most desired designer handbags could fetch tens of thousands in auctions, but this one wasn't terribly rare, and the closing price likely wouldn't be more than fifteen hundred.

"This is all rubbish," Hunt muttered, and for once I agreed with him.

It wasn't the items as such; we would sell the antique pieces in our shop—small inexpensive items were our bread and butter—and I could personally use the handbag. It was the fact that wealthy people had gone through their closets and donated what for them was useless trash.

We reached the last item, and it wasn't the book. Baffled, I looked around, about to head to the steps off the stage after the other guests, when I realised there was one more display case. I could just about detect it out of the corner of my eye, but I instantly wanted to look away. I raised a hasty shield, and the effect went away. The book appeared.

Kane smiled at me. He was standing by the display case, yet I'd ignored him too, as if he weren't there. "You noticed the spell."

I rounded the case to him so that the people could move past me. "That was a clever addition." I glanced quickly around, but no one was paying any attention to us, the spell effectively shielding us too. Nevertheless, I leaned closer not to be overheard.

"Battisti called. He'll definitely be here."

Kane looked grim. "Did he say when?"

"No, but he said he's taken precautions so that we won't capture him. Hunt believes he's taken hostages. Have you seen Amber and Giselle?"

"Yes, they're over there, handling the champagne."

I looked over the vast room. It was dimly lit to make the most of the coloured walls, and it took me a while to locate them among the crowd. Relief washed over me.

"It's not any of us, then."

"Not yet." His ominous statement made me lose what little appetite I had. Then he smiled, warmly. "You look lovely."

I almost blushed. "Thank you. If I die today, I'll die pretty."

He took a hold of my arm. "No one is dying today," he said sternly, then leaned down and kissed me. I may have clung to his labels rather embarrassingly, until Hunt cleared his throat behind me.

"No kissing my date, Archibald."

Kane shot him a fierce look over my shoulder. "You keep her safe."

Magic by the Book

"Of course."

A gong chimed, indicating that everyone should take their seats. With a last squeeze of Kane's hand, I followed Hunt to our table—only to have the biggest shock of the night.

"AUNT EMILIA, UNCLE JOHN! What are you doing here?" I stared at my family members in dismay. It wasn't that I didn't like them, but their presence complicated matters tenfold.

Aunt Emilia was, in fact, my cousin, the daughter of Dad's older sister, Aunt Clara, but since she was thirty years older than me, and had a daughter my age, I'd started to call her my aunt when I was little.

John Radcliffe, her husband, leaned down to kiss my cheek. He might be my only uncle, but he was my favourite. "Phoebe! What a lovely surprise." He turned to Hunt with an expectant look, and I hastened to introduce them.

"Uncle John runs the family business," I added. He'd taken over after my father had a heart attack. "This is Morgan Hunt."

I paused, awkward, when I realised that I had no idea what Hunt's main business was. It wasn't running nightclubs. Luckily, Uncle John knew who Hunt was, and offered a hand to him with a smile.

"It's a pleasure to finally meet you. We belong to the same club, but I've never managed to catch you there."

Hunt's smile was the most pleasant I'd yet seen during our brief acquaintance. "I'm an infrequent visitor. It's nice to meet Phoebe's family."

The comment caused Aunt Emilia's eyes to flash in interest and my stomach fell. She'd tell Mother I was dating Hunt if I didn't correct her immediately.

"Mr Hunt is doing a favour for my boss, who is overseeing the auction, by inviting me here."

Hunt's lips twitched with a quick smile, but he didn't correct me. Aunt Emilia hid her disappointment well. "That's kind of you, Mr Hunt. And it's a lovely surprise to have you here, Phoebe. If I'd known, I would've purchased seats for Olivia and Henry too."

Her daughter Olivia had recently married Henry Sanford, after a bunch of mages almost ruined the whole thing. Incidentally, the dress I was wearing was bought for their engagement party. Aunt Emilia gave it a critical glance but didn't make any comments.

We were introduced to the rest of the table, three middle-aged couples who were acquaintances of both Hunt and my uncle from the business world—no celebrities for us—and we took our seats. Hunt manoeuvred us so that we sat facing the case holding the book, so we'd know the moment Battisti arrived. Uncle John sat next to me and proceeded to engage Hunt in a conversation I had no interest in.

Whether it interested Hunt or not, he kept up the conversation easily. No scary vampire for these people.

I wouldn't have been able to concentrate on the conversation anyway. My attention was on the stage. Kane and Simon had retired to their seats to have dinner too. Luca and Ashley were at their spots near the book, standing in calm rest, studying the people. Grady and one of his wolves were on the opposite side of the stage near the door.

Magic by the Book

The book was as secure as it could be. I tried to relax and force my attention back to our table, but when the first course was brought in I was startled by its sudden appearance, not having paid any attention.

"Everything's ready at our end," a voice murmured by my ear, and I realised only then that it was Amber.

"Battisti called and he will be here," I murmured back.

The hand placing the salad plate in front of me wobbled a little. "This is it, then."

For the duration of the dinner, though, nothing happened. Everything proceeded smoothly, the staff accustomed to handling such large dinners. Everything that was placed in front of me looked beautiful, but I couldn't say if it was good, because I only tasted dust. I tried not to drink too much of the excellent wine that was regularly poured into the glasses, but I was starting to feel lightheaded. Or it could be the hyperventilation that crept on me as the auction drew near.

It was slated to take place before dessert. When the plates were being cleared after the last course, my aunt stood up and gave me a pointed look, which I correctly interpreted as a command to join her.

I didn't need to visit the ladies', and I didn't want the third degree that it was intended for. Moreover, I wanted to stay in the great hall, in case Battisti showed up. But I rose obediently, murmuring my excuse to Hunt. To my surprise, he pulled me closer and spoke to my ear.

"Keep an eye on her—and for Battisti."

Everything I'd eaten threatened to come up when I realised what he meant. Battisti might take my aunt hostage.

With stiff legs, I followed Aunt Emilia across the floor, joining the several other women who'd had the same idea. As I neared the door, I sought Grady's gaze, hoping to convey the urgent need of protection with my eyes. He gave me a small nod, easing my nerves a little. Whatever happened, the building was full of people who could handle it and protect my family.

My aunt leaned closer to me as we made our way downstairs. "You should be nicer to Mr Hunt. He'll think you're not interested."

I hadn't realised I hadn't been nice, but I didn't really have a good grasp on the past couple of hours. "That's because I'm not."

"Phoebe … how can you say so," she admonished me. "Don't you know he's an important man. And isn't he handsome too?"

Since I couldn't tell her Hunt was a scary, centuries-old vampire, I blurted out the truth: "I'm seeing my boss now." My heart was beating fast for the confession, but it felt good to get it out.

She gave me an askance look. "Is it wise?"

Not the reaction I was hoping for. "We'll make it work. We share the same interest in art and antiques." Not to mention magic, but again, I couldn't tell that.

"Hmmm…" was all she said, but it sounded disapproving. Hopefully it was only disappointment for Hunt and not because she genuinely though Kane and I wouldn't be able to make it work. Either way, Mom would call me tomorrow—provided I was there to be called.

A surprisingly many women had decided to pop to the loo; the queue reached to the foyer. Good thing I didn't have an urgent need to go myself—though I would, to avoid embarrassment when the action started.

People were popping outside for a smoke too. My back was towards the door, and every time I heard it open, I tried to surreptitiously check if Battisti had arrived.

"Are you waiting for someone?" my aunt asked acerbically, noticing my twitching.

"No, I'm ... checking if I recognise any celebrities."

She didn't quite roll her eyes, but she came as close as she was able to. "Useless lot. None of them will bid for anything, mark my words."

"Are you interested in any of the lots?"

She pursed her lips. "Not really. Why, is there anything worth bidding for?"

At least she had confidence in my professional skills.

"No. And definitely nothing over a thousand pounds."

"Well, we can always drive the price up. For charity, of course."

"Of course."

No one attacked us in the ladies'—unless you count the woman who jumped the queue ahead of me, taking the stall I'd been about to enter. I contemplated casting a water spell and dousing her, but that was surely the first step on the path to the dark side, so I simply took the next one that freed up and held my tongue.

I couldn't see my aunt as I was washing my hands, which caused a brief adrenaline spike, but she was waiting for me in the lobby. I barely refrained from chastising her for being reckless. She would've thought I'd lost my mind. Besides, I noticed the wolf guard I'd met at the safehouse loitering near her.

As we made our way up again, my phone buzzed inside my clutch, indicating a message. "I'll check this before I go in," I said to my aunt, digging the phone out. She nodded and headed in ahead of me.

"Don't be long."

I hoped for a message from Kane with important information, or to say he missed me. What I got were two photographs from an unknown number. My entire body froze when I saw the contents.

In the first, Aunt Emilia and I were queueing to the loo, taken in the foyer. I hadn't even noticed. Panic rising, I looked around to spot Battisti, in case he was watching my reaction, but there was no one near me. I hurried into the great hall, opening the second photo as I went, only to stop dead in my tracks.

It was a photo of Mrs Hayling and Camillo. They were sitting on a stone floor, huddled together in fear, their hands intertwined as they held onto each other tightly, looking at the camera with panicky eyes. Their surroundings looked mildly familiar, like a manmade grotto, but I couldn't immediately place it.

The reason for their fear was standing behind them. He looked like a very large man at first glimpse, his bare upper body grotesquely muscular and slightly green in hue. There was a vicious grin on his face, baring a row of razor-sharp teeth like shark's, and I knew I wasn't looking at a human.

Battisti had summoned a demon after all.

"What's wrong?" Kane asked right by me, startling me into almost dropping the phone. Wordlessly, I handed it to him. His eyes grew large and he cursed.

"Battisti has made his first move. And his timing is impeccable. The auction is about to begin."

Twenty

GRADY CAME OVER TO US, EYES sharp. Even in a black suit that fit him better than many of the other men's here, his silver hair in a sexy hipster do, he seemed scary and a little wild. The police-grade handcuffs peeking under his jacket didn't make him any cuddlier.

"Is there a problem?"

Kane showed him the photo and he studied it with his head tilted like a curious wolf's. "Who are they?"

"The pair looking like they're about to wet themselves abducted Mr Hayling," I told him, and he startled.

"Battisti captured them for you?"

I hadn't thought of it that way. "I kind of think he's using them as leverage."

"And the muscle?" His eyes narrowed and he leaned closer. "Is that what I think it is?"

Kane looked grim. "Yes. And if I remember my demonology correctly, that's likely the grade of demon that's captured inside the book."

That was not good. "Dare we hope he's learned to control them these past centuries?"

"He'd better, because that particular demon has a taste for human flesh."

I couldn't help glancing at Grady. He noticed and a slow, wolfish grin spread on his face, showing too many teeth. "I mean, meat is meat when you're hungry…"

I pinched my eyes closed to ward off the image. "I don't really care for Camillo and Mrs Hayling, but we can't let them be harmed. And who knows what will happen if that demon gets loose."

Grady nodded. "Do you know where this is taken?"

"No," Kane and I said in unison, and his brows knit with worry.

"If it's somewhere in this building, we'll all be in danger if that thing goes on rampage."

Kane shot Grady a questioning look. "Do we need to start evacuating?"

Grady studied the room and the festive people who had no idea something bad was about to happen. The energy he constantly emanated spiked, causing hairs on my arms to shoot up.

"We don't know that this photo was taken here. But I'll send men to look. A demon should be easy to sniff out. If it's here, I'll ring the fire alarm and start evacuating."

Kane nodded. "Tell them not to engage, if they find the demon," he cautioned. Then he looked around and heaved a fortifying sigh. "And since we're trying to lure Battisti here with the auction, we should go on with it."

"Unless he's counting on us emptying the building so that he can take the book while we're not paying attention," Grady said.

"We'd best handle this fast, then."

Hoping that Grady's men would be able to handle things, I hurried back to my table. Kane went to Simon and likely told him to speed things up, because the auctioneer instantly sprang into action.

I showed the photo to Hunt under the table. He gave it a surreptitious look and his brows shot up. "Should I know these people?"

"They're Battisti's leverage." I should be worried for them, but knowing he hadn't harmed my friends was such a relief that I was a bit dizzy. I lowered my voice further. "And that's a high-level demon. Grady sent men to look for it, but if it gets loose here, none of us is safe."

"Stay alert," he said, and I rolled my eyes.

"I'm nothing but alert." There was so much adrenaline coursing through me I was about to start zooming around the room like a hyperactive five-year-old.

I turned my attention to the stage as Simon began the auction. The guests quieted, but the room didn't fall completely silent, the alcohol having loosened everyone's tongues. Behind him, on a large screen, a video was rolling, showing starving children in a drought-ridden African country. I found it moving, but there were quite a few cynical faces around me.

When the video ended, Simon launched into his opening spiel about the purpose of the auction and how it would proceed. "Bids are fifty pounds until we reach a thousand, after which they're a hundred pounds each. The house will be forgoing the usual commission, so you don't need to hold back in fear of extra costs. May the competition be fierce."

There were some polite laughs. Kane went to the first lot and took out the miniature painting to show it to the audience, though a picture of it was displayed on the screen too. Simon kept a steady stream of talk as the bidding started.

I always found this part exciting. I sat straighter, leaning towards the stage as the price got up, people getting into the spirit of bidding. The closing price for the miniature was almost three thousand pounds, which was a lot more than I'd expected.

Other items fetched fairly well too. There was a veritable war over the cruise, the winner a celebrity TV presenter who looked utterly satisfied for the purchase.

"Do you want that bag?" Hunt asked me when Kane took the Louis Vuitton out. He could probably read the answer from my eager face, so I nodded.

"Yes. But I won't bid for it." And not because I couldn't afford it, having blown my account with the magic books. I didn't need a bag that would sit on a shelf to be admired and not be used.

"I could buy it for you."

I gave him a startled look, then shook my head decisively. "Absolutely not."

His lip curled in an amused smirk as he turned to face the stage again. He made a few bids anyway, like he had bid for almost every item, bowing out before the price rose too high.

The bag fetched two thousand pounds. Much too high a price for it.

I kept an eye on the clock. The auction had proceeded at a good pace, but who knew how long Battisti could control the demon. I strained my ear, fearing I'd hear screams of terror from the hallway every time the door opened, but there were no unusual sounds.

As Kane took out the last item before the book and the bidding began, my tension returned with a vengeance. Hunt leaned closer. "Calm the beating of your heart. You'll give yourself a coronary."

Magic by the Book

I didn't ask how he could detect my heartbeat over the excited noise in the room. I only growled in return. "Exactly how do you suggest I do that?"

He huffed and took a hold of my wrist under the table. A moment later, calmness poured into me, forced on by him. I would've freaked out, but I was too mellow to. "Now, concentrate on your magic and shield up."

With the tension gone, I was able to find the spark of magic inside me. I closed my eyes to concentrate as the bidding went on around me. As Simon knocked the gavel for the closing price, I had the shield up and I opened my eyes.

A portal formed by the last display case and Battisti stepped out.

He looked exactly like his portrait from four centuries ago; he hadn't aged at all. His hair was still dark and long, and fastened to his neck with a silver clip. Only the Vandyke was gone, his face cleanly shaven. His dinner jacket was modern and exactly like all the men here were wearing. Still, he looked very Italian and striking, completely unlike the middle-aged Englishmen attending the party. I should've spotted him in the foyer.

A startled murmur washed through the audience, followed by excited applause, as people thought his appearance was a very good trick. They were cut short when Battisti waved his hand, freezing the entire crowd, their mouths included.

Fear tightened my bones. He had to be stupendously powerful to be able to control three hundred people without breaking a sweat.

My shield held, amazingly enough, and I was able to move. Or it could be Hunt was shielding me as well. But we both sat still, letting Battisti believe he had all of us subdued.

On the stage, Simon had frozen facing the book. His eyes were still moving, and he studied Battisti with keen curiosity. Kane was nowhere to be seen, and I hoped he was merely concealed by the spell he'd put on the display case. I tried to look around to see how my friends were faring, but it was difficult without turning my head.

No one came in from the kitchen or the hallway, even though people had been moving about throughout the auction. Had Battisti frozen the staff and the smokers, or was there a ward on the doors, blocking them out?

I hoped Amber and Giselle weren't stuck in the kitchen. We might need their help too.

Battisti gave a cool, appraising look at the room, before turning to the display case. This was our chance. I had no idea what I would do—what could I do?—but I pushed up, the heavy chair making only a little noise on the carpeted floor, and headed to the stage as silently as I could. Hunt was even more silent, and I only realised he'd followed when he walked past me. Was he after the book or Battisti?

I was almost at the steps to the stage when I noticed I was holding the clutch tightly in my hand, but it was too late to discard it. Maybe I could throw it at Battisti to distract him. With the phone and mirror inside, it might do some damage.

The warlock didn't pay any attention to us, his focus on the wards. With a sneer not unlike what Hunt had worn in the same position, he dismantled them and stepped to the book. He checked the display case for more wards and then, surprisingly carefully, opened it and lifted the book out. The look on his face was almost ... reverent.

He clearly cherished the book, so why had he given it to Camillo?

Holding the book under his arm, he stepped back, only to be stopped by Kane's wards. He swivelled around with a snarl, ready to handle whoever was trying to detain him. A baffled look spread on his face when he realised he was held by wards he'd already taken down, but his mood instantly turned to fury when he saw us.

We'd climbed on the stage. Hunt and I stood side by side facing him, and Kane appeared on my other side. Luca and Ashley were behind the display case, and Amber and Giselle showed up too, taking their places in the circle.

"Release me, mages," Battisti demanded. He hit the wards with his free hand, but he couldn't get out without putting the book away and using both his hands to break the wards. He couldn't form a portal out either. The space inside the wards was too small for it.

Kane nodded. "The moment you tell us where you've hidden your hostages."

"And call off the demon," Amber added.

"Also, you have to promise not to imprison people inside the book anymore," I stated, my voice firm despite my fast-beating heart. Then I reconsidered: "Or give the book to others for the same purpose either."

Fury distorted his face. "I did not give the book to them. They stole it."

"That was brave of them..." Hunt drawled. "Or careless of you."

I agreed, though I wasn't stupid enough to say it aloud.

"They will pay for it," Battisti hissed. Kane leaned closer.

"And they will. But there's no reason to put all these people in danger too."

"Ah, you realised they're here."

My bones threatened to turn liquid for the confirmation of my fears.

Battisti nodded, coming to a decision. "The only time I've used the book as a prison is when I captured the demon. You have my word it won't happen again. And you'll get the whereabouts of the deceitful pair when I'm out of here."

We glanced at each other, unsure if we could trust him. But we really wanted to get rid of him and the book, so Amber nodded at Kane.

"Release him. The faster he calls off the demon the better."

We retreated a little, but not so much that Battisti could instantly create a portal and flee when the wards came down. With an elaborate gesture, Kane dismantled them.

Everything happened so fast I barely registered it. Hunt lunged at Battisti, who stepped back and pulled the book out of his reach. Turning away from Hunt, he opened the book and my stomach clenched in horror. He was facing Kane now, clearly speaking a spell. Was he releasing the original demon? Kane wouldn't stand a chance if it came out full of fury.

I didn't consider. I pushed Kane to the side as hard as I could as the spell took effect. I glimpsed the horrified look on his face, and then…

Magic by the Book

I PAUSED ON THE SMALL landing outside my flat and dropped the luggage that had turned heavier with every floor I'd dragged it up. The late August day had been long and hot, and I'd been travelling since the early morning to return home from my holiday in France. I was exhausted.

As I inserted the key into the lock, I had a brief foreboding that things wouldn't be well inside, but then again, I often did. My flatmate, Nick, wasn't exactly the most reliable of people.

I pushed the door open and listened, but everything was quiet. Maybe he wasn't home. Glad for the brief respite, I carried the luggage in and closed the door, only barely refraining from slumping against it in exhaustion.

The flat smelled stale and of garbage going ripe. Nick probably hadn't been here the whole time I was in France. I went to check his room, but it was empty. The kitchen was littered with discarded takeout packages and dirty dishes, but not three weeks' worth. The fridge contained more takeout food, some with their own ecosystems.

I threw the door closed, disgusted. I didn't have energy to deal with it now.

I carried the luggage to my room and dropped my handbag on the bed. I was about to remove my shoes when something about the bag caught my attention. My brows knit.

Why had I travelled with my silver evening clutch? It made no sense, and not solely for its looks. I couldn't remember packing it in the first place. I had no use for it on a summer holiday in Southern France.

That wasn't the only oddity. I was wearing high-heeled silver sandals. They matched the clutch, but weren't exactly suitable for travelling either. No wonder my feet hurt. And was I wearing a cocktail dress? I spread the skirt wide, as if it would help make the outfit make sense. Whose dress was it anyway? I'd never seen it in my life.

I sat on the bed, baffled. Why couldn't I remember dressing in these this morning? And how on Earth had my mother allowed me to leave wearing clothes this inappropriate for travelling?

She wouldn't. Yet I was wearing them anyway. Had I hit my head after coming home and had dressed up for an evening event without remembering it? I poked my head carefully, but nothing hurt.

I glanced at my wrist to check if I'd lost time since entering the flat, but I wasn't wearing a watch. I stared at my empty arm in disbelief. I never travelled without my wristwatch, as I tended to check the time obsessively to make sure I didn't miss my connections. Had I lost it somewhere?

The thought saddened me. It had been a graduation present from Aunt Clara, an antique piece that had belonged to my grandmother. I didn't want to lose it.

Hoping I'd stowed it in the clutch for safekeeping, I upended its contents on the bed. A lipstick, phone, and a silver compact mirror dropped out, but no watch.

I picked up the phone, but there was no connection. It was late in the evening, which suited the theory of lost time, but not the early evening sun outside my window. Was it showing Central European time still? But it was only an hour's difference to London.

Stymied by all the discrepancies, I picked up the mirror, only to yelp in surprise and drop it on the bed when it zapped me. Silver was the best conductor of electricity, but there was no source where it could've come from. I wasn't an expert on static electricity, but I didn't think that was to be blamed here.

Magic by the Book

Yet another mystery.

I poked the compact with my index finger, but it didn't zap me again, so I picked it up to study it closer. It was a beautiful art deco mirror, handmade, if I was any judge of antiques. And it wasn't mine. So what was it doing in my purse?

Gingerly, anticipating another electric shock, I opened the compact to find a slightly darkened mirror. I angled it to study my reflection, and almost dropped it again.

Staring back at me from the mirror was the face of a strange woman.

I blinked, and the reflection blinked too. It was a woman maybe a decade older than me, with downturned green eyes and faint lines at the corners. The expression staring back at me was powerful and slightly disdainful—nothing I recognised ever wearing on my face. The face was dainty and sharp-chinned, the hair was mahogany, short at the back and longer at the front, falling asymmetrically past the left eye.

I would never cut my hair short, so I made the only conclusion I could. I hadn't hit my head; I'd swapped bodies with someone.

"What the hell?" I exclaimed aloud.

"Indeed," my reflection answered in a dry tone. With a shriek, I threw the mirror on the bed. My heart was beating so hard for the fright, I had trouble breathing.

"Pick up the mirror, Phoebe," the woman in the reflection said.

Timidly, I obeyed, and turned the mirror to my face again. The reflection still showed a strange face. "How do you know my name?"

The woman in the reflection gave me a slow look. "Did you hit your head or something?"

"I ... maybe?" I stared at the reflection askance. "Are you my face?"

She looked heavenwards, as if asking for strength. "No, I'm not. Don't you know what you look like?"

"I thought I did," I said, defensive. "But then your face appeared in the mirror."

"That's because it's not currently a mirror."

I blinked. "It's a video call?" I turned the mirror in my hand, but it remained a perfectly normal silver compact.

"No, it's a spell."

"Get out of here!" I exclaimed. "Who do you take me for?"

"I used to take you for an intelligent person..." She pinched the bridge of her nose. "What's the last thing you remember?"

"I ... just returned from my summer holiday at my parents' in France."

"*Summer* holiday? What month do you think it is?"

"August?"

"It's November."

I stared at her, stunned. She ignored me and addressed someone outside the view in French. "Call Archibald."

"How do you know my boss?" I asked, as a man appeared in the view over her shoulder, looking put out. He was in his early forties, maybe, and handsome in a stark, French way.

"Do I have to?" he grumbled in French. Then he spotted me and gave me a surprised look. "Hello, Phoebe. What are you doing in the mirror?" he asked in English.

"That's what we're trying to find out, so call Archie," the woman ordered before I could answer, or figure out how he too knew who I was.

Magic by the Book

The man tilted his head and his dark eyes sharpened. I could've sworn they flashed eerily. "I think she's in some kind of alternate dimension."

The woman looked as stunned as I felt, but less disbelieving. "Voluntarily?"

"People seldom are," he said dryly.

"How can you tell?" she asked, all business now. They both ignored me.

"Can you see that haze around her?" She squinted her eyes, studying me. She nodded, and he launched into a lecture in French that I understood every word of yet didn't comprehend at all. He was in all earnestness talking about magic, spells, and pocket dimensions or something.

"Let me see…"

He told her to hold the mirror so that it faced him. Then he gestured with his hands and fingers, and said words in a language that I didn't know but which sounded simultaneously harsh and sibilant, and made shivers of fear run down my spine.

When he finished the last word, the surface of the mirror rippled like water. In front of my fascinated eyes, he pushed his hand into the mirror on his side—and through to me.

Twenty-one

THE HAND SHOULDN'T HAVE FIT through the mirror, yet it did. The fingers wiggled. "Take my hand," he ordered.

"What? No!" I didn't know these people.

"Do you want to be stuck in there for the rest of your life? Take the hand."

"I'm not stuck, I'm home."

"That's not your home," the woman said somewhere in the background, the voice clear despite the hand blocking the mirror. "It's your memory of it."

I don't know why I even considered obeying. It had to be all the oddities that had led to the woman appearing in the mirror, the strange clothes and the mirror zapping me.

I had my phone in one hand and the mirror in the other, which didn't leave anything to take the man's hand with. I considered leaving the phone behind, but if the woman was right and this wasn't a real place, I wouldn't be able to come back for it.

With no other place for it, I pushed it inside the corset top of my gown, where it stayed snugly. I had no room for the clutch, but it hadn't been expensive. I could abandon it. If it even was real.

Holding the mirror tightly, I took the hand. It was cool and dry, but didn't zap me like I half feared.

He pulled. I was sure nothing would happen—hello, it was impossible for me to fit through the mirror—but there was a lurch that made my stomach roil, followed by a dizzying swirl of blackness that made me close my eyes tightly. It didn't help.

I dropped on my bum with a painful thump and opened my eyes.

"We should've put the mirror on the floor," Danielle said dryly. I stared at her with my mouth open, gasping for breath, fighting nausea. She and Laurent were looking at me with as much concern as a warlock and his evil apprentice could.

I was still somehow holding the compact, as if it had turned inside out like a piece of clothing through the mirror, but now it showed me my pale face and startled eyes.

"How… why…?" I looked around and realised I knew the place. It was the living room of Danielle's house in London. There was no mistaking the Laura Ashley wallpapers and flower-patterned chinch sofas. For an evil woman, she had a really romantic taste in décor.

"How did I end up here?"

"Do you know who we are?" Danielle asked, and I nodded, still bewildered. "What's the last thing you remember now?"

My head was in a swirl. The memory of returning from my holiday was so strong, yet there was an even stronger memory. "The auction! Battisti!"

Laurent startled. "Giovanni Battisti, the warlock?" he asked as if the Italian was the only warlock in the world. When I nodded, his brows furrowed. "*Merde*! That's bad news."

"What time is it? I need to go back to help my friends."

"Go back where?" Danielle demanded. "How did you end up in a pocket dimension in the first place?"

"The Guildhall. They're fighting with Battisti, and he captured me inside an ancient book." I shuddered when the realisation of where I'd been hit. Without the mirror and Laurent, I would've been captured forever. "And he has an insanely high-level demon guarding hostages somewhere in the building."

I began to push up, ready to rush out of the house and run the ten or so kilometres across town in my heeled sandals if needed.

Laurent offered me a hand and pulled me rest of the way up. "I'll take you. I've always wanted to meet Battisti. Where exactly are they?"

"The great hall," I said.

"Picture it in your mind as clearly as you can," he ordered, and placed a hand on the side of my head.

I tried to imagine the stage, the display cases and where everyone had been standing. He nodded. Then, with a simple gesture, he drew a large circle in the air with his hand, and a portal opened. On the other side was the edge of the stage.

"Go," he ordered.

I didn't need to be told twice. I stepped through the portal and into chaos.

A BATTLE WAS IN FULL swing. Kane was attacking Battisti with blue energy balls, forcing him to retreat towards the other end of the stage. Battisti zapped a black bolt at him in return, but Kane lunged to the side just in time. It hit the floor instead, creating a smouldering crater. At Battisti's flank, Hunt took the opportunity to attack him, but Battisti's shields held.

Behind Battisti, Ashley was lying prone and unconscious. She was in her wolf form, so whatever hit her must have been powerful. She was breathing and guarded by Grady, who had shifted into a huge silver wolf.

He was keeping a sharp eye on Battisti's retreat, snout in a deep snarl, body coiled and ready to attack the moment he had a chance. But when he lunged at Battisti, he only collided with shields that Battisti was able to hold all around him while flinging attack spells.

But he couldn't control the people anymore. Everyone's mouths were free, and screams of fear filled the huge space. Some of the guests were able to move, and they were rushing to the door, only to be blocked by wards.

Amber, Giselle, and Luca had opted for crowd control instead of attacking Battisti. They were at the door, guiding people to the back of the room that was empty of tables. Judging by the meek fashion in which they were obeying, Luca was using his suggestive skills on them.

Simon had unfrozen too, and he was busy collecting the lots before the battling mages destroyed them. He had his hands full, and since I didn't know what else to do, I went to help.

I was still holding the mirror. I didn't want to lose it, so I pushed it inside my corset under the phone, the two creating a large rectangular lump on my chest. It was ugly and uncomfortable, but as long as they were secure, I didn't care. This wasn't a beauty pageant.

I raised my shield as best as I was able to and placed myself between Simon and the mages. Together, we carried the lots to the opposite side of the stage from where Battisti was headed.

"I'll guard these, you go help Archibald," Simon said.

"I doubt I'll be much help," I muttered, but I rushed back to Kane.

While I'd been distracted, Danielle and Laurent had come to Kane's help. But they weren't aiming to subdue Battisti. They were hitting the floor in front of him, forcing him to step back, driving him towards a portal that Laurent had created behind him. Wherever it led to was dark, and I hoped it was a dungeon able to hold a warlock.

Demon dimension would do too.

"Release Phoebe," Kane was bellowing at Battisti, his face fierce with fury as he threw another energy ball at the warlock, only hitting his shield.

I needed to tell him I was safe, but I didn't want to distract him and give Battisti a chance to hit him. I didn't want to be hit either, so I strengthened my shield, briefly lightheaded for the energy drain, and walked to the line of mages attacking Battisti.

Battisti noticed me instantly and his eyes grew large. He lifted a hand to point at me, his attention not on the people attacking him. That was all Laurent needed.

He flung the largest energy bolt I'd ever seen—and I'd seen a fair few magic battles already. It hit Battisti's shield straight at his chest. It wasn't enough to break the shield, but it had enough force to make Battisti lose his balance and stumble through the portal right behind him.

The moment he was through, the portal closed, leaving us staring at the empty stage, bewildered.

"What did you do that for?" Hunt demanded Laurent, gesturing at where Battisti had been. "We needed the book."

The warlock gave him a cool look. "It was the fastest way to end the battle. He won't come back from there before I release him."

"But what about Phoebe?" Kane asked, his voice low with fury and the exhaustion of the battle. "He has to release her!"

"I'm here," I said. He swivelled toward my voice, his face full of disbelief that turned to relief. With a couple of long strides, he crossed the stage to me, pulled me into his arms, and kissed me for all that he was worth.

"It's really you," he said in awe when we came for air. He studied my face, and wiped away a tear of relief that was falling down my cheek. "Are you hurt? How did you get out?"

"I'm not hurt. Laurent got me out. For some reason, my mirror connected with Danielle's." I turned to her. "How did it happen anyway?"

She spread her arms. "It started to buzz in my bag. I took it out and there you were. But how the mirrors connected, I have no idea."

"Your great-great-grandfather put a spell on them almost a century ago," I told her. Her brows shot up.

"I had no idea."

"As fascinating as this is, we have bigger concerns," Amber said, addressing us from the floor below the stage. She made a sweeping motion with her hand over the room that had erupted into chaos the moment Battisti left and the spell keeping everyone immobile dissipated.

"We need to get the wards on the doors down and calm these people before they get hurt. And someone needs to go deal with the demon."

I'd forgotten about it. A panic washed over me when I thought it might have released the moment Battisti disappeared.

Laurent frowned at the panicking people, then made an almost offhanded gesture that froze them again. It was no less frightening that he was able to control three hundred people than when Battisti did the same.

He addressed Hunt: "You handle their minds, I'll handle the doors."

Without waiting for an answer, he strode to the door, took one look at it and portalled to the other side. Hunt watched him go with dismay, only to shrug it off.

"Right, then. I believe I'll remove the past fifteen minutes. The auction was a success, everyone should take their places, and now it's time for dessert."

He glanced over his shoulder at us. "You should shield."

Hastily, we obeyed, and he faced the room again. The tightening of his face indicated it took an effort to capture the minds of so many people at once.

"Tell Dufort to release them."

Amber relayed the news through the door and a portal appeared again, showing fed-up Laurent who waved a hand at the people, before disappearing as it closed. It occurred to me that he could've let us out through the portal to hunt for the demon, but he clearly had other priorities.

Moreover, I really didn't want to go after the demon without him.

When the people were free to move, Hunt gave them a command to take their places. Like zombies, the people ambled to the correct tables and sat down. I studied them worriedly until I found my aunt and uncle, both unharmed.

Almost all seats were filled, so there weren't that many

people missing. That made our task a little easier, though I feared there might be furious people on the other side of the door who hadn't been able to get back in.

Was it evil of me to wish Laurent had dealt with them?

Once everyone was seated, Hunt pointed at Luca. "You take that end of the room, I'll take this."

They hurried to alter the minds one by one—or a table at a time in case of Hunt. We headed to the door that Laurent opened just then.

"Where to?"

I had given it some thought already. "To the Roman amphitheatre."

LAURENT IN THE LEAD, we headed down the stairs with Kane and Danielle, Grady keeping the rear still in his wolf form. To my amazement, there were no people angrily demanding to be let in, nor were there people in the foyer. Had the demon already got to them?

Nausea hit me, but then I figured there would be more blood and gore if it had.

We hurried downwards, past the crypts on the lower ground level, both of which were empty and dark, all the way to the amphitheatre below ground. Lights were on there, and that's where we found the missing people.

The stairs ended at a glass-covered viewing balcony over the Roman ruins that had been preserved as a museum. Below our feet, leaning against a section of ancient brick wall, were Camillo and Mrs Hayling. And around them, standing stiff and looking terrified, were the dozen or so missing people, Grady's men who had been sent to look for the demon among them.

The source of their fear was standing in front of them, meaty arms crossed over its large chest, a vicious glower on its face as it stared at them. I was briefly relieved that it hadn't got free when Battisti disappeared, followed by the horror of realising we would have to deal with it ourselves.

"How do we get down there?" Kane demanded, looking for stairs.

Grady began to sniff around, and with a commanding bark, hurried down a dark corridor. We followed and soon found a spiral staircase to the museum.

"Watch for boobytraps," Kane said as Grady was about to shoot across the floor. The wolf ground to a halt, his claws skidding on the stone floor.

"We can't just barge in there," Laurent said. "That demon needs to be taken down first. I sincerely doubt we can kill it."

"Can't you create a portal and send it away?" I asked, and he gave me a slow look.

"Naturally, but where would I send it? I can't create portals to demon dimension."

"The same place you sent Battisti?"

A smile spread on his face, and it was not nice.

Kane had been studying the room with his head tilted. "Good news is the demon is held with wards. Bad news is the people are inside the wards with it. I think it's a similar trap than what I created around the book. You can get in, but not out. So be careful."

They crossed the floor and I followed, a bit wobbly in my high heels, my energies almost spent. We paused well away from the demon, and Laurent gestured with his hands. A colourful wall of complicated wards appeared between us and the demon—and it finally noticed us.

It turned around and studied us with cold, inhuman eyes, as if we were specimens under the microscope. Then it opened its mouth into what was probably a grin, showing us the rows of fangs. It took a step closer to the wards and leaned a hand against them. They began to sizzle and pop, as if it was an electric field, but if the wards hurt it, the demon didn't react.

A wave of terror washed over me and I whimpered.

"We can't release that thing," Danielle said with a shudder. Grady bared his teeth and growled, but the demon's attention was on Laurent, as if it could tell he was the biggest threat.

For his part, Laurent looked excited. He was all but rubbing his hands together.

"Could you create a portal inside the wards to get the people out?" Kane asked, but the warlock shook his head.

"The best we can do is to make sure the demon doesn't leave this room." He glanced at Danielle and conjured a couple of pieces of chalk from somewhere. "You can draw a demon trap. Show Archibald so he can help."

Kane didn't look happy about the idea of learning warlock magic, but he took the offered piece of chalk and began to draw a complicated pattern on the floor in front of the wards. They were nothing like what we used in our spells, and I'd witnessed enough dark magic already to know what they were.

"What should I do?" I asked.

"Maybe go back to the great hall," Laurent suggested dryly. I knew he was right, I'd be safest there, but I didn't like it.

"I can feed energy to the trap," I stated, just as my legs decided this was the perfect moment to give up on me. I plopped down on a piece of ancient wall and pressed my head between my knees. Everyone was ignoring me, too busy with their tasks, and I recovered soon enough. I wouldn't be feeding any spells though.

"Damn that man and his complicated wards," Laurent muttered in French.

"Maybe you should bring Battisti back to deal with them," I suggested and received a withering look in return.

The demon watched Laurent work with keen eyes. I had no doubt that the moment it was free, it would attack him. And once the biggest obstacle was taken care of, it would deal with the rest of us.

"My men and I can keep that thing in rein for long enough," Grady said behind me, startling me. I made to turn, but a glimpse of naked torso made me hastily change my mind.

"That's two thousand years of history and several hundred lives you're staking on that."

"I didn't say we can win…"

There was a flash behind me and a moment later, Grady's silver wolf took a spot next to Laurent. Apparently he was strong enough to shift whenever he wanted. Inside the wards, the two wolf guards began to strip before the bemused eyes of the humans. They shifted and the humans scrambled as far away from them as possible, huddling together in fear.

"We're ready," Danielle said, straightening. Kane did the same, his eyes tightly on the demon. They began to feed energy into the trap, and it started to glow faintly. I wanted to join them, but I had nothing to give.

"Almost there," Laurent said. "Stand back."

The command was for me, because Danielle and Kane were busy with the trap. I pushed onto my tottery legs, but they wouldn't carry me, so I dropped behind the piece of ancient wall I'd been sitting on. That thing had lasted two thousand years; maybe it would survive a demon too.

With one final pull of the wards, the barrier came down. Laurent didn't wait but created a portal behind the demon even as Grady lunged at it from a side, teeth bared. The demon made a sweep with its hand, but the wolf swerved at the last moment. Then there were three of them attacking.

The demon was trapped between the wolves, the portal, and the demon trap. It bellowed in anger, and I almost wet myself.

The wolves and Laurent with his energy bolts pushed the demon to the edge of the portal, but the damn thing stood its ground and wouldn't step through.

I searched frantically for a way to help, but I couldn't create attack spells. But the levitation spell had worked before.

Creeping closer behind the wall, I gathered all the energy I could muster. I yanked the spark of magic inside me—no time to carefully coax it—added the fear and fury I had in me, and cast the levitation spell. I threw it at the demon and to my amazement, met my mark.

I hadn't turned into a master mage overnight. The demon didn't rise in the air. It barely moved. But it lost its balance briefly just as Laurent hit it with a huge energy bolt, and staggered backwards through the portal. With a wave of Laurent's hand, the portal closed.

Disbelieving silence fell. I collapsed in relief and exhaustion. That had gone better than I'd hoped. "Do you think Battisti will survive it?" I managed to ask.

The warlock shrugged. "The demon should still be in his command. And he has the book. All he needs is to capture the demon inside."

Maybe the two demons could keep each other company from now on.

The captured people finally realised the threat was over and they were free. They made a frantic rush towards the stairs, only to be stopped by Laurent's freezing spell. How he had energy for that, I had no idea. Kane and Danielle looked utterly exhausted for keeping the demon trap active.

Laurent gave the people a cool look. "We'll need the vampire here to alter their minds."

Kane took out his phone and called Hunt. Then he came to me and helped me up. I leaned on him heavily. "Are you all right?" he asked, as if I'd been toiling with the wards. "That levitation spell was ingenious," he praised me warmly. Then he looked around, his brows furrowing.

"Where are the prisoners?"

We hadn't paid attention to Camillo and Mrs Hayling. They weren't among the people frozen in the middle of the floor. If they'd run off the moment the wards came down, they could be anywhere by now.

I swivelled on my heels to see if they were hiding behind the ruins, and came face to face with Mrs Hayling—and a pistol pointed at my heart.

She didn't waste time for declarations of intent, and I had no time to even be afraid. She fired the weapon, her aim true. The impact made me fall backwards and collapse against Kane. The last thing I felt before everything went black was his arms wrapping around me.

***

I CAME TO WITH Kane patting my cheeks. "She's been unconscious for too long." He sounded frantic. "I don't understand. There's no blood, and I caught her before she would've hit her head."

"Maybe she collapsed with exhaustion," Luca suggested. How he was here, I couldn't fathom.

"There's a hole in her clothes."

The hands patting me stilled. Then, carefully, Kane pulled out the phone and mirror I had stashed inside the corset for safekeeping. I opened my eyes to see him slump in relief.

"These stopped the bullet."

The phone was cracked through, with the bullet lodged into it, and the mirror was slightly dented too. Kane's eyes were glistening when they met mine.

"You're safe."

I tried to push up, but the impact of the bullet had bruised my chest and I winced in pain. It was best to stay where I was, on Kane's lap. "What happened?"

"After you were shot? Dufort took Camillo and Mrs Hayling away. I would've liked to see to their punishment, but maybe this is for the better."

He helped me up and my legs held. The room had emptied while I was out for count, but Luca and Hunt were there, having altered the minds of the humans. They were studying me with concern. Then the latter smiled.

"I think everything worked out well in the end. How about some dessert?"

Epilogue

AFTER EVERYTHING THAT HAD happened, settling down to have dessert was maybe the oddest thing I'd done that evening. Odder still, I ate it with gusto, the first time that evening that I even tasted what I was having. All around me, people behaved like everything was normal, the auction and the evening a great success.

But I was too exhausted to linger afterwards, even though there would be a live band and dancing. Hunt looked drained too, not that he would admit it. My aunt and uncle followed us when we left.

As we were helping them into a cab, my aunt paused and gave me a puzzled look, as if she didn't quite understand why she was telling me: "Remind me to talk about your Aunt Beverly one of these days." With that curious remark, she closed the door and they drove away.

Hunt saw me home where the rest of the household soon arrived too, Ashley still in her wolf form, but conscious and in good spirits—as far as I could tell. Kane came with them, and even though we were exhausted, we settled down with tea to go through the events of the night.

"Grady will let Mr Hayling go tomorrow," Kane told us. "But I really don't know what to tell him."

"Maybe we could alter his mind one more time," Luca suggested.

"And hope Laurent won't let his wife go?" Amber asked in a dubious voice. Luca shrugged.

"He doesn't strike me as a lenient man. For all we know, he gave the pair to Battisti."

I found myself wishing that Battisti would lock the two in the book.

Kane had given me Monday off. I woke up around midday to a strange ringtone buzzing by my bed. Bleary, I fumbled for the phone, only to stare at it, baffled. It wasn't mine.

It took a moment for me to remember that Luca had given me one of his old phones to replace the one that had saved my life. The caller was Mother, who wanted to know all the details about my relationship with Kane. At least Aunt Emilia had left Hunt out of her account.

"That does it, we'll spend Christmas in London," Mother declared. My heart fell.

"Do you have to? I was looking forward to spending it in France."

"It's high time we take a firmer look at your life," she stated, the words no woman closer to thirty than twenty wanted to hear.

I spent the day recovering and felt better by the next, which was good, because I had my presentation to the Mages' Council. After everything that had happened, facing a dozen stern-faced mages was a walk in the park, and my pulse barely sped up as Kane led me before them. One by one, I performed all the spells asked of me, and didn't light unwanted fires anywhere.

Magic by the Book

The mages deliberated briefly afterwards, while Kane waited with me in the adjoining room. He smiled at me warmly. "You did very well. I'm proud of you."

His confidence turned out to be well-founded, and without much ado I was accepted as a mage. I should've felt more excited than I did, but I was still reeling from the weekend. I struggled to focus when the mages wanted to know everything that had happened at the auction, and to give a concise account.

"I would've preferred you hadn't let the responsible people go, Mage Boyle," an older man with thick white sideburns said to Amber with a grumble when we'd finished talking. "Especially with a warlock."

Amber nodded calmly, as if she'd had any say in how the events unfolded. She was their leader and took responsibility. "I judged that it was more important to protect the humans than start fights with warlocks."

After some talk, the mages agreed it had been for the best. But they also declared that the book should be acquired for the council's safekeeping.

Good luck with that.

Little by little, the world returned to normal. Kane and I finally managed our first date in a proper restaurant without interruptions. And a week later, after another successful date, I finally stayed the night at his place.

After all the delays and build-up, I was more nervous than I usually was in these situations. Kane wasn't any calmer. But once we started kissing, our bodies took charge, and I forgot my nerves.

I can't say it was smooth and passionate like in the movies—it was more about fumbling hands and trying to choreograph each other into a position—but Kane's body was everything I'd believed it to be, and once he got over his nervousness, he knew how to make the most of it, taking me on a ride with him.

Second time was even better.

"Stay till morning," Kane said after we'd were recovered a little. Since I really wanted to, I nodded and cuddled next to him.

I woke up to the scent of coffee and noises from the kitchen that indicated he was making breakfast. Smiling, I got up, made a quick pitstop to freshen up, wrapped myself into his much too large bathrobe, and went to find him.

He was standing by the stove, dressed in black boxer briefs and a T, a sexy sight that made my mouth water. My heart skipped a beat when he smiled. "Good morning. I was ready to bring you breakfast in bed."

I smiled in return and went to give him a kiss. "I can go back to bed if you want me to."

"Oh, I want you to…"

Our kiss was interrupted by a knock on the front door. His brows knitted in annoyance. "Who's calling this early on Saturday?"

He switched off the stove. I was wearing his robe, so he pulled on a raincoat from the rack and went down the stairs to answer the door. I stifled my curiosity and didn't peek over the railing to see who it was, not even when he exclaimed in surprise. But when a woman spoke in an urgent voice I had to creep closer.

Before I managed to get a good look, there was a bright flash of light that briefly blinded me. When I was able to see again, and the black spots dancing in my eyes had cleared, I leaned over the railing.

Kane and the woman were gone.

About the Author

SUSANNA SHORE is an independent author. She writes *Two-Natured London* paranormal romance series about vampires and wolf-shifters roaming in London, *P.I. Tracy Hayes* series of a Brooklyn waitress turned private investigator, its spin-off series *The Reed Files*, and *House of Magic* paranormal mysteries set in London. She also writes stand-alone thrillers and contemporary romances. When she's not writing, she's reading or—should her husband manage to drag her outdoors—taking long walks.

If you want to find out when Susanna's next book comes out, subscribe to her newsletter on her website:

www.susannashore.com

Made in United States
North Haven, CT
03 April 2023